BARBARA NADEL was born and brought up in the East End of London. She has a degree in psychology and, prior to becoming a full-time author, she worked in psychiatric institutions and in the community with people experiencing mental health problems. She is also the author of the award-winning Inspector Ikmen series. She lives in Essex.

@BarbaraNadel

By Barbara Nadel

Bright Shiny Things

BRIGHT SHINY THINGS

BARBARA NADEL

Allison & Busby Limited
12 Fitzroy Mews
London W1T 6DW
allisonandbusby.com

First published in Great Britain by Allison & Busby in 2017.

A CIP catalogue record for this book is available from
the British Library.

First Edition

HB ISBN 978-0-7490-2013-2
TPB ISBN 978-0-7490-2146-7

Typeset in 11.5/16.5 pt Sabon by
Allison & Busby Ltd.

The paper used for this Allison & Busby publication
has been produced from trees that have been legally sourced
from well-managed and credibly certified forests.

Printed and bound by
CPI Group (UK) Ltd, Croydon, CR0 4YY

To Senan, with love

PROLOGUE

As the body hit the floor, some of the dead man's blood caught the side of her face and she gasped. It was still warm.

She made herself look down. Drawn to the source of the blood, she fixated on his torso, which was a mass of red punctuated by deep, black stab wounds. Then she looked at the face. Which she recognised.

ONE

'He shit his pants! I'm telling you, I was there!'

Abbas al'Barri was drunk. He'd been drunk in 1991 when they'd first met. Twenty-six years later, he was drunk again.

'I'll admit he pissed himself,' Lee Arnold said.

'And shit! I'm telling you, man! He shit his pants! I saw it and I smelt it!'

Lee shrugged. There was no point arguing with Abbas when he was rat-arsed. The bottle of whisky he'd opened when Lee had arrived was half empty. And Lee didn't drink.

'Fucking "elite" Republican Guard!' Abbas said. 'Fucking Ba'athist scum!'

Although it still, sometimes, haunted his dreams, the First Iraq War was over for Lee Arnold. Since he'd left the army, shortly after the War in 1992, he'd first joined the Metropolitan Police force and then set up in business as a private investigator. The bloody battles against Saddam Hussein's Republican Guard were not memories he liked to invoke. But he hadn't come to this smoke-filled house in East Ham for his own amusement. Abbas was laughing but that was only because he was shit-faced. And he was shit-faced because he was still there in his mind. All the time.

On the night of 26th February 1991, Lee had been driving a Challenger 1 tank into battle against the 52nd Iraqi Armoured Division. As a corporal in the 7th Brigade of the British 1st Armoured Division he'd been part of the multinational force that had been sent to recapture Kuwait from Iraqi occupation. He'd been sweaty with fear, hoarse from smoking too many fags and he'd also had a passenger on board. One of the Brigade's Iraqi interpreters, Abbas al'Barri was a Shia dissident from the northern Plain of Ninevah. He'd been arse'oled before he'd even got on board.

The first thing he'd ever said to Lee had been, 'I'm a very bad Muslim. But what in the name of God are you to do?'

They'd hit it off straight away and when what became known as the Battle of Norfolk was over, they'd gone out drinking together in the southern Iraqi city of Basra. There, for the first time, they'd discussed how many Republican Guards had pissed or shit themselves, or both. Back then, a good night out for Lee Arnold had meant a bottle of vodka and a 'ruck'.

Abbas had been handy in a fight all those years ago too. But, although the drink was still in his life, the fight had gone. That had disappeared the day he'd discovered that his eldest son, Fayyad, hadn't gone to Ibiza for a booze and birds holiday with his mates, but had joined the Islamic State Group in Syria. Lee remembered that day well because it had been the first time that Abbas had called him for years.

When Lee had returned to the UK in 1992, Abbas and his family had also left Iraq. Like most of those who had translated for the foreign coalition, the al'Barri family would have been at risk from Saddam Hussein had they tried to stay. So Abbas, his wife Shereen and their children Fayyad, Djamila and Layla had been settled in a council house in East Ham. Two years later the al'Barris' youngest child, Hasan, had been born in Newham General Hospital. Lee and Abbas had 'wet the baby's head' for two days of happy drunkenness. The next time they'd seen each other, Abbas's name had been all over the newspapers as the father of the latest ISIS recruit. And his drunkenness was dark.

Now, it was even darker.

Hasan and Lee put Abbas to bed when he finally became unconscious. The boy, unlike his mother, was embarrassed. Shereen was furious. Later, sitting down in her kitchen with Lee and a jug of strong coffee, she told him why Abbas had really wanted to see him.

'We got this in the post on Monday,' she said as she pushed a large Jiffy bag across the table.

Addressed to Abbas, the postage stamp was Dutch.

Lee opened the bag and frowned. 'Ivory?'

'No,' Shereen said. 'It's the tooth of a whale.'

Lee removed it. About ten inches long, it looked like a massive incisor from a chain-smoker. The surface of the tooth was rough and, when Lee held it to his nose, it smelt of damp.

'So . . .'

'Lee, may I have one of your cigarettes, please?' Shereen asked.

He didn't think she smoked any more. But he said, 'Course you can, darlin'.'

He offered her a fag and took one for himself. Once her smoke was alight, Shereen said, 'You know that we come from Ninevah. Do you remember?'

'Yes,' he said. 'The Ninevah Plain used to be full of all sorts of people before ISIS. Shias, Christians, Yazidi people . . .'

'That's right. Many, many mosques, churches, monasteries – holy places of all kinds. Even under Saddam. The monks even

11

taught our children. But that was then,' she said. 'Now these monsters my son has chosen to join . . .' She threw her arms in the air. 'Since when were we Sunni? Tell me, Lee, since what time did my son become someone else?'

'I don't know.'

Her eyes filled with tears. 'What did I do, eh? We always kept the children away from religion. We saw this madness coming. What did I do for . . . this?'

He said nothing. The poor woman was confused and who could blame her? Her son had chosen to go to a lawless country to fight for a cause she couldn't understand.

Shereen shook her head. 'But . . . Look,' she said, 'we've not had a word from Fayyad since last August. Not one text, not one phone call. Then . . .' She pointed at the Jiffy bag. 'This.'

'It's his handwriting?'

'Yes. But more significant is the content,' she said.

'A whale's tooth?'

'Yes. But not any whale's tooth,' she said. 'This is the tooth from the whale that ate the Prophet Jonah.'

'In July 2014, ISIS blew up the Mosque of the Prophet Yunus, which is our name for Jonah,' Shereen said. 'It contained the tomb of the prophet as well as a relic, which was a copy of the Tooth of the Whale.'

'A copy?'

'Yes. Given to the shrine by American soldiers in 2008. We were so embarrassed.'

'Why?'

Shereen had switched off the harsh neon lighting strip in the kitchen in favour of candles, which gave off a softer light. She was beginning to get cataracts and candlelight was more comfortable for her eyes. But Lee noticed that it also made her look older. The light and shade the candles threw picked out every hard-won line and crinkle on her beautiful face.

'The Americans believed the story we told about the tooth being stolen,' she said. 'It was a story that the people of the Ninevah Plain created to protect our relic. Even then there were people coming onto the Plain who meant us harm. Al-Qaeda, Salafis, madmen. The imam of the Mosque of Jonah gave the tooth to the monks of the Monastery of Mor Isak. High up in the mountains behind the Christian town of Bartella, it is a hard place to get to. And it is big. Now there is only one monk, but in the past there were thousands. Brother Gibrail put this tooth into the wall of the monastery. He told no one the exact location, not even Brother Serafim, his only companion at that time. That way if anyone came and asked where was the tooth, no one but Brother Gibrail would know and he would kill himself before he would give that secret to the madmen. In December of last year he did just that.'

'He took his own life?'

'Yes.'

Now the low light was eerie. Shereen was calling back the memory of Iraq far more powerfully than her husband. She spoke of a place Lee remembered as a pressure cooker of the fanatical. One day he saw a huge group of men, Shias someone had told him they were, beat themselves with chains until they fainted from blood loss. It was an act of devotion apparently. But to what?

'ISIS came and they blew up Mor Isak,' she said. 'Brother Serafim escaped. He said that they left not one stick of furniture intact, not one plant in the garden alive. There is a woman who lives in Dagenham that I know, Nasra. She is a Syrian Christian from Ninevah. She told me that everyone was saying that the tooth was lost. And I believed it to be so, until this arrived.'

Lee held the artefact up to the light. 'You're sure this is the real deal?'

'Lee, I grew up looking at that tooth,' she said. 'And so did my two eldest children. The tooth was very precious to both Fayyad and Djamila. One of their favourite things as little ones was to go to see the tooth when it was in the Mosque of Yunus. When we heard it was moved to Mor Isak, my Fayyad cried.' She touched the rough surface of the dark-brown object lovingly. 'Abbas and I believe that our son has had a change of heart.'

'About ISIS?'

'Why else would he preserve something those madmen find abominable?' She leant towards him. 'Lee, Fayyad is reaching out to us. He wants our help.'

'To do what?'

'To come back to us!' she said. 'The Tooth of the Whale tells me this more powerfully than any letter.'

'Maybe he just sent it home for old time's sake,' Lee said. 'Shereen, love, I don't mean to rain on your parade, but this needn't mean anything. Worse, it could be a trap.'

'A trap?'

'To give you false hope. You know how twisted these bastards are! They encourage these young blokes to reject their families, to actively torment them in some cases. You're "infidels" now, why should he care about you?'

Shereen looked down at her hands.

'I can see it's crossed your mind,' he said.

'But not Abbas's.'

'Well, no.'

'Lee, if Fayyad doesn't come home, Abbas will drink himself to death,' she said. 'He can't take it. He just can't.'

'Have you told the coppers?' Lee asked.

He saw the candlelight flicker in her slightly milky eyes. It gave them a vaguely sinister, unearthly look.

'Oh, no,' she said. 'Abbas is adamant. No coppers. He wants you to find Fayyad.'

'I said I'd finish my A levels and I will.'

The gangly girl sprawled across the sofa didn't take her eyes from the TV as she spoke. Shazia Hakim was, to the annoyance of her stepmother, addicted to dark, Scandinavian crime dramas. Wasn't there enough gloom in everyday life? She was also, in Mumtaz Hakim's opinion, being dangerously casual about her own future.

'If you go in under the graduate entry scheme . . .'

'I don't want to wait that long,' Shazia said. 'I've already taken an extra year for my A levels. And, anyway, I want to go in as an ordinary constable. I want to learn from the bottom.'

'Shazia, you know that, at that level, you may face . . .'

'Racism and sexism. Yeah, I know, Amma.' She shook her head. 'You've talked about it, Lee's talked about it, Vi's talked about it. And as I've said to all of you, if Asian girls don't go in and change it, then who will? Anyway, if I join up when I've finished my A levels I can start earning and you won't have to worry about nine grand a year uni fees.'

Mumtaz put the book she'd been trying to read down. Science fiction had never really been her thing but she was giving it a go because her cousin Aftab had recommended it.

'Shazia,' she said. 'As I've become tired of telling you, don't think about money. I have that covered.'

The girl looked, briefly, away from the TV. 'No you don't.'

Mumtaz ignored her. 'What about your application to Manchester University? What happened to that?'

'You know what happened.'

Shazia turned back to the TV and Mumtaz said no more.

The subject of the Sheikh family and what they had done to Mumtaz and Shazia was a closed book. Shazia's late father had been in debt to the Sheikhs, a local crime family, when he'd been stabbed to death on Wanstead Flats nearly four years earlier. A gambler, a drunk and a womaniser, he'd habitually raped both his first wife and Mumtaz. He'd also abused his own daughter. Shazia hadn't cried when her father died. She still didn't know that Naz the spoilt favourite nephew of the Sheikh family patriarch, Wahid-ji, had been the one who had killed him. And now that Naz himself was dead, theoretically that information had died with him. Except that Mumtaz knew it hadn't. Because she'd been there when Naz had killed her husband. She'd let him get away as Ahmet had lay dying. She'd let him die. Then the Sheikhs had begun blackmailing her.

The two Hakim women had secrets from each other that neither of them barely dared to even think about. Shazia carried guilt, Mumtaz did too, but there was also fear because the Sheikh family hadn't finished with the Hakims. Only one person apart from Mumtaz knew about the Sheikhs and that was her business partner, Lee Arnold. And even he didn't know the whole story.

Fayyad was not the skinny boy that Lee remembered. Now a tall, muscular man in his thirties, he had a beard and carried a semi-automatic rifle. In this picture he was smiling. Lee pointed at the computer screen. 'How'd you find this?' he said.

'They have websites dedicated to getting brides for their fighters,' Shereen said.

'But this is Facebook.'

'Read it,' Shereen said. 'He says he's looking for a wife.'

Lee had heard that one of ISIS's most powerful recruiting tools

16

amongst Muslim women was its stable of young, fit, handsome fighters. Pictures were put online to draw in those already in the early stages of radicalisation. A handsome face and a set of muscles like Fayyad's could clinch it. Lee barely recognised him. He called himself Abu Imad. All the fighters had new names signalling their 'rebirth' as adherents of ISIS.

'When did you find this?'

'We've been looking online ever since he left,' Shereen said. 'Djamila found this a few days after we got the tooth.' She touched his arm, desperate for him to believe. 'You see he's reaching out online and by post.'

'Yeah, reaching out to entice some vulnerable girl to go and join him in Raqqa,' Lee said.

'No! No! Lee, you don't understand!'

'I think I do,' he said. 'Shereen, love, I know you want to think—'

'He sent the tooth from Amsterdam,' Shereen interrupted. 'ISIS people use Amsterdam as a transit point to go on to Istanbul and then into the Middle East. They come into Europe via Schiphol Airport and they leave from there too.'

'How do you know this?'

'Because I have read everything there is to read about these bastards!' She began to cry.

Lee let her and then he said, 'Whatever's going on here, you have to tell the police. I can't help you. I'm not an expert on terrorism. I'm not an expert on much.'

'But you work with a covered lady,' Shereen said.

Lee frowned. 'How's that relevant?' he said.

TWO

Mrs Butt's husband, Nabeel, was indeed having an affair with Mrs Kundi who ran the Fatima Convenience Store in Manor Park, just as Mrs Butt had suspected. Mumtaz had photographs of twenty-five-year-old Nabeel locked in a passionate embrace with the sixty-year-old widow who was, it had to be said, extremely well preserved for her age. She was also loaded. As well as the convenience store on the Romford Road, her late husband, Sadiq, had left her one massive house in Forest Gate plus a string of flats all over the East End, which were rented out. Mrs Butt, a pretty twenty-three-year-old with two small children, shook her head.

'He has had more money lately,' she said. 'Must've got it from her. Silly old bag! He's been buying the kids computer games they're too young to use. Course he plays them himself.'

Nabeel Butt was a very handsome young man whose main fault, apart from unfaithfulness, was his complete refusal to work. That was down to his wife who toiled most of the day and part of the night in her father's launderette in Plaistow. Her mother looked after her twin girls while Nabeel pleased himself and, apparently, Mrs Kundi too.

'What will you do?' Mumtaz asked. It had to be hard to see a photograph of your husband being pleasured by a much older woman half hidden behind a stack of Coca-Cola bottles. Getting that shot hadn't been easy. Standing in the rain for hours, waiting for the convenience store to close.

'I dunno,' the young woman said. 'I'll have to think about it. Me dad'll go bonkers once he knows. But then he might blame me. You know how it is.'

They shared a look. Oh, Mumtaz knew how that was. Girls who wanted to divorce errant husbands were often accused of not being 'good' wives, which either meant they needed to work harder, have more children or allow their husbands sexual favours they found distasteful. Not that her own father had behaved like that. Baharat Huq had been as glamoured as everyone else by the lies handsome and apparently successful businessman Ahmet Hakim had told so that he could marry Mumtaz. But after Ahmet's death, when she'd finally managed to tell her father about the beatings and the rapes she had endured, he had been mortified. He had blamed himself.

'I can't advise you,' Mumtaz said. 'It's not what private investigators do.'

When Mrs Butt left the office, Mumtaz had her lunch at her desk. Lee was out with a prospective client who had looked as if he'd had a very rough night. They'd gone to the Boleyn pub at the other end of Green Street which, given the client's state, hadn't seemed like the best idea. But what did she know? The client was, apparently, one of Lee's old friends from the First Iraq War. An Arab, by the sound of his name.

'Shereen told me everything,' Lee said.

'She said. You think we should go to the police,' Abbas al'Barri said.

19

'I know you should,' Lee said. 'You should also stop drinking too. You look like shit, mate.'

Abbas looked at the double whisky in front of him.

'Hair of the dog.'

There weren't usually many people in the Boleyn. There never had been that many on weekday lunchtimes in recent years. But at least up until the previous football season, the pub had done well on match days. Now West Ham United had moved to the Olympic Stadium in Stratford even that trade had disappeared. And when the property developers who'd bought the old Boleyn ground started to demolish it and build posh flats, the pub was probably for the knacker's yard.

Lee said, 'I know he's your son, but Fayyad openly admits he takes part in ISIS activities in Syria. He's a terrorist.'

'He's trying not to be!' Abbas said.

An elderly man looked up from behind his copy of *The Sun*, sniffed and then walked out to have a fag on Green Street.

'You don't know that.'

'And you don't know that he isn't reaching out!'

'No. I don't. But what I do know is that those counterterrorism officers who worked with you when Fayyad took off for Syria are the best people to help you.'

'This looking for a wife thing is nonsense!' Abbas said. 'He never wanted to be married!'

'How do you know?'

'He never discussed it with me.'

Lee sipped his Diet Pepsi. It was probably rotting the hell out of his guts but it was better than the booze and painkillers he'd slung down his neck for more years than he cared to recall. At least Pepsi didn't make him behave like a twat. Like Abbas.

'Shereen told me you've got some idea about contacting him on Facebook.'

'Yes! You—'

'I can't do it,' Lee said. 'Outfits like ISIS monitor social media. Assuming for a moment that Fayyad does want to come home, then I might inadvertently say something to him that would get him into trouble. They could kill him.'

Abbas looked into his whisky glass.

'You had a family liaison officer, didn't you?'

'A Sikh woman.'

'Then contact her,' Lee said.

He shook his head. 'She just made tea and said comforting words. She was about twenty at the most,' he said. 'What can such a person know? And we can't contact him, Shereen or me. We can't bear it. What if we're wrong? What if this is some sort of cruel joke? Lee, I know you work with that Muslim lady . . .'

'Mumtaz isn't getting involved,' Lee said. 'I won't have it.'

'She works for you. She must do what you tell her.'

'Not if what I ask her is bad for her,' Lee said. 'And this would be. Believe me, Mumtaz's got enough shit in her life without getting inside the head of someone who's been fighting in Syria. It's fucking dangerous. You should know that.'

Abbas didn't answer.

'Go to the police and tell them,' Lee said. 'There's nothing me or Mumtaz can do for you.' Then he stood up. 'I'm going out for a fag,' he said.

As he passed him, Lee heard Abbas say, 'You owe me.'

She was right, the old man was looking at her.

'You think that old bookie want to give you some lovin'?' Grace said to Shazia.

The girls were sitting on the wall outside Newham Sixth Form College. Shazia was eating a KitKat while Grace smoked a fag. Grace's mum and dad belonged to what she called the 'happy clappy' church next door to Tesco's on the Barking Road. They didn't approve of smoking. Which was why Grace had to do it.

'You know him?' Grace asked. 'He, like, an uncle or something?'

'No.'

He wasn't and Shazia didn't know him, as such. But she had seen him, often. And whenever that happened he always seemed to be staring at her. Was it just paranoia? A lot of girls dreaded being spotted by a single or widowed, much older man. Being taken a fancy to by an old guy with money sometimes meant that an offer of marriage would be received. The only consolation for Shazia was that her stepmother would never agree to such a match. Shazia knew that to the bottom of her soul. What she also unfortunately knew was that her amma was also skint, beggared by those bastards her dad had been in debt to. The old man walked away.

'So you comin' down the chicken shop after college?' Grace asked.

Grace had the hots for a local bad boy who called himself 'Mamba'. Like Grace, he came from a God-fearing and intensely moral Nigerian family. No one knew what Mamba – whose real name was Benjamin – was like at home, but on the street he was all 'gangsta'. Grace was besotted.

Shazia shook her head. 'Nah.'

'Oh, girl, why not?'

'Got work to do,' she said. 'If I don't do it, mum'll give me shit.'

'She just your stepmum,' Grace said dismissively.

'Yeah, but if I'm ever going to get out of Newham, I have to get my exams.'

'To go uni, yeah.'

She hadn't told Grace, or anyone apart from her amma, that she was actually going to join the police. If she was. She'd started to rethink her plans in the past few days. Maybe going to university and then joining the police was the way forward? If nothing else it would put off the evil moment when she had to tell her friends that she was going to become a 'fed'.

'There other ways to get out this shithole,' Grace said.

'Yeah.'

Grace caught the downbeat tone in Shazia's voice. 'I don't mean becoming some gangsta's baby mama. I ain't doin' that.'

'Unless Mamba asked you.'

Laughing, Grace pushed her, 'Cheeky bitch!'

'Just sayin',' Shazia said.

The girls chatted on until it was time for their afternoon sessions to begin. But when, later, Shazia came out onto the street to go home, she saw that the old man she'd seen earlier had reappeared. Once again, he stared at her. Who was he and what did he want?

DI Violet Collins might be the rough side of fifty and as curvaceous as a stick, but she knew how to give a bloke a hard-on. Lee put his hands on her waist to guide her as she rose and fell on his erection. When they'd finished and were laying on his bed smoking post-sex fags she said, 'That's set me up for a few weeks. Ta, darling.'

He smiled. Then noticing that her cigarette had a long and precarious piece of ash on the end he said, 'Don't get it on . . .'

'The duvet. I know,' Vi said as she flicked it off into an ashtray on the bedside cabinet. 'I know you, remember? Like no one else.'

She did. As well as being occasional lovers, 'fuck buddies' as Vi liked to put it, they'd worked together for ten years when Lee had been in the Met. Also, long ago, she'd saved him from himself. The First Gulf War had left Lee Arnold a wreck. Addicted to booze and painkillers, he'd been on the road to self-destruction until Vi had turned up one day with a cage containing a mynah bird. As she'd handed it over to him, she'd said, 'You might want to kill yourself, but this poor innocent sod doesn't deserve to die. Look after him.'

The bird, who Lee named Chronus, hadn't been the prettiest pet on the block but he was bright and had very quickly learnt all of Lee's favourite West Ham United songs and team lists. He also, just by his presence, made Lee clean up his act. Although the fags remained, the booze and the drugs went. But at a price. Lee Arnold spent at least four hours every day cleaning his small flat in Forest Gate. Nightmares about Saddam Hussein's Republican Guard had been replaced as the enemy by dust.

But although, as ever, mindful that Vi could be sloppy with her fags, Lee wasn't thinking about dust as he lay next to her, naked, staring at the ceiling. His mind was still on Abbas al'Barri. Absolutely convinced that his son was reaching out from the heart of ISIS-controlled Syrian territories, Abbas was a man in torment. What he wanted, which was for Fayyad to come home in one piece, was almost impossible. Occasionally someone managed to escape, but those people were always under suspicion, which Lee could understand. However horrific the methods used by ISIS were, recruits to their cause had still gone to them knowing, and approving, of their philosophy. Runaways were watched by the security services, probably, in many cases, with good cause.

Like Abbas, however, Lee was intrigued by the Tooth of Jonah's Whale. It was the sort of thing the ISIS boys would automatically destroy. Anything that could be considered even remotely idolatrous was either smashed up or, if it was worth something, flogged to some greedy collector online. Had Fayyad sent the tooth to his parents for old times' sake? If he had, he wasn't a very good ISIS member. And what, if anything, did his appearance on Facebook so quickly after sending the tooth home mean? If anything? Was he 'reaching out' or was he simply trying to reel in young female recruits using his good looks and big muscles as bait? And why was Lee even thinking about it, anyway? He'd told Abbas he couldn't and wouldn't help him and he'd advised him to go to the police. He looked at Vi who appeared to be sleeping. Should he tell her?

Lee knew why he was thinking about Abbas and that was because, as Abbas himself had pointed out, he owed him. The Iraqi translator had taken a bullet in the leg for his British soldier friend and Lee knew that, even now, the nerve damage it had caused troubled him. It wasn't the only reason that Abbas drank, that had all started when he'd got himself banged up in one of Saddam's prisons in the 1980s, but that catastrophic leg wound hadn't helped.

'You're very quiet, Arnold,' Vi said. 'Penny for 'em.'

She always knew when he was worried about something. She usually knew when he was keeping something from her. Even her own DS, Tony Bracci, called her a fortune teller. It's what her Gypsy mum had been.

Lee knew he should tell her about Abbas. Protocols existed to deal with these situations, protocols that were there for a reason. But he was hesitating and he knew he was doing that for a reason. Coppers, even the exalted graduate types who tended to drift towards sexy jobs like homicide and counterterrorism, sometimes got it wrong. Sometimes people who weren't villains got banged up, sometimes people, whether innocent or guilty, died. None of it was, usually, deliberate. The coppers were under pressure for results and shit happened. But shit couldn't happen to Fayyad al'Barri. When the family had finally managed to get out of Iraq in '92, Lee had gone to Heathrow to meet them. He still remembered the sight of Fayyad solemnly carrying his one precious possession, which had been a Frisbee. It was all the ten-year-old had left. Djamila, his eight-year-old sister, had run into 'uncle' Lee's arms but Fayyad had held himself aloof. He'd already been too damaged by war to risk outward shows of affection. But over the years Fayyad had learnt to smile again and, when he'd left to join ISIS, it had come as a shock to everyone, including Lee. Fayyad couldn't be put at risk, he was too precious.

And Lee Arnold owed his father. He looked at Vi and said, 'I'm alright.'

It was nearly midnight when the front doorbell rang. Shazia was asleep. Mumtaz felt a tiny jolt of fear. The old man had agreed to wait until Shazia had finished her A levels before coming to formally make his disgusting proposal. That was still three months away.

She spoke into the intercom. 'Who is it?'

'Lee.'

She let out a shaky breath and buzzed him in.

Mumtaz made 'English' tea with milk, which they drank in her darkened garden so that Lee could smoke. He told her everything about Abbas al'Barri, his family and his son Fayyad.

'Seems it's normal for these ISIS fighters to go online and use their well-developed pecs as bait,' he said.

'I've heard of such things, yes,' Mumtaz said. 'I know several ladies who are worried about their daughters. Not clients, just people I see around. The Internet, useful though it is, has some lethal downsides.'

Lee looked at his glowing fag end. 'Shopping,' he said.

'Shopping?'

'Being a bit glib, I s'pose, but Jodie's racked up over a grand's worth of debt online shopping,' he said. 'So her mother tells me.'

Lee's daughter Jodie lived with his ex-wife in Hastings. To Lee's horror the nineteen-year-old was, like her mother, interested in little beyond shopping, tanning and celebrities.

'You're not going to pay it off, I hope,' Mumtaz said.

'Couldn't even if I wanted to.' He smoked. Then he said, 'If I pose as some little Muslim girl already in love with the idea of sodding off to the caliphate and marrying a fighter . . .'

'You'll never get away with it,' Mumtaz said. 'On Facebook you might just get away with it. But, from what I've heard, these men want to see what they're buying before they buy it.'

'Buy?'

'It's a figure of speech,' she said. 'They want to know what these prospective brides look like. They want to be sure they're not too old or scarred, fat or have, I don't know, big noses or something. They want young, pretty women they can breed with. So they use Skype.'

'Fayyad is on Facebook.'

'Yes and if a girl with a pretty photo on her page contacts him then he'll want to Skype her,' she said. 'And even if you cover and say you're way too religious to show your face on Skype, your voice and your size will give you away.'

'So I have to find a girl . . .'

'A woman,' Mumtaz said. 'Girls are way too vulnerable. Spending time inside the head of a man who, even if he is now a reluctant terrorist, may have killed people, is not something with which a girl could cope. The police have people who will be able to do this sort of thing.'

'I know,' he said. 'But Abbas doesn't trust them. And he's sick, in his head. I've never seen him so bad. He thinks they'll do so many checks to make sure they're not being duped that they'll lose him. And that may happen.'

'And it may not,' she said. She paused. 'But I know that in your awkward, round the bushes British way, you're asking me if I'll help you and I will.'

'No.'

'Yes. I know you owe Abbas your life and I owe you.'

'You owe me nothing,' he said. 'I haven't done anything. Not yet.'

'But you will,' Mumtaz said. 'You will speak to my brother Ali and persuade him to change his ways and I know you're gathering intelligence on the Sheikhs.'

'I—'

'I've seen your files!' she said. 'Don't try to tell me you're doing nothing!'

He didn't. He just sat.

Having beggared her for her husband's gambling debts, the local crime family, the Sheikhs, were now coming for Shazia. Although the girl hadn't killed him, Shazia had been with the family's favourite son when he'd been stabbed. She hadn't known that it was Naz who had killed her father, but she had been aware that he had been taking money from Mumtaz. And so in spite of the fact that Naz had been killed by a Pole employed by a rival Asian gang, because Shazia had been at the scene, Sheikh family honour had to be satisfied. This was to be done by Mumtaz giving Shazia in marriage to the current head of the Sheikh family, seventy-year-old Wahid. If she failed to deliver the girl when she finished her A levels the Sheikhs would inform the police on Mumtaz's brother, Ali, who was giving shelter to radicalised young men in his house on Brick Lane. Lee had offered to help. But what he didn't know was that Mumtaz and Shazia had more in common than he thought. Even Shazia didn't know that her precious stepmother had watched her father bleed to death when Naz Sheikh had stabbed him. In that moment, she'd had enough. The Sheikhs had never let her forget that or the idea that they could tell Shazia her secret any time they wanted.

'I don't want you to do this,' Lee said as he lit another cigarette. 'You've enough on.'

She ignored him. 'So this Abbas and his wife,' she said. 'What do they do? Do they work?'

'Abbas works for the BBC Arabic service, Shereen teaches maths.'

Mumtaz leant back into her chair and looked into the candle flame on the patio table.

'I saw when ISIS blew up the Mosque of Jonah on the news,' she said. 'Whatever one may feel about relics they have value for a lot of people. Whether they are genuine or not is almost immaterial. People make an emotional investment in such things and it is that which makes them meaningful.'

'With your psychology grad's head on,' Lee said. 'What about as a Muslim? How'd you feel about the Tooth of Jonah's Whale with that hat on?'

She shrugged. 'The al'Barris are Shia, I am Sunni. We are more austere in our relationship to buildings, tombs, relics. But some amazingly ornate monuments are Sunni and we do revere the inanimate. What is the Holy Kaab'a in Mecca if not an object of veneration? Ordinary Sunni people have no problem with any of this. Difficulties arise with people like ISIS who have this notion that any form of man-made structure, any artefact that is revered is an abomination. Their caliphate, as I perceive it, should it come into being, will be a twelfth-century environment with selective modern graft-ons like mobile phones, modern weapons and the Internet. Without those things they couldn't survive, which is, of course, one of their great weaknesses.'

'So what are their strengths?' Lee asked.

She thought for a moment and then she said, 'Their ability to get inside people's heads. The message ISIS sends is uncompromising and takes no prisoners. It is sure, it is certain and there is great comfort in it.'

'Comfort?'

'Yes,' she said. 'Any kind of certainty is comforting. What ISIS offers is right and wrong, heaven and hell with no ambiguity. Break the rules and you will die both here on earth and in heaven. But do everything we tell you and we guarantee you will have dominion over all others and you'll go to heaven too. What's not to like?'

THREE

'Rajiv-ji!'

For a moment the tall, leather-clad man kept on walking. As one of the few Hindu traders on Brick Lane as well as being the only openly gay man, Rajiv Banergee was deaf to any sort of approach on the street. And even though the caller had addressed him politely, Rajiv spat back a venomous 'fuck off!' just in case. But when he did turn around he saw a friendly face and he blushed.

'Oh, Baharat-ji!' he said. 'I do apologise for my language! I am so, so sorry.'

The old man, Baharat Huq, smiled. 'You get a lot of unwanted attention, Rajiv-ji,' he said. 'I would do exactly the same myself if I had to put up with these terrible boys round here.'

'Them?' he laughed. 'They're a joke, Baharat-ji. I don't worry about them.'

He looked at a small group of teenage boys wearing shalwar khameez and kufis. Some of them he recognised as members of a street gang known as the Briks Boyz. All of Pakistani and Bangladeshi heritage, they fancied themselves as guardians of

31

Muslim pride in the Spitalfields area. In reality they were at best anodyne, at worst, thuggish.

'Rajiv-ji, I wanted to speak to you,' Baharat said.

'Oh.' He frowned. 'Nothing bad, I hope.'

The old man smiled. 'Don't worry,' he said.

Rajiv brightened. 'Oh well, come to the shop,' he said. 'I'll get my boys to make tea.'

Rajiv had inherited the Leather Bungalow from his father when the old man had died back in the 1980s. Back then Rajiv had cross-dressed with pride, but now although still as slim as a whip, he contented himself with a little eyeliner, some mascara and an assortment of large, very dressy rings. The world had changed and, to Rajiv's way of thinking, for the worse.

Sitting in the dingy little office at the back of the leather shop, the two men made idle gossip until one of Rajiv's assistants brought them tea. Once the boy had gone the old man said, 'Rajiv-ji, I understand from my friend, Mr Berman . . .'

'Ah, Lionel, yes.'

'I understand from him that yesterday you were abused in this your own shop by a boy who is currently staying with my son, Ali.'

'One of the Arab boys?'

'Yes.'

Rajiv laughed. 'Oh, yes. He put his head around the door and shouted "Faggot". Then he ran away. It was pathetic. Actually it would have been funny if Lionel hadn't been so upset about it.'

'Yes, well I too am upset about it,' Baharat said. 'And I wish to apologise. Ali will not, as you know. I have told and told that boy that what he is doing with these riff-raff he takes in is not in any way advancing the cause of Islam, but he takes no notice. I tell him, real Muslims do not persecute any creature, human or animal. But he continues with this, excuse me, shit, about my being taken in

32

by "Zionist lies". One day the police will come for him. I know it! How can a man have two such wonderful children in Asif and Mumtaz and then such a ridiculous boy like Ali?'

Rajiv shrugged. He didn't have any children, what did he know? But he did like Baharat's daughter, Mumtaz. In an attempt to change the subject, he asked after her.

'Still working as a detective,' the old man answered proudly. 'And her stepdaughter is doing very well with her A levels. She will go to university. I tell you, Rajiv-ji, it is a good job that girl has my daughter as her mother. That waste of space, her father, put the child into a private school and forgot about her. Mumtaz takes an interest. But then, she is a clever girl.'

'She always was, Baharat-ji.'

'Indeed. Worth ten, no, a hundred of that vile trickster I gave her to.' He shook his head. 'There are days, you know, Rajiv-ji, I find it hard to live with myself. My Mumtaz has endured such hardships because of that man! And you know, sin though it is, I am happy that Ahmet Hakim is dead. May God forgive me.'

Uncomfortable with 'God talk' Rajiv again changed the subject. 'Well you tell Mumtaz and Shazia to come in when they visit you next time,' he said. 'If the little one is going to university she will need a nice stylish jacket. I see all the smart girls wearing leather bombers these days. And no charge, Baharat-ji.'

'Ah, but—'

'No, it will be my pleasure,' Rajiv said. 'Truly. Only cost will be a chat with the lovely Mumtaz.'

It was only when Baharat looked closely that he saw the shadow of a bruise on Rajiv's right cheek, underneath his foundation.

He wasn't her type. Mumtaz had never been attracted to musclemen and Fayyad al'Barri was clearly muscle-bound. She preferred thin, aquiline men, like her late husband, like Lee Arnold. Also, Fayyad had a wispy beard that he'd dyed red. A lot of the ultra-religious men did that. But in spite of that, she could see why people would find him handsome. He had full lips, almost like a girl's and the most soulful, large green eyes. Predictably his profile was an exercise in bragging. He was a 'warrior', a 'sword of God' and 'fearless'. His life was exciting, meaningful and 'almost perfect'. The only thing he lacked was a pious, obedient wife who would give him a lot of lion-like sons and daughters whose beauty would only be matched by their chastity.

Mumtaz looked away from the screen and said, 'Yuck.'

Lee laughed.

'This guy could get a degree in self-aggrandisement,' she said. 'The kind of woman he wants is a cipher.'

'Then that is what poor little Mishal must be,' Lee said.

Abbas al'Barri had come to the office that morning. Delighted that Lee had changed his mind about helping to, hopefully, get Fayyad home, he'd hardly listened to the list of conditions his friend had put on the operation. Lee was sure that Abbas still didn't know that if Mumtaz felt threatened at any time she'd be able to just stop it. And that was a real possibility.

It had been once Abbas had gone that they'd come up with the name Mishal for their phoney jihadi bride-in-waiting. On the basis that it was about the youngest that Mumtaz could pull off convincingly, they'd decided that Mishal was eighteen. Like Mumtaz, of Bangladeshi heritage, she lived with her parents and two brothers on Brick Lane where her father worked as a minicab driver. It was important to keep as many details as possible close to Mumtaz's own life story. That way she was less likely to make mistakes in her conversations with Fayyad.

Although ideally they would have wanted her to have an

arranged marriage, Mishal's parents didn't approve of coercion and were happy to consider any suitable young man she may suggest. Mishal found that very disappointing.

'They're being affected by the beliefs of the non-Muslims around them,' Mumtaz said.

'Mishal doesn't approve.'

'She's tried to talk to them about it but she finds challenging authority difficult,' Mumtaz said.

'Mmm. That's good. Showing disapproval for their outlandish beliefs but also respecting them because they're her parents.'

'Fayyad, or rather Abu Imad, to use his jihadi name, will expect her to transfer that kind of loyalty to him,' Mumtaz said. 'He'll reel her in because she's questioning her parents' authority – her dad also takes the odd beer – she's hormonal, she's studious and quite lonely. She has recently started to break her parents' rules, however, by going on Facebook.'

'So we'll have to give her "friends" or she'll have no "profile". Christ, I sound as if I know what I'm talking about!'

'Yes, but kids are quite indiscriminate about who they "friend",' Mumtaz said. 'I can "friend" a clutch of Shazia's distant acquaintances in the certain knowledge they will reciprocate even though they have no idea who Mishal might be.'

Lee sighed. 'That's so weird to me.' Then he asked, 'Does she cover her head?'

'Yes, but only in the same way I do. She'd like to go further but she's worried about what her parents might think. She may well change into niqab when she goes to college.'

'Does that happen?'

'Yes,' Mumtaz said. 'And in the other direction too. Girls from pious families uncover when they get to college. Shazia has got two friends who do that. One of them has a Lithuanian boyfriend.

Lee, do you know anything about Fayyad's interests? If Mishal is going to make contact with him, then he has to find her, doesn't he? I mean if she contacts him he may well become suspicious.'

'He's the one touting for a bride.'

'I know, but I think that if he can find her online that will be a lot more convincing than if she contacts him.'

It was a good point. But it would take time. Also, were he in fact reaching out, it may be time they didn't have.

Lee hadn't seen Fayyad for at least five years. He said, 'He was always a big Hammers fan. I don't know whether that all went out the window when he got religion. And would a girl like Mishal be into football? Wouldn't it be a bit undignified for her to be looking at all those men's knees?'

'Her father is a fan,' Mumtaz said. 'She was brought up with the Hammers. She is enormously loyal to the team. But her devotion does give her problems. Only God should be worshipped and Mishal feels that she should really drop her interest in football because she fears it may be sinful.'

Lee shook his head.

'I know it's weird,' she said. 'But this is how radicalisation, be it Islamist or some other form of brainwashing, works. Gradually the "victim" is distanced from whatever makes her herself until only the ideology is left. If Fayyad is actually trying to make contact with a view to coming home, he will respond to mention of West Ham. It'll probably be negative, for the sake of his ISIS masters, but it may well mark Mishal out from other potential brides.'

'As well as her photograph,' Lee said.

Mumtaz put a hand up to her head. 'Oh, I'd forgotten about that.'

'I don't know how you do modest but sexy . . .'

'Oh, not sexy! No!' she said. 'God, will I be attractive enough for him . . .'

'If you're not then he must've lost his mind . . .'

'Be serious!' she said. 'And will he believe I'm eighteen? Lee, I am thirty-four! That is geriatric for these people!'

'Yeah, but you can do younger. I think.'

'But eighteen? God, this is madness! What am I doing?'

'You don't have to do anything,' Lee said. 'We'll stop it. I'll do it. I'll—'

'You can't!' she said. 'And you won't!'

He said nothing. They sat in silence, stumped by their own fears. However much Lee felt that he owed Abbas, this was proving too hard. It was also potentially dangerous both psychologically and, possibly, physically. ISIS killed people and their reach was long. But then he remembered something.

He said, 'Photography.'

'Yes, it's a problem,' Mumtaz said. 'We know that.'

'Yes, but it could also be another way in,' Lee replied.

He hadn't even tried. Shereen threw the graffiti-spattered homework book on the floor. 'Suk my Cock', 'Ass-Fuck' – it wasn't even good graffiti. Juvenile and boring. But Shereen knew that the author was far from being a child. Harrison Yates at fifteen was the product of an alcoholic mother, an absent father and a life hanging around the periphery of street gangs, none of whom would accept him. He was one of only five white British boys in Year 10 and he was about to become a father. Why should he bother with his maths homework?

She looked at the photograph of Fayyad she kept on her desk. She touched it. That was the real Fayyad; beardless, smiling. As soon as they'd arrived in London everything had gone right for that boy. Of course, he'd put the time in to master the language and get to university, but he'd worked at getting in with the right people at school and had made brilliant friends who would have stayed with him for life had he not gone off to join ISIS. Shereen still saw Dwayne who had become a plumber as well as 'Mo' Mohammed who was married and had two little daughters. Nice, normal boys who had done well for themselves. Why had he rejected them? And for what? What had happened to the boy who had once dreamt of being an officer in the British Army?

Shereen picked Harrison Yates's book up off the floor and wrote 'See me' where his homework should have been. If he even turned up to her class it would be a miracle. Why would he when most of the other boys in his set didn't bother? These days Shereen seemed to teach almost exclusively girls. Sometimes every head in her class was covered. She knew that as long as the girls were happy, it didn't matter. But Shereen was still at heart a part of Saddam Hussein's Iraq which, for all its faults, had allowed women to choose how they dressed. She had never covered and neither had her mother. Covering, in Shereen's head, was something your grandmother did.

She looked at the clock. It was almost five, which meant that she had just over an hour to finish marking and organise dinner. Layla was going out with her friends and so it would just be Abbas, Hasan and her. She went to the fridge to see what she could assemble with ease, when there was a knock on the front door.

'That's my mother's garden.'

Mumtaz thought that it looked more like a patio. Plants she couldn't identify grew in pots and old oil drums while, in the middle of the space, an attractive woman in a sundress sat beside a fountain.

'And that's my mother,' Shereen said. 'She was a biologist.'

She could have been almost anything. Italian, Spanish, Portuguese.

38

'Fayyad liked photography too?'

'When he and Djamila were little, I used to take them with me every time I went out with my camera,' Shereen said.

'Portraiture.'

'I always liked that,' she said. 'Black and white medium was my favourite. And you know that on the Nineveh Plain we had such a wide range of subjects. We had tattooed nomads, Kurds, Assyrian Christians, Yezidis.'

She showed Mumtaz a photograph of an old woman whose face was so wrinkled and sun-blasted it looked like oak. She wore the most extraordinary earrings in her long, stretched lobes. They appeared to be bundles of coins.

'That lady was the wife of a Yezidi sheikh,' Shereen said. 'She believed that photographs stole people's souls. But she let Fayyad take her picture. He was eight years old. A long time before he decided that he wanted to work in banking, he wanted to be a photographer and, for a while, a soldier. I always encouraged him. Photography is what I would have done had my life gone differently. When he left, we had not talked about photography for years.'

Mumtaz looked at Lee. He'd brought her to the al'Barris' home when he'd remembered Shereen's photography. In spite of their strictures against the deification of images, ISIS fighters liked photography. There was, it seemed, nothing they enjoyed more than photographing each other, the land they conquered and their victims. All for the purpose of propaganda. An interest in photography could well single Mumtaz/Mishal out from the other girls intent upon catching the eye of Abu Imad.

'Why do you need to know about my photographs?' Shereen asked.

He'd had two reasons. But he told her just one.

39

'You're so good, I wondered if you'd take some shots of Mumtaz,' he said.

Coming to Shereen wasn't ideal, the less she and her family knew about how they planned to make contact with Fayyad the better, but Mumtaz was nervous about her ability to look eighteen and Lee knew that if anyone could help her do that, it was Shereen.

'Of course,' she said.

She didn't ask what for, but of course she knew. Lee said, 'An innocent look, you know?'

'I know,' Shereen said. Then she smiled. 'You know, Fayyad never brought a girl home here to meet us. When I think of that, it makes me sad.'

It was *Fight Club*. He'd grown up with that film, he knew that. He was well aware of the 'rules'.

Brick Lane was less than a mile from the sky-piercing tower where he worked making unimaginable amounts of money for people already so rich they didn't notice the odd billion either way. He'd met a few. When he'd first started with Vanek Brothers he'd wanted to become one. But then, in spite of the amazing salary he earned, and the bonuses, Amir Charleston began to come to the conclusion that he was unhappy.

As he jogged past Spitalfields Market, he saw a few faces he recognised from work, one or two he vaguely recalled from Eton. But they didn't notice him in his black Club R.W.R. T-shirt and shorts. He could have been any one of any number of high-functioning private equity fund managers out for a power-run. And that was good. Because had he been recognised he might also have been followed. Only by colleagues. But he didn't even want them to know what he was doing. This was his thing.

Amir turned down Fournier Street, past the Ten Bells pub and

40

into the streets of old Huguenot houses that had once characterised almost all of Spitalfields. But the houses didn't interest him. Headed to Brick Lane and beyond, Amir had an appointment with the only thing in his life that was making any sense to him. The only thing that was making him happy.

Rajiv grabbed Ali Huq's sleeve.

'This isn't you,' he said.

Ali Huq squirmed as he tried to pull away.

'What happened to you, eh?' Rajiv said.

Under his breath the younger man said, 'Get off me, pervert!'

Rajiv shook his head. 'I know you, remember,' he said. 'Why have you turned against your friends? Your family?'

'That's none of your business.'

'It is my business if I get this,' he pointed to the bruise under his eye, 'from one of those boys you allow to stay in your house.'

Ali said nothing. He was a tall, good-looking man of forty whose once smiling face was now almost always frowning.

'I don't know whether those Arabs you've taken in are here legally or not,' Rajiv said. 'And frankly I don't give a shit. I also don't give a shit about what they believe or where they're from. The only thing that bothers me is what they do. That little bastard with the birthmark on his face punched me when I was on my way home. I know it was him because earlier in the day he'd stuck his head round the shop door and called me a faggot.'

'If you don't behave appropriately . . .'

'Appropriately!' Rajiv said. 'This, from you! Listen to yourself! I'm not one of you, I can do what I like. And your dad knows about the "faggot" incident. He came to apologise to me. I didn't tell him about the punch, though. We don't grass each other up here. But I expect you to put a stop to it. Those fuckers are hassling girls on

41

the street. And they are serious. Not like the Briks Boyz, I can deal with them. Sort it out!'

'Or you'll do what?' Ali said.

'I don't know,' Rajiv said. 'Come round your house and put shit through your letter box? Who knows? But I tell you one thing, Ali-ji, you don't want to get on the wrong side of a furious tranny. There are laws to protect us these days. And if they don't work, we can have the loosest lips in town.'

Ali Huq's face reddened.

FOUR

'This is mine.'

He put his hand on the bonnet of the armoured car and smiled.

'By the Grace of God captured from Assad's thugs. Now a tool of the Caliphate, inshallah.'

Abbas al'Barri looked blearily at his wife and his daughter and said, 'I haven't got time for this. I have to get to work.'

'This is our son!' Shereen pointed at the laptop open on the kitchen table. 'Look at him!'

Drunk again the previous night, Abbas tried to concentrate. Fayyad looked like a younger version of Abbas's late father, who had been a goatherd.

'What is this?' Shereen asked her daughter.

The young woman, Djamila, closed the laptop and put it in her bag. 'YouTube,' she said. 'ISIS vids are all over it.'

'YouTube? Why can't they shut it down?'

'Abbas, it's the Internet,' Shereen said. 'It just is. Nobody can control it.'

Abbas al'Barri looked at his daughter. 'How did you find it?'

'He's my brother, Dad,' she said. 'I look for him. It isn't hard.'

'Hah!'

'I have to go to work now,' she said. She left.

Abbas looked at his wife and said, 'I will ring Lee.'

There was so much blood that, at first, Doris thought that it had to be red paint. She told Stan.

'Last week bloody Chinese takeaway up the wall, now this,' she said.

She wheeled him down the passage to the front door. He liked to sit in the sunshine.

Doris went into her small front garden. 'All up the gate!' she said.

They lived in a council house at the top end of Brick Lane, as it turned into the Boundary Estate. Long ago, Stan had lived in one of the Huguenot houses in Princelet Street. His dad had rented two rooms, which had just about accommodated all eight members of the family. There'd been rats and fleas and Stan had been made to go to Hebrew school but he remembered it with love. Back then he'd been able to walk . . .

'Oh and look, Stan, some little sod's left his bleedin' jacket on the path, all covered in it!'

She went out into the street. 'How am I going to clean all this up for Gawd's sake?'

Stan said, 'Call the council. They're the landlord, let 'em work for the rent for once.'

And so she did. She said there was red stuff all over her gate and on a leather jacket dumped on the pavement. They said that the police would be with them as soon as they could. Seemed like a bit of an overreaction to Doris. They didn't explain why.

Bob ticked off the East End stereotypes in his head. Boozer waving a two-litre bottle of White Lightning and stinking of piss, hipster with a green beard wearing a deerstalker, yummy mummy holding her infant in a baby sling looking anxious, lots of Asian men, staring.

DI Montalban had told him to 'move those fuckers out the way', which Bob had done. But they'd all come back. They always did.

The body had been found around 3 a.m. by a young advertising exec rolling home to his funky Arnold Circus apartment after a heavy night at some rooftop bar in Shoreditch. The sight of a dead body with its face stamped to a pulp on the old Arnold Circus bandstand in the middle of the Boundary Estate had caused the adman to bring up yesterday's bento box, which still lay beside a wooden bench next to the tent SOCO had erected over the stiff. Now they'd just got a call from the council to say that a tenant in one of their Brick Lane properties had phoned to let them know there was a leather jacket lying on the pavement outside her house. Rajiv-ji had never gone anywhere without his leather jacket.

Like DI Ricky Montalban, Constable Babar 'Bob' Khan had been born and bred on Brick Lane. As a kid he'd been fascinated by the exotic, and some said dangerous, owner of the Leather Bungalow. With his eyeliner, his flashy rings and his slim, leather-clad body, Rajiv Banergee had been like a being from another world amid the uniform shalwar khameez that dominated the Bangla Town end of the Lane. Bob's dad had hated Rajiv, claiming, on no evidence at all, that he was a bad influence on children. But Bob was pretty sure his old man hadn't got so far as murder. Sadly, though, he knew plenty of men who might have taken that path.

Montalban, a dark, heavy-set man in his late thirties, walked over to the staring Asian men and said something that made them scatter. The yummy mummy too took fright.

'What was that about, guv?' Bob said when Montalban came and stood next to him.

'A bit of gentle persuasion.'

Montalban's dad had come from what remained of the small group of Spaniards who had once lived at the top end of Brick Lane. He'd been called Felipe and, even in old age, everyone had been afraid of him. Bob's dad truly believed a story that had been around all Bob's life about Felipe Montalban punching rats the size of cats to death in the dark days of the 1970s. Back then, when everyone in Spitalfields had been poor, not only rats but also white supremacists had walked Brick Lane. Bob's dad said that Asians got their heads kicked in regularly in those days. Now in the twenty-first century, here was another Asian, dead with his head smashed in.

'So, Bob, son, think the Briks Boyz are up to doing this?'

Bob, at only twenty-four, knew the eighteen-year-old leader of the local street gang. Vicious but pathetic, like all of them.

'The Boyz are little shits . . .'

'Little shits who don't like anyone who isn't like them, yeah,' Montalban said. 'Give 'em a tug, Mr Khan. A hard one.'

'I've no idea what'll happen if you "like" it,' Lee said. 'Maybe nothing. He may not even notice. But if you press that button then Mishal is committed.'

Mumtaz's finger hovered over her mouse button.

'I know.' But she still paused. Then she said, 'Lee, are the al'Barris paying us?'

He sighed.

'They're not, are they?'

'No,' he said. 'But it's not because I'm doing my mates a favour. Or rather it is, but there's another reason, which is that the coppers should be involved.'

'I know.'

'But Abbas is on the edge and so if we can somehow work out what Fayyad is really up to maybe we can make the coppers aware of it and, at the same time, stop any bad things happening.'

'Like what?'

'Like Abbas drinking himself to death or sodding off to Syria.'

'I thought you said that Abbas felt he couldn't get involved?'

'Not online, but if he carries on thinking about that tooth and what it might mean, in the end he won't be able to stand it any more and he'll go out to Syria himself. His drinking's off the fucking scale, we have to stall him at the very least. What we can't do is profit by it. If the coppers do find out, they could finish us. We'd lose our ABI memberships, we'd be unemployed. I should've done this speech before but . . . Look better or worse, I'll do it on me own . . .'

'No!'

'You know we're up to our necks in process serving . . .'

Mumtaz's phone rang. She looked at the screen.

'It's my dad. Can I take it?'

'Course.'

'Abba . . .'

To Lee her conversation was just a rattle of unintelligible Bengali sounds. She rarely spoke her parents' language. He got up to go out and have a fag and leave her to it. But then, as her conversation progressed, he saw that she had tears in her eyes. He sat down again.

When she'd finished, he said, 'What's the matter? You need to go home?'

Mumtaz shook her head.

Lee wanted to comfort her but he didn't know how. He let her recover herself. She wiped her eyes. Then she said, 'I apologise, Lee.'

'No problem.'

She put a hand on her chest. 'A family friend has died,' she said.

'I'm really sorry.'

'A man called Rajiv, a Hindu. He ran a leather shop. He's been in Brick Lane forever. Abba just told me that the police found his body this morning. He was beaten and stabbed to death.'

'On Brick Lane?'

'In Arnold Circus,' she said.

'That's all yummy families and trust fund artists these days, isn't it?'

'Mainly, yes,' she said. 'But that doesn't mean the local thugs don't hang out there too. Crazy jihadi kids who hate everyone. Rajiv was homosexual, flamboyant. He has been threatened many times. Most recently by those boys my brother takes in.'

'Oh.'

In spite of himself Lee speculated about how the questioning of Ali Huq's guests could pull the rug out from under the Sheikh family's plans to use her brother's extremist tendencies to get their hands on Shazia. If the police were made aware of the boys Ali had given shelter to, perhaps that particular problem would go away.

'Abba doesn't want to go to the police, but feels that he has to. We don't grass,' she said.

'No.'

'No, but we also don't let down our friends. Rajiv was a dear man. God will not be happy with his death.'

'Mumtaz . . .'

'I told Abba I will go to the police,' she said.

She was very pale and didn't look right. Lee said, 'Are you sure? I could—'

'No.' She stood. 'I should have alerted the police to what Ali was doing a long time ago. I can't leave it any longer. A good man has died and I could've prevented it.'

48

'You don't know that,' Lee said. 'This might have nothing to do with your brother.'

'And it also might,' she said. Then she pressed the 'Like' button on the YouTube clip.

'There,' she said, 'Mishal likes that crap that Abu Imad spouts, she thinks it's inspiring.' She pressed the share icon. 'And she wants the world to see how fit he is.'

Then her legs became wobbly and she sat down. Then she cried.

Bob had Sultan Ibrahim's number. Sixteen, overweight and sullen, the boy was the pampered only child of pious, well-meaning parents who thought that the sun shone out of his arse. His expensive 'street' gear – hoodie, Nike trackie bottoms and massive white trainers – made him look soft, which wasn't the idea. Sultan, although near the top of the Briks Boyz hierarchy, wasn't a player, mainly because he was fat. But he always had money, which was why the Boyz let him hang with them. Whether the Boyz also knew that Sultan was, potentially, their weakest link, Bob Khan didn't know, but he hoped they didn't. And he hoped that he was right.

Sultan sat between his enormous mother and etiolated father on a vast royal blue sofa. His father, Parvez, was well beyond retirement age and shook. Maybe he had Parkinson's? Poor sod looked as if he was about to drop. Not that he spoke.

'My boy is a good boy,' Mrs Ibrahim said. 'People are jealous. That's the truth of it. They make things up about my son because he has the best of everything.'

It wasn't easy. Even though Bob didn't have any sort of connection with the Ibrahims he didn't feel able to just say *Look! Your kid's a shit who runs with a gang of little bastards who give people grief!*

Instead he said, 'Sultan, I need to know where you were last night.'

'Last night!' his mother said. 'He's a child! Where do you think he was? In his bed!'

'With respect, Mrs Ibrahim, I need Sultan to tell me.'

At least the Ibrahims spoke English. Bob's Bengali was shit.

'Well?'

The boy didn't even look at him. 'It's as Amma said. I was here,' he said.

'Why do you want to know?' Mrs Ibrahim said. 'You think my son had something to do with the death of that hijra?'

News travelled fast in Bangla Town.

'I'm not at liberty to talk about the crime that was committed last night,' Bob said. 'But I can assure you that no transgender person was involved.'

'Rajiv Banergee was hijra!'

Bob ignored her. Although born and bred on Brick Lane, Mrs Ibrahim was the kind of woman who liked to live as if she was a moralistic grande dame in some Sylheti village back in the 1960s. Not for her the new Muslim radicalism, rather a brand of old-fashioned bigotry rooted deep in the village culture of Bangladesh where the 'hijra' or cross-dresser was a figure of contempt and abuse.

'Sultan, I know you run with the Briks Boyz,' Bob said.

Mrs Ibrahim's face flushed. 'Briks what? What are you talking about, Officer? What is this idiocy . . .'

'Prove it,' Sultan muttered.

'I don't have to prove it,' Bob said. 'I've seen you. Hassling girls on the street, shouting obscenities at shopkeepers not halal enough for you, writing racist graffiti, homophobic graffiti . . .'

'I'm a Muslim,' Sultan said.

'Yes,' Bob said. 'Which is why you shouldn't do such things.'

'We are persecuted.'

'Everyone's persecuted,' Bob said. 'You're doing better than most. As your mother has pointed out, you have everything. Just tell me where you were last night.'

'I was—'

'And before you just say "here" again, let me tell you that if I'm not satisfied with what you tell me, I can take you down the station.'

Mrs Ibrahim fanned her face, 'Allah!'

Everyone in the flats must have seen Constable Khan arrive. If they then saw him leave with Sultan and his parents, what on earth were they going to think?

'I ain't done nuffink . . .'

'Speak properly, for God's sake!'

The boy visibly trembled. It was the first time his old man had spoken.

'You are neither a cockney nor are you from the Caribbean,' Mr Ibrahim said. He looked at Bob. 'Elocution lessons I pay for! Why?'

'Abba, I was in, you know—'

'I do not!' the old man said. He pointed at his wife. 'You say he will grow out of it, my wife, but so far he is not.'

'Parvez-ji . . .'

'You prattle about how this idiot does what he does because he is such a good, pious boy!' Mrs Ibrahim began to cry. Her husband addressed Bob. 'I know it is Rajiv-ji that has died,' he said. 'I never knew him, but what I do know is that taking any life is wrong. My son was out last night, Constable. Between eleven and midnight. In spite of his great fat belly he gets out of his bedroom window on many nights to go and be with that Chaudhuri boy.'

Zayn Chaudhuri was the Boyz uncrowned emperor. At eighteen he was older than the rest of the crew. He was also vicious, prejudiced and venal. Zayn was known to all the local coppers. Many of them had also had the pleasure of meeting his crackhead of a father. His mother, a white girl originally from Norwich, had buggered off years ago, leaving her son to stew in his own resentment about being both half English and the son of an unbelieving crackhead. Zayn had eventually resolved this existential crisis by creating his own version of fundamentalist Islam via the medium of a street gang. It attracted every disaffected kid in the area. Zayn had God and he knew the word 'sharia' and he had a knife. He also said it was OK to rob people who weren't Muslims – and some who were.

'Daddy-ji!'

Sultan began to cry. Had Bob suspected that the kid was the Boyz weakest link, just because he was fat? He didn't like to think so. But then again he knew he was kidding himself.

The old man leant across and raised a shaking hand in front of the boy's face. Then he slapped him.

'Mummy's boy!' he said. 'Stupid, spoilt, mummy's boy!'

'Ricky Montalban's on it,' Vi said. 'Took over from Kev Thorpe last March.'

Lee had been at DI Thorpe's retirement do. With over forty years' service to the people of Tower Hamlets under his belt, Kevin Thorpe had deserved to get so plastered he put himself in A&E. He'd been well looked after by a big, dark bruiser of a bloke called Rick.

'Looks like a bull?' Lee asked.

'He's Spanish, of course he looks like a bull,' Vi said. 'They all do.'

'Bit racist.'

'So sue me,' she said. 'To answer your question, it's Ricky Mumtaz'll see. I'll have a word.'

It was typical of Mumtaz that she'd phoned Limehouse CID as soon as she'd made up her mind. Lee had heard her say that she had information about a family member, possibly in connection to the murder of Rajiv Banergee. Then she'd left.

Lee finished his call to Vi Collins and looked at Mumtaz's computer screen. There was something in Mishal's private inbox.

To his amazement she already had a message from Abu Imad. It said, '*Hi. Like that you like me.*'

FIVE

A lot of blokes boxed. The sport was particularly popular amongst the public schoolboys. But Amir still felt nervous. His left eye had almost closed up it was so swollen.

Guys patted him on the back, gave him knowing looks. Contact sports were huge, he knew that. But he couldn't rest until he'd spoken to someone.

The number in his phone was for someone who insisted he call him 'Grasshopper'. Amir knew his real name, but the guy liked the cloak-and-dagger stuff. That was OK. Quite exciting, really. Grasshopper – apparently related to some TV martial arts programme back in the 1970s.

He dialled.

A testy voice answered. 'What do you want?'

'Er, I just feel a bit exposed today,' Amir said. 'My eye's, well it's closed . . .'

'Really? Well, big diddums. Get used to it or get out.'

Amir hadn't expected that. Grasshopper had been, well, polite every other time he'd met him. Maybe he disliked using the phone?

He said, 'OK . . .'

'This number's for emergencies,' Grasshopper said. Then he cut the connection.

If Amir hadn't still been buzzing from the night before, he would've chewed Grasshopper out for that. That was rude. But, in spite of everything, he was on top of the world.

The Sheikhs still had her. Her brother Ali and his radicalism had only ever been a footnote. The Sheikhs knew the darkest chamber of her heart.

Her husband, Ahmet Hakim, hadn't been simply murdered, he'd been allowed to die. Not only had Mumtaz seen the handsome Naz Sheikh coming towards Ahmet with a knife, she'd not even tried to warn him. Then when the deed had been done, she'd allowed the boy to get away, while her husband bled into the ground. By the time the ambulance arrived he was dead and she was glad. Unlike Shazia, who lost not just her abuser, but her father, Mumtaz lost nothing except pain.

Shazia could never know. Apart from the love of her parents, the love of that girl had been the most important relationship in Mumtaz's life. Shazia had no one else. If Mumtaz didn't protect her, no one would. And if this meant also shielding her from the truth, then so be it.

DI Montalban put a cup of tea down in front of her. A few years her senior, Ricky Montalban had been to Cass Infant and Junior School with Mumtaz and her brothers. As he sat down, he smiled.

'Not seen you for a good few years,' he said.

He'd always been a big lad. Now he was overweight. But he was still the same old Ricky. She'd been relieved when she'd been told she'd be talking to him.

'What you been up to? I heard you got married.'

He had to know what had happened to Ahmet.

55

'I'm widowed,' Mumtaz said.

'I'm sorry.' He sipped his tea. 'I did hear a rumour.'

'But every cloud, you know,' she said. 'I've inherited, if that's the right word, a wonderful stepdaughter.'

'And you're a private detective,' he said. 'You was always a clever girl.'

She smiled.

'So you might have some information about our dead man.'

'Possibly,' she said. 'I knew Rajiv Banergee.'

'We all did.'

'He had a lot of trouble in recent years.'

'Yeah, although he didn't complain to us as often as you might think or as frequently as maybe he ought,' Montalban said. 'He moaned about lack of police presence, but he was never up for pressing charges if he had any trouble. He said it was just kids having a pop at him and they'd grow out of it. I told him I didn't think that homophobia and racism were things what was going to go away.'

Mumtaz shook her head. For a moment, just before she entered Limehouse Police Station, she had questioned what she was doing. People on Brick Lane didn't grass and yet here she was, about to dob in her own brother.

'Ricky—'

'Look, I don't know what you want to tell me but I can see it ain't easy for you,' he said. 'So let me say this: at this stage whatever you tell me is just between us. Depending on what you say, it might stay that way.'

'I'm fairly sure it won't,' she said.

'In that case it must be serious.'

She drank some tea. What was best? To lead up to it slowly or just to come out with it?

She kept her eyes on her teacup. She said, 'My brother Ali is taking in people from the Middle East.'

'So are a lot of people,' Ricky said. 'Legally or illegally, it's a fact. We deal with what we find. What we talking here?'

'I've no idea whether the young tenants in Ali's house are legal or illegal,' she said. 'But . . .' She stopped. She felt a bit sick. She swallowed. 'Ali is not the person you remember from school,' she said.

'Who is?'

She looked up. 'Ricky, his views are extreme now.'

All his levity disappeared.

'He is virulently anti-Semitic and homophobic,' she said. 'He's not like my brother any more. He rarely speaks to any of our family now. Having said that, Asif won't speak to him. Now he takes in these boys . . .'

Ricky leant forward. 'This is hard for you.'

'We don't grass,' she said. 'You know that.'

'And you haven't,' he said.

'Yes, I have. I've just told you my own brother has been radicalised.'

'Yeah, which I knew,' Ricky said.

'You knew?'

'We've been watching his place for . . . a while,' he said.

'So do you know who those boys are?' she said.

He smiled again. 'You know I can't tell you anything,' he said.

She did. She also knew that he was trusting her not to alert her brother.

'If and when the law is broken, we will take charge of the situation,' he said. Then he sat upright again and changed the subject. 'You're working with Lee Arnold.'

'Yes.'

'Got quite a reputation when he was at Forest Gate nick,' he said. 'Before my time, but I know of him. Think he worked with DI Collins, didn't he?'

'Yes,' she said. 'Do you know her?'

'Oh, yes,' he said. 'I know Vi very well.'

And that was how he ensured that she didn't warn her brother.

'Much as I appreciate you coming in today, as far as I'm concerned you was never here, Mumtaz,' Ricky said as he stood up.

Did he think any less of her for dobbing in her own brother? As a one-time resident of Brick Lane, he probably did. But as a copper he understood completely – and he was grateful.

Just before she left, he briefly took her hand. He had to know that men shaking hands with covered women was usually haram. But he also knew Mumtaz.

She knew, for her part, that he would keep her in the loop.

Maybe Fayyad answered all his 'Likes'? The idea seemed ridiculous, but stranger things happened. And ISIS, as an organisation, was busting a gut to get new recruits. They'd recently taken some defeats and were struggling.

Lee stopped looking at Mumtaz's computer and picked up a large brown envelope. He had to serve notice to quit on a couple in a flat in Forest Gate. They hadn't paid their rent for six months. But paradoxically, they'd been out every time anyone had tried to serve notice on them. Under the landlord's instruction, Lee had watched the flat and had got to know what Chelsea Myall and her boyfriend Stanislaw Kanapka did during the course of a normal week. In the case of Stanislaw, that was working on a building site in Kent, where he slept with a load of other Polish men in a Portakabin. Chelsea busied herself spending Stanislaw's money and not paying the rent. She drifted about all over the place.

However, the one regular thing she did do was take her mum to bingo in Stratford every Wednesday.

Lee picked up the brown envelope. Today Chelsea was going to get more than a full house.

Just about to leave, he wrote a note to Mumtaz, which said, *Mishal has made contact. You've a message in Mishal's private inbox. Don't do anything until I get back. Lee.*

Very few people could remember the last time Susi Banergee was on Brick Lane. Baharat Huq was one.

'Look! Look!'

He beckoned his wife, Sumita, over to the window and pointed to a tall, shapely figure on the street.

'Who's that?' Sumita said.

'Susi Banergee, Rajiv-ji's older sister. Don't you recognise her?'

'Maybe . . .'

She did. But Sumita wouldn't admit it. She'd never liked that woman.

Susi Banergee had to be seventy and yet she looked twenty years younger. Dressed in a figure-defining silver sari, Susi at almost six feet tall cut an extraordinary figure in Bangla Town. Heavily made-up and with her thick, black hair piled high on her head, Ms Banergee's arms, neck and earlobes dripped with gold and diamond jewellery.

'Ah, I think she is alone,' Baharat said. 'Look! Standing in the street with no one to assist her.'

He went outside immediately. When Sumita heard Susi's piping voice she cringed. That woman had always been a man-eater! But then she had to be nice. Susi had just lost her brother in the most awful way imaginable. She went into the kitchen to make tea.

* * *

There was more than one message in Mishal's inbox. Mumtaz counted thirteen. They almost all said the same thing, but in different forms.

Hi. Like that you like me. Can I be your friend?
Love your like.
Happy you like me.
Your Like made my day.
My heart sings for your Like.
Like me again.
Like me, I like you.
Salaam alaikum sister!
You are Muslim?
Happy I bring a smile to your face.
Like me again!
Your Like comes from a pure heart.
Like you.

She felt slightly breathless. If this happened when she'd simply liked his video, what would he do when she made contact?

Bombardment was a well-known tool in the armoury of extremist organisations. It worked particularly well on young people who could be flattered by constant and apparently earnest attention. Together with support for their nascent aspirations, this was a method that cults like Jim Jones's People's Temple had used to reel in young followers back in the 1970s. On an intellectual level, it was interesting but it also made Mumtaz wonder how she was going to cope with Abu Imad. If he was this keen now, what was he going to be like a few days down the line? And if, as his family believed, he was reaching out with a view to coming home, then why reach out to Mishal?

In her heart, Mumtaz hadn't really believed he would get in touch. Girls 'Liked' extremist videos all the time. Why had he chosen her? Or was she just one of many that he bombarded? Was that in fact his 'job'? And if it was, did he fight too or did he just recruit?

Who, if anyone, was watching what he did?

Mumtaz had to fight to stop herself visualising them. Another message dropped into her inbox:

Like to see a video of you.

'Do you remember the Montalbans?'

Susi Banergee had always smoked Sobranie cigarettes, even as a teenager. The one she was smoking now was turquoise.

'Yes, yes,' Baharat said. 'My children went to school with Richard and the girl, Carmel. Richard went into the police. Was it him who came to see you?'

'He did.' She sipped her tea. Then she looked at Sumita and smiled. 'Much cardamom,' she said.

She didn't like it.

Sumita smiled back in spite of herself. Baharat ignored the tea.

'Such a shock!' he said. 'Rajiv-ji was greatly loved.'

'Clearly not by everyone,' Susi said.

Most women would have just lowered their eyes. But Susi Banergee had always been a very forthright person. She'd probably had to have been. Baharat remembered her father, Krishna. He'd 'dressed'. Baharat could clearly remember Krishna-ji swinging down Brick Lane in a black and silver sari singing tunelessly back in the early 1970s. He'd got beaten up, mainly by the white National Front who had stalked the streets of Spitalfields back then. Everyone had been amazed when, a few years later, Rajiv had wandered around in even more flamboyant clothes than his father.

61

'Do the police have any suspects?' Baharat asked.

'They didn't say.'

Susi seemed very calm. As a girl she'd been known for her hot temper. But that wasn't in evidence. Maybe the lawyer or doctor or whatever he was she had married who had taken her to live in a mansion out in Essex had tamed her. But then perhaps she was simply holding her emotions close. There would be much for Susi to do in the weeks and months that were to come. Not least would be to decide the fate of the Leather Bungalow.

'Have you parked your car somewhere safe?' Baharat asked. 'You are welcome to use one of my residents' parking passes.'

'Oh, that's very kind,' she said, 'but the police brought me. I will go home in a taxi.'

He had rescued her from isolation in the street but now Baharat got the impression that Susi didn't really need anybody. It seemed unlike her. A drama queen from her head to her toes, his recollections of her consisted of many men running about doing her bidding. Perhaps the shock of Rajiv's death had made her humble.

'I didn't know the boys who worked for my brother,' she said. 'I have not yet been to see Rajiv's business. But through the police I have told them to not come to work this week.'

'Of course.'

'But I have no idea when my brother's body will be released to me,' she said.

Like Muslims, Baharat knew that Hindus usually liked to, in their case, cremate their deceased loved ones in less than twenty-four hours after death. He also knew that in the case of a suspected murder that was impossible. Tests would have to be done, forensic material collected. Mumtaz had told him all about it.

'The Antyeshti rites should be enacted soon.'

Baharat didn't known what they were.

Susi put out her turquoise cigarette and lit up a yellow one.

'It should be done by the eldest son,' Susi continued. 'But my brother had no son. I can't think who to ask. Who would be appropriate?'

She had no other brothers and she didn't mention that she had any sort of child.

Sumita said, 'Your husband?'

Susi ignored her. 'My cousin Prakesh had a son. But his mother is English.' She put a hand up to her head. 'This is awful,' she said. 'Just awful.'

But she still didn't cry. Baharat imagined that she'd probably do that once she got home to her mansion in Essex and her husband.

SIX

Grace had said that she was going to go to some bar on a rooftop in Shoreditch. Apparently a lot of white posh people went there so they could mix with black gangstas. It was said that the boy Grace fancied so much, Mamba, went there.

Shazia wouldn't have gone to a place like that anyway, but still, stacking tins of vegetables on Cousin Aftab's convenience-store shelves was well grim by comparison. At least she got paid. A lot of girls she knew worked in shops for their dads or uncles and didn't get a penny. They were just expected to do it.

Aftab was on a cigarette break when the old man she'd seen staring at her several times in the last month came into the convenience store. As well as smoking, Aftab was also talking to the Turkish man who ran the kebab shop next door and so Shazia stopped what she was doing and went behind the till.

The old man was quite sweet in a 'granddaddy' sort of way. Small and rather delicate-looking, he put his head on one side and said, 'Do you please have any Gummy Bear or Haribo halal sweeties?'

He had a thick Bengali accent and moved his head from side

to side when he spoke like a comedy Asian. That was annoying.

'Yes,' Shazia said. 'There.'

She pointed to a display that was right in front of him.

'Oh, yes.'

He looked, talking to himself in Bengali as he investigated his options. That, too, was annoying. But at least he wasn't staring at her this time, which was an improvement.

After what seemed like an interminable amount of time, he chose a bag of Haribo Red Cherries and gave Shazia a five-pound note. Then, as she counted out his change, she saw that he was staring. Should she challenge him on it? She wanted to but she also didn't want to make trouble for Cousin Aftab. He wasn't actually her cousin, but the relative of her amma, so there was no blood between them. This meant he didn't owe her a job or anything, really. But Aftab was naturally kind as well as being the most cockney Asian she had ever met. He made Shazia laugh. She kept her mouth shut.

But as she passed coins across the counter to the old man, he spoke.

He said, 'Young lady, I know your stepmother.'

'Oh,' she said. She smiled.

Maybe he was an ex-client of the Agency.

'Yes,' he said. 'Please do send her my good wishes, if you will.'

'Of course.'

He started to leave when Shazia realised that she didn't know who he was. She asked him.

Turning and smiling, he said, 'My name is Wahid Sheikh.'

He left.

Just the sound of that surname made Shazia's heart race. Sheikh? Was he one of *them*? If he was, why had he wanted to send good wishes to her amma?

Then she remembered the last time she'd seen a Sheikh in the flesh. That had been Naz. Thankfully he'd been dying.

Mishal's inbox was pinging and pinging. Mumtaz would have shut the laptop down ages ago. But she knew that Mishal wouldn't. Young people were always connected, they were addicted to connection.

It did it again. All she wanted to do was lay on the sofa and watch *Master Chef* but, even if she put the laptop in her bedroom she could still hear it. If that was Abu Imad then he had to be wondering why Mishal wasn't answering. Kids always answered, often straight away.

She called Lee. When he picked up the phone she heard his mynah bird, Chronus, in the background.

'Up the 'ammers!'

The poor thing had been coached in West Ham United songs and chants ever since he'd been given to Lee.

She heard Lee yell, 'Chronus! Wind it in for a second, will ya!' Then he spoke. 'Mumtaz. Hello.'

She told him about the laptop and the pinging.

'So switch it off,' he said. 'Do Abu Imad good to sweat about what Mishal's thinking for a bit. You accepted him as your friend so this is going to happen.'

'Yes, but Lee, kids like her are always online. They're plugged in morning, noon and night.'

'Yeah, but remember that her parents aren't into this radical stuff and so she has to be careful. There are going to be times when she can't get back to him. You're gonna have to chill.'

Mumtaz sighed. 'I know. I'm both pleased we've made contact so easily and nervous we might lose him.'

'Which is why you can only be in contact when I'm with you,'

66

he said. 'You should've waited for me this afternoon, but . . . You're the psychologist, I don't need to tell you that.'

'I know.'

There was a pause, then he said, 'You heard from the Sheikhs?'

'No,' she said. 'Wahid-ji has kept to his agreement to leave us alone until Shazia has finished her A levels. Have you found anything?'

'They're a slippery bunch. They pay their taxes and keep their noses clean. But there'll be something, trust me. I know their type. What happened at Tower Hamlets nick?'

She told him about Montalban and how she knew him. 'He knows about my brother,' she said.

'Great!' he said. 'Bloody marvellous! That means that the Sheikhs have got nothing on you. Result. Why didn't you ring me up immediately? I've a couple of possible leads, with working girls, which I can go for if you want me to. Old Rizwan Sheikh used to have a threesome with one of the ladies plus a bloke, before he got ill.'

'Yes . . .'

'Yes!'

Had he detected the caution in her voice? Of course the Sheikhs still had her. While Shazia needed to be shielded from what she had done to her father, they always would. But she couldn't tell him that.

'I . . . I just want them brought down,' she said.

'They will be.'

But when? And how? And why wasn't she letting Wahid Sheikh do his worst and tell Shazia? She could deny it. But she knew she didn't trust herself to do that. How could she, when in her own mind she was as guilty as hell?

The laptop beeped again. This time, Lee heard it.

'Switch it off!' he said.

'OK.'

She powered the machine down and shut the lid.

'You know, Lee, if my brother Ali has anything to do with Rajiv-ji's murder my parents will never recover,' she said.

He paused for a moment, then he said, 'Mumtaz, you need to get support from your other brother. He's not like Ali, is he?'

'No, no. Asif lives with a white girl in south London,' she said. 'He fell out with Ali a couple of years ago. He'll go mad when he finds out what's happened.'

'He doesn't know?'

'No. He used to work on the Lane, but now he's got a job in the City.'

'Which isn't far,' Lee said. 'Talk to him. Get his support with your parents. And remember, we don't know whether Ali's involved in Rajiv Banergee's death or not. He probably isn't.'

'You think?'

'From what you've told me about him, he sounds like a decent geezer at heart.'

'He was always a good Muslim.'

'So he's lost his way,' Lee said.

'Yes, but so have all these other men from decent families, and they kill,' she said. 'Look at Fayyad.'

'I know, but we do have to trust, just a bit,' he said. 'If we don't, we lose the plot. And this is England, remember? Innocent until proven guilty? That applies to your brother just like everyone else.'

'You shouldn't keep looking at it.'

Djamila put a hand on her mother's shoulder. Shereen had been sitting at the kitchen table looking at the Tooth of Jonah for hours.

'It's my meditation,' Shereen said. She looked up at her daughter.

'Do you remember when we used to go to see the tooth at the mosque when you and Fayyad were both little?'

'Of course.' She sat down. 'Mum, Fazil and I are going to meet Monika and her new man. Will you be OK on your own?'

Abbas had passed out drunk hours ago.

'Yes, of course,' Shereen said. 'Hasan is in.'

'Is he?'

'I know you'd never know it,' Shereen said.

'He's not still playing Call of Duty is he?'

The young man standing behind Djamila said, 'It is addictive.'

'Yeah, Fazil, right,' she said. 'Just as long as CoD is all he's doing up there.'

Shereen took her daughter's hand. 'Djamila, darling, don't you think that I watch him all the time? After what happened to Fayyad?'

The young woman sighed.

'I know how those people can worm their way into people's homes,' Shereen said. 'I had to learn that the hard way.'

Djamila kissed her. 'As long as you're sure.'

'I am.'

Shereen's daughter and her boyfriend left for some club in the West End. Once she was certain they had gone, Shereen returned to her meditation.

Zayn Chaudhuri had gone to ground. Predictably. A weeping, snivelling Sultan Ibrahim had finally told Bob Khan about as many of the places where the Briks Boyz 'hung' that he knew about, but clearly he didn't know them all. Or he was lying.

Ricky Montalban knew Zayn's dad, Suleiman, of old. A crackhead with a fancy for hard-core porn, he lived in a filthy flat on Old Montague Street. His son spent very little time there. But he did, sometimes, go home to sleep. Ricky knocked on the door. Through a small window beside the door he could see light from a television flickering in the darkness. He knocked again. Suleiman was always off his neck and so it would take him a while to register he had visitors.

Ricky looked at Bob and shook his head. Bob shrugged.

Ricky knocked again. 'Oi! Suleiman! It's Rick Montalban! Open up!'

A couple of minor members of the Briks had been picked up earlier, but they'd had alibis for Rajiv Banergee's death. All tucked up in bed according to their parents.

'Police! Open the fucking door!' He banged on the door again. This time, the lights from the TV went off and a light in the hall came on.

'Come on, Suleiman, I ain't got all night.'

The door opened slowly.

'Fuck me.'

Suleiman Chaudhuri looked bad even by crackhead standards. He wasn't big anyway, but he was also emaciated. Ricky had him down as forty-nine but he could have easily been sixty – or eighty. Having no teeth, yellow skin and tatty, salt-and-pepper hair didn't help. He wore a shirt and only a shirt.

Ricky pushed past Suleiman and went inside.

'Smells like a bog in here, Suleiman,' he said.

Bob joined him. His 'guv' wasn't wrong.

'I don't have no nothing.' Suleiman had a weak, whining voice. He shuffled past the officers and into the room with the television and one, greasy sofa.

'You been wanking, Suleiman?'

Ricky picked up the TV remote control and turned it on. Writhing, barely identifiable flesh flashed onto the screen accompanied by guttural groans.

'Avert your eyes, Mr Khan,' Ricky said. 'This stuff'll make you go blind.' He turned the TV off. Then he said, 'I'm not here about rocks, Suleiman, or even about your taste in porn. Wanna know where Zayn is.'

Suleiman sat down on the sofa. 'What's he done?'

'What do you think he's done?' Ricky said. 'Oh, and if you can't put any pants on will you cover your knob with something? It's making me want to fucking throw up.'

Suleiman put a hand over his shrivelled genitals. 'I dunno,' he said. 'He ain't here.'

'Mind if we look around?'

'Knock yourself out.'

Bob took what he imagined was a bedroom. There was a single mattress flung on the floor surrounded by random clothes and dodgy-looking tissues. There was nothing else. The bathroom contained all the usual bathroom fittings but with extra grime. As far as Bob could see there was no soap. He opened the door to a cupboard, which contained an old water tank and a load of newspaper. There were no towels. Did the old man dry himself on copies of The Sun? Bob shut the cupboard door. He met Ricky in the hall.

'Nothing,' he said.

'Kid's bedroom's remarkably clean,' Ricky said.

'But no kid, guv?'

'No.'

They went back into the living room. Suleiman, still sitting on the sofa with his hands over his genitals said, 'So?'

'So I need to speak to Zayn,' Montalban said. 'And with or without you, I will Suleiman. But if you help us out it'll be better for you, know what I mean?'

'If you like.'

'I do. And believe me, it'll be better for both of you if you bring him in.'

'What's he done?'

'Dunno yet. Until he answers my questions I won't know. Do you know where he was last night, Suleiman?'

'Here.'

'You seem very sure of that for a bloke who's usually off his neck by teatime.'

'I know when me son's in.'

'Good for you. You're obviously improving, Suleiman.'

They left.

Suleiman left it a good fifteen minutes before he went and pulled Zayn out of the space behind the old water tank in the bathroom. That fucking Bob Khan had always been a daft kid, couldn't see for looking, stupid little cunt.

Once Zayn was out, Suleiman said to him, 'So what did you do then, you useless fucker?'

SEVEN

Mumtaz opened her laptop. That photo that Shereen had taken of her must have impressed Abu Imad. There were so many messages she couldn't possibly read them all.

Lee, staring at the screen, said, 'You can pull out of this now.'

'I know,' she said. 'But we've made contact and who knows, maybe he's in touch with a lot of other women. Maybe he's seeing which fish will bite.'

'Makes you wonder when he's got time to fight.'

'And yet that video appears to have been shot in the Middle East,' she said. 'He's out there or he's been out there. What do we do now?'

Lee sat down. 'Send him a message.'

'Saying what?'

Lee had been a copper and he'd fought in Iraq, but he had very little knowledge about the ISIS mindset. But then who did? Talking heads on the telly claimed to have insight but did they really? Both politicians and community leaders seemed to be at a loss to stem the flow of young people out to the caliphate and so, logically, it seemed that they couldn't know much.

He said, 'Well, let's think it through. Mishal's seen Abu Imad's video, which she liked enough to Like. This means she has to have extremist sympathies, plus her hormones are ruling her head.'

'Even coming from a fairly liberal family, she will not have had sexual contact with boys,' Mumtaz said. 'Her understanding of sex will be . . . Well, it could be minimal or it could be distorted. Some girls are very clued in, in spite of what you may think.'

'But not Mishal.'

'No,' she said. 'I see her as one of those who has on the one hand a sort of Mills and Boon romantic fantasy about relationships while at the same time being afraid of sex. Many girls are raised with the expectation that it's something to be endured. And yet they still have feelings and so many of them live in hope that their husbands will be different.'

Lee wondered whether Mumtaz had felt like that before her marriage, but he didn't ask. As he saw it, there was a line between himself and Mumtaz that he couldn't cross. Whether that was real or not, he didn't know. She was the only Muslim woman he had ever worked closely with. She was certainly his only Muslim female friend. He wished she could be more . . .

'Mishal is a virgin,' Mumtaz said.

'Yeah, well I imagined . . .'

'Not all Muslim girls are,' she said. 'You might be surprised. And you know that a lot of our men know that. Abu Imad does.'

'How do you know?'

'Because in amongst all the pleas and protestations and nonsense he has sent to Mishal, he also asks her if she is a virgin.'

She showed him on the laptop.

Mishal, the message read, *I know that you are pure. But just to put my mind at rest, can you confirm to me that you are a virgin?*

* * *

74

'I had nothing to do with the death of Rajiv Banergee.'

Ali Huq began to walk away from his father. But Baharat, in spite of arthritis, sore feet and all the ills that attended his seventy-five-year-old body, hobbled after him.

'Don't you walk away from your father!' he roared. 'I don't care how old you are, you're still my son and you will listen to me!'

Baharat Huq was a man of conscience but his sense of appropriate timing was poor. To challenge his son about the death of Rajiv Banergee in Ali's own shop was a mistake. And although the Islamic clothing outlet had once belonged to the old man, it had been in the hands of his son for ten years. It was also full of customers.

'I will speak to you later, Abba,' Ali said.

'You will speak to me now, you insolent monkey!'

Ali pushed past two apparently outraged boys and said, 'I did not kill Rajiv Banergee and neither did anyone I know!'

'And yet you argued with him,' Baharat said. 'People saw you. And one of those terrorists you give shelter to abused him!'

'Abused him? How?'

'Running into his shop and shouting obscenities!'

Ali ignored him . . .

'And someone beat Rajiv-ji before his death,' Baharat said. 'I saw a bruise on his face the last time we spoke.'

'Nothing to do with me.'

Baharat shook his head. 'When the police ask, I will tell them everything I know,' he said.

'So tell them.' Ali took his father's arm and pulled him into the small office at the back of the shop. He shut the door. 'How dare you come here and accuse me of these things!' he roared. 'For your information, I do not shelter terrorists!'

'Oh, no? Then why do you have those boys living in your house?'

'They are refugees from Syria!'

'They cause trouble,' Baharat said. 'Saying bad things to girls! Writing bad words about Jews!'

'They have been traumatised! They don't understand this country where women walk about half naked! They are observant . . .'

'Which makes their bad behaviour alright?' the old man sat down. 'I have spoken to you of this before. Ali, my son, there are Muslims who are bad . . .'

'You!' he said.

Baharat's whole body jolted backwards.

'You drink and smoke and you have no idea about what is happening for young Muslims in this country,' he said. 'You're what black people call an "Uncle Tom", an apologist for this Islamophobic country, a friend of the Christians, a—'

'Oh and listen to the "good" Muslim as he abuses his father!' Baharat said. 'Those Arabs you shelter are not right. They are friends to no one, least of all you. I wish I knew who you got this idea that you are superior to everyone else from, but if I find out I will thrash that person. This is not you! Being cruel and discriminating—'

'The Holy Koran teaches—'

'The Holy Koran does not teach hatred!' Baharat shouted.

Through the office door both men could see Ali's customers looking and listening.

Baharat waved an arm at them. 'And you can all shut your ears, you nosy parkers!'

'Abba . . .'

'If I find that you have had anything to do with the death of Rajiv-ji, I will put you down like a dog!' Baharat said. 'You? A

76

good Muslim? You just bring shame to Muslims! You bring shame to your family! And you make your mother cry.'

'I'm helping refugees,' Ali said. 'Displaced children.'

'And how do you come to get these children?'

'There are Muslim aid organisations.'

'Oh, are there?' Baharat said. 'And they chose you, a single man with hatred in his heart for anyone who isn't like him to look after children? Don't you think that is a little odd? I do. But then, maybe these good people do not know that you are a bigot.'

Ali looked at the floor.

'Until four years ago, you were my good son, Ali,' Baharat said. 'What happened to you? And do not blame our religion for this. Whatever you are doing, it is not from faith. This is politics. This is Jews against Muslims, Muslims against homosexuals. This is war.'

Ali looked up. 'Yes,' he said, 'you're right, Abba. This is war. But it isn't the one you think is happening.'

'Oh?'

'No,' he said. 'This world is filthy and corrupted. This is a war for the soul of a world that will descend into chaos unless mankind bows to the Will of God as it should. When all the world accepts that the laws of God cannot be broken, all this horror will stop.' And then, suddenly, he cried, 'If this doesn't happen we will all burn! We'll burn and it will be terrible!'

As Baharat watched him, his son sank to his knees and then lay on the floor weeping, just like he had done when he was a child. Confused, but also full of tenderness for the vulnerable child Ali still clearly was, the old man put a hand on the side of his face and said, 'Ssshh. Ssshh.'

I feel as if I should apologise for sending you so many messages but, at the same time, I make no apology for my love. And love it is, my perfect Mishal. How can I not love someone who watches my video? Especially someone as beautiful as you! I saw immediately from your Facebook that you are a Muslim. That makes me so happy! Do you like what you see? Tell me that you do!! Knowing that you appreciate me will make me stronger!!!

Abu Imad had contacted Mishal before she could get in touch with him. Was it all too quick and ardent to be true? What was happening? How could they find out?

Lee scanned articles about radicalisation online. Was doing all this for mates' rates, in Abbas's case, worth it? Of course it was! But . . .

'I'll have to get back to him soon,' Mumtaz said.

'Yeah, alright. It says here . . .'

'I've got *Hello Abu Imad. Wow, I can't believe so many messages from you!*'

'You've probably got to use youth speak,' Lee said. 'Fayyad is in his thirties but he thinks that Mishal is a teenager. So all that LOL, reem stuff . . .'

'Reem's *The Only Way is Essex*,' Mumtaz said. 'He won't say that!'

'Won't he?'

'No,' she said. 'He's religious.'

'Yeah, but what I'm reading says that they use youth speak.'

'Yes. LOL, emojis, ROFL . . .'

'ROFL?'

'Rolling on the floor laughing,' she said. 'But I doubt he'll do that.'

Lee threw his arms in the air.

'You have to be proper excited he's so into you,' he said.

'While at the same time being modest,' she said. 'If I'm overkeen he'll go off me. Trust me.'

Lee shrugged. Alongside trying to get as much information as he could about men in Fayyad's situation he was also attempting to get his accounts up to date.

Mumtaz thought, wrote, and then thought some more. Eventually she said, 'How about I add this?'

He looked up. 'Shoot.'

'*Hello Abu Imad. Wow, I can't believe so many messages from you! I didn't think you'd contact me. I really appreciate your time. Thank you.*'

'Is that it?' Lee said.

'Yes. Why?'

'Bit short. Shouldn't she be a bit more into him?'

'Not if she wants him to think that she's a nice girl,' Mumtaz said.

'Do you *really* think he wants a nice girl?'

'Did Fayyad like nice girls?' she asked.

'As far as I remember Fayyad's sex life didn't exist,' Lee said. 'But then that's according to my knackered memory, who knows?'

'Well in his guise as an ISIS fighter, he will only be able to like nice girls,' Mumtaz said. 'And so that is what we will give him.'

Ricky had seen it happen.

'She looked him straight in the eyes and then hissed like a snake.'

'Did you manage to catch the boy?'

'Yeah.'

Chief Superintendent Vine always wondered about local coppers. On the one hand their knowledge of their manor was excellent, while on the other he sometimes wondered where their loyalties lay. Less so with Montalban who, though Brick Lane born and bred, didn't actually belong to any sizeable group as far as Vine knew. Which was a fair bit. Although originally from

West Yorkshire, Vine had made it his business over the years to get under the skin of the London Borough of Tower Hamlets.

'He's called Akbar Maan,' Ricky said. 'I know him of old.'

'One of the Briks Boyz?'

'Nah. Just a lone scrote. Done a bit of shoplifting, bit of weed . . .'

'Do you think he's vulnerable to radicalisation?'

'Nah. Says his prayers but likes getting pissed. He's just a twat.'

'So what was he doing in the Leather Bungalow when you were escorting Rajiv Banergee's sister around the premises?'

'Probably looking for a new jacket, sir,' Ricky said. 'He's a chancer. Mind you, that'll be the last time he goes on the rob for a while, I reckon.'

'Because of Mrs Chopra.'

'She frightened me!' Ricky said. 'Thought Akbar was gonna shit hisself. Hissin' at him like that!'

'Did you ask her about her behaviour?' Vine said.

'No. I remember her from when I was a kid. The whole family was a bit weird. The old man, like the victim, used to cross-dress. Susi Banergee was never someone you messed with. But when she got married, years ago, she left the area. Never seen her since. It's said she's got money. She'll have a bit more now.'

'Is she the victim's only heir?'

'As far as we know.'

'So what about the problems Mr Banergee had in recent years?' He opened a file on his computer. 'Criminal damage, 1999, criminal damage 2005, a couple of instances of minor assault, homophobic graffiti . . .'

Ricky sighed. Here it was. He knew there was some truth in where Vine was driving but he also knew that Rajiv Banergee had had a complicated life.

'My first thoughts when we found Mr Banergee was Muslim kids,' Ricky said. 'You and me both know what goes on. I was straight onto the Briks Boyz, particularly Zayn Chaudhuri. Dunno where he's crawled away to but he's on the missing list.'

'Can you see Zayn as a killer?'

'Yeah, but only him,' Ricky said. 'The others are just all mouth. Also they come from decent homes, most of 'em. Zayn's old man's a crackhead. The kid's basically dragged himself up. I can't work out whether someone radicalised him or he decided that religion was a good way to control people. But he's all over the evil West stuff, calls people poofs, anti-Semitic graffiti a speciality. More worrying for us is that Zayn has spent some time with a bloke we're watching who's taken in some Syrian refugees. Now he is a person of interest.'

'Mmm. Ali Huq. Yes?'

'Yes, sir.'

Mumtaz leant against the side of the bus stop. Shazia had seen her, but she'd guessed she was working and had turned away. She was a good kid. So were the girls she hung around with, even if that Grace wore skirts so short you could almost see her knickers.

Whenever she had a job that required observing a kid at Sixth Form College, Mumtaz had 'issues'. Because Shazia studied there it was always possible her target was a youngster that she knew. But not in this case. Soni Kaur was in the first year of her A-level studies and, as far as Mumtaz could tell, was part of a group of other Sikh girls plus a couple of white kids. They were a loud and excitable bunch and Mumtaz hadn't been able to find anything worrying about Soni's behaviour.

Parents worried about what was actually a narrow range of problems. Drugs, booze, sex and 'getting in with the wrong crowd' covered most of it. Soni's parents had a notion their girl was smoking cannabis. But, so far, there was no evidence to suggest that she or any of her group indulged in spliff sessions. What they did do was hang out around the chicken shop at the Green Gate rather more than was good for them. But then so did young Grace. So did a lot of kids. Supposedly 'safe', in terms of being both halal and beef-free zones, chicken shops were where a lot of Asian kids gathered. White and Afro-Caribbean youngsters liked them too and so they were good places to arrange to meet outside college. Unless you were Shazia.

Chicken and chips was not an expensive meal, but for Mumtaz and Shazia it was a luxury neither of them could often afford. Although she'd railed at the unfairness of having to take a packed lunch to college every day and eat at home in the evening, Shazia knew she had no choice. Her earnings from Cousin Aftab's convenience store had to go on clothes and books. It was what the children of debtors had to do and she knew it. And Mumtaz had been very quick to point out that her skin was all the better for avoiding fried food.

Mumtaz's phone beeped.

Soni and her friends stopped chatting on the pavement and began to walk in the direction of the chicken shop. Mumtaz looked at her phone. Something for Mishal.

You are the girl of my dreams.

EIGHT

People came to the Leather Bungalow from all over. Some cousins and an ancient uncle from Brentford, the husbands, wives and children of other cousins from Redbridge, Brentwood and Hertford – an aunt from Brighton. The Banergee diaspora had abandoned their Brick Lane home turf a long time ago.

As she sat in the middle of the sales floor in a chair that looked like a throne, Susi Banergee heard what they said. Cousin Indira, who had always been a massive bitch said, 'Why was Rajiv living here still? How did he make money from this old place? Hidden away in all these so-called curry houses.'

A young girl that Susi didn't know replied, 'All the bankers from the City come to Brick Lane.'

'For curries, yes,' Cousin Anita said. 'Not for leather jackets. They'll go to Prada or bugger off to Dubai or something. You know that my neighbour is forever over to Dubai. Handbags. All fake, but cheap and you'd never know.'

It was only the keen, if ancient eyes of Uncle Chandresh that noticed someone was missing. Or at least he was the only one who said anything.

'So where is Dilip?'

Susi felt her face drain.

'He is in surgery today,' she said.

She saw Cousin Indira narrow her eyes. 'And he couldn't be spared when his wife is bereaved?'

When they'd all been children, Indira had possessed a reputation for being a busybody. She knew everything and everyone and the Muslim kids had thought she was a witch. Did she know something now?

'Orthopaedic surgeons are not ten a penny. He had no choice,' Susi said.

Indira knew what she was really saying and she retreated to the back of the room. Her husband, Max, was a lowly GP in Golders Green. And he was a Jew.

The relatives milled. Arriving all the time, there were so many, Susi didn't know who half of them were. But she accepted their condolences with grace and they, in turn, availed themselves of the food and drink she had managed to persuade Dilip to pay for. He had liked Rajiv.

'So what do the police know so far?'

Fat, short and sweaty, Cousin Gangi's husband Vipul was not a man to mince his words even in the face of death.

'Do they think it's one of these Muslims? Rajiv had problems with those bastards, didn't he?'

'Yes, but whether they killed him, I don't know,' Susi said. 'In this instance the police have been very good. They have largely left me alone to grieve.'

'That's good.'

It was.

He went back to Dilip's whisky. Greedy little grocer!

Susi looked around the room. In fact her whole family were

greedy – drinking liquor as if their lives depended on it, stuffing pakoras into their fat mouths. Fat and complacent and entitled. They'd laughed behind her father's back all his life because of how he dressed. And Rajiv. But they'd never laughed at Susi and they never would.

Lee stayed over. He didn't sleep, but then neither did Mumtaz. Shazia, watching *Game of Thrones* in her room, was blissfully unaware of what was happening in the living room.

You must give me your Skype address. I need to see you.

Mumtaz shook her head.

'For a wanted man Fayyad is moving fast,' she said. 'I've gone from being no one to the girl of his dreams, to someone he has to see, in just over a day.'

Lee frowned. Did Fayyad know what was happening? Was he making contact with a view to getting out of Syria as his parents believed?

'But then men from the subcontinent and the Arab world are accustomed to making their minds up about women quickly,' Mumtaz continued. 'Some of them, even now, have only to look at a girl to propose marriage. It's the mothers who find out about a girl's character. The man just looks and if he likes what he sees, the deal is done.'

Lee didn't comment.

'I really don't want to show my face to this man, not yet,' Mumtaz said.

'So cover your face.'

'Mishal doesn't,' she said. 'Her parents won't let her.'

'Yeah, but in her room she can do as she pleases.'

'Well, she would if she had a niqab,' Mumtaz said.

'That's the . . .'

'The thing that covers the face, yes,' she said. 'I don't have one. Mishal, were she really serious, would have bought one on the sly.'

'Maybe her parents confiscated it.'

'Maybe. But if I don't talk to Abu Imad in niqab he may think I'm not a nice girl,' she said. 'And besides can I really pass for eighteen in the flesh? I don't know.' She shook her head. 'I'm going to say there are too many people about to Skype.'

'OK. But I don't think you need to worry about how you look,' Lee said.

She ignored him.

Mum, dad and brother not leaving me alone. They'll hear me Skype. If they hear me type, they won't think anything. Can we just do this?

She made them tea while she waited for a reply. Lee went out into the garden to smoke. When he came back she was sitting in front of the computer looking troubled.

'What is it?' he said.

'It's like a job interview,' she said.

Where do you live? What do you like to do? Were you born Muslim? What do you want from your life? Do you like children? Are you a virgin?

'He's asked me if I'm a virgin before.'

Do you have a boyfriend?

Lee said, 'We must be careful what we tell him.'

'In what sense?'

'Tell him too much and he'll be suspicious. Tell him too little and he'll lose interest.'

Mumtaz typed what she thought he might want to hear.

For some hours after that it seemed as if the only thing that Abu Imad was interested in was Mishal's devotion to West Ham United. She told him she enjoyed photography, but he ignored that.

86

Oh wow! You're a Hammer! So am I!

Lee took over. Abu Imad was as sad as he about the move away from the Boleyn Ground at Upton Park to the Olympic Stadium at Stratford.

It isn't the same! Boleyn is our home!

Mumtaz interjected here. *Yes, but at least it means that I'm not getting called Paki every time I go down Green Street on a Saturday any more . . .*

Abu Imad agreed that was a good thing. Then he wrote, *Just hope they don't now move the Bobby Moore statue to Stratford too. That would be really sad. Hey, Mishal, did I ask you whether you have a boyfriend?*

'He's insistent, I'll give him that,' Lee said.

It was 1 a.m. and they were both tired. But Abu Imad still appeared to be as fresh as a daisy.

Mumtaz typed. *SMH. Of course I don't have a boyfriend! I'm saving myself for my husband.*

'SMH?'

'Shaking my head,' she said. 'I've been mugging up on youth acronyms.'

'God.'

Of course you are, Abu Imad responded. *I'm sorry, Mishal, I'm just so anxious that having found you, you really are as perfect as I think. You haven't told me whether or not you're a virgin yet and it's making me nervous.*

'God he's obsessed! I've told him twice! What's he trying to do, catch me out or something?' Mumtaz shook her head. 'Yetch! He wants a child-bride. Sick!'

'Yeah, but she's eighteen,' Lee said. 'Legal.'

'Just. I've told him I'm saving myself for my husband, but it's not enough for him.'

'So tell him you're a virgin one more time.'

'You think?'

Abu Imad's response was instant.

You have made me so happy, Mishal. A Muslim sister and a virgin! And a Hammer! Oh, you know what I wish? I wish you could be with me here in our wonderful Caliphate. Of course, only as my wife. There are no unmarried sisters here. But many warriors are alone. Like me. You know you'd love it here. We have everything. Beautiful apartments, fantastic shopping and we have no bills! Everything is provided. You'd love it.

Mumtaz leant back in her chair. 'Shopping, home, bills, children, sex – not necessarily in that order,' she said. 'God!'

'Well he's not going to be a feminist, is he?'

'No, but it's all so – primitive!'

Lee wondered whether her husband had also been 'primitive' but he didn't ask.

'Was Fayyad like this before he was radicalised?' she asked.

'Not that I know of,' Lee said. 'His parents have always been very liberal as far as I know. Grandparents too. His sister works for that designer label . . .'

'Which one?'

'Alexander something . . .'

'Alexander McQueen!'

'Yeah, in a shop up west somewhere,' he said. 'She don't make dresses, she sells them.'

'Even so . . .'

The computer beeped.

Where are you, Mishal? Has what I said about you becoming my wife been too much for you?

Mumtaz looked at Lee and said, 'I think I've just been proposed to.'

* * *

88

Both boys were online. Contacting Muslim brothers back in Syria he imagined. So why did Ali Huq feel unsettled? And why was he so concerned that his Arabic wasn't up to following all their conversations?

They'd both been out when Rajiv-ji was murdered. He hadn't asked them where. He didn't know how they'd react if he did. The younger of the two, Qasim, was quite approachable but the older boy, Nabil, was a closed book.

He'd been told by Aziz the tailor that they came from Aleppo, which had been all but destroyed. But neither of the boys had ever alluded to it. They just said that they were Syrian, they were Muslims and they wanted to go back. Sometime. Aziz the tailor, who co-ordinated the settlement of Syrians on and around the Lane, said they'd go when they were ready.

Although it made him feel guilty, Ali knew he wanted them to go. He'd never encouraged them to hurl abuse at Rajiv-ji, much less punch him in the face, but he had turned a blind eye to their activities. He'd had to.

Rajiv Banergee had always been 'wrong'. A man who dresses as a woman, a man who has sex with other men. It was an abomination. It was especially wrong when Rajiv deliberately set out to tempt Muslims, which he did. Ali knew who, and that knowledge made his skin go cold. Because he also knew that someone else knew that too.

A lot of Asian families had one or two members who pioneered their way out of districts where they were related to everyone, and into places that were 'white'. In Bob Khan's case, this was his Uncle Tanweer. Now residing in suburban splendour in Esher, Uncle Tanweer was fond of saying, 'You will never be your own man in the ghetto', whenever he came back to Brick Lane. However, for a police officer like Bob, there were consolations. Knowing 'everyone' could be useful. In this case that person was his second cousin, Yasin, who lived in the same block of flats as Suleiman and Zayn Chaudhuri.

While not wishing to actually 'dob' the Chaudhuris in, Yasin had alerted Bob to the fact that Zayn was in and out of his dad's flat and back to his old petty drug-dealing activities. He just didn't go very far.

And so Bob waited. Just another Asian bloke with his hood pulled down over his eyes, mooching around the streets, smoking and drinking from a box of mango juice. Montalban was at the end of a phone and so, as soon as Bob saw Zayn enter the flat, he'd get onto the blower.

But as the dead of night turned into the early hours of the morning, with no Zayn in sight, Bob began to become suspicious. Yasin had definitely seen Zayn leave at just before 9 p.m., but he hadn't been back to the flat since. Where else could he be? All his well-known haunts were under surveillance. He'd just vanished. Had he been tipped off by someone? And, if so, who?

Yasin claimed not to know. But before Bob left in the morning she did say, 'You know that the Huq family on Hanbury Street knew Rajiv-ji well.'

'Baharat-ji's family?'

'Yes. The daughter, Mumtaz, was at John Cass School with me. She got married to a man up Forest Gate who was murdered.'

Bob remembered something about that.

'A Hakim?'

'Yeah. Well, she's a private detective now. She might know a thing or two.'

As, according to Montalban, did her brother Ali. But Bob didn't tell Yasin that.

* * *

Why was she still awake? Susi knew that with Bertram in charge of the place, no one could get her unless she wanted to be got.

She remembered this particular Huguenot house well. Halfway down Fournier Street, when she'd been a girl it had been lived in by a family of Jews. She'd gone to school with the daughter, Adelaide Silver. But when her family left, the house was up for demolition until it was bought first by a reclusive artist and then by Bertram Carney, who turned it into a boutique hotel.

Furnished with a mixture of expensive antiques and distinctly odd ephemera, the Weavers Boutique Hotel was, according to Bertram a 'queer's vision of a Victorian bordello'. And given that Susi had, in the past, brought attractive men, and boys, to the Weavers for some afternoon – or evening – delight, it had just the right vibe. It also had discretion. Even when Dilip had challenged Bertram at reception about his wife's whereabouts, the old queen had said nothing. She'd been in this same room with an eighteen-year-old Moroccan. Maybe that memory was keeping her awake? Or perhaps it was the knowledge that Dilip, in spite of everything, was paying for her bed and board at the Weavers.

But then he had an ulterior motive. Looking good in court was going to earn him Brownie points when the divorce hearing happened. He had supported his wife when her brother died in spite of her infidelity. For her part, she would cite his impotence and his reluctance to do anything about it. Too 'ashamed' to go to another doctor for help! What nonsense. He didn't care. Far too interested in his golf and his cars and vintage fucking wines. What had she been supposed to do with that? Rot away in a corner? Probably. Her best friend Miriam had taken lovers when her husband had lost interest and then, in court, she'd been punished. Banished from a five-bed mansion in Epping to a one-bed flat in Ilford. And not a store card remaining.

Susi had always liked Arab boys best. Because so many of them were sexually repressed, when the floodgates opened, they were beyond eager. One, who she had called 'Saladin', had been her best. In his thirties, he was tall, handsome and had a cock like a battering ram. She'd had him often until he'd gone to Bradford for some strange reason. She suspected it was to get married. She wondered what his, no doubt, timid young wife would make of his addiction to oral sex. How would her prim little mouth cope?

But then Rajiv's face appeared in her mind and Susi began to cry. Maybe if she cried hard enough the vision would disappear? She wanted it to.

NINE

Word was all the Boyz were going to be taken away by the feds. But not Zayn. He'd die rather than let them feel his collar. That fuckin' Jake, Khan, had got him proper vexed, though, even if watching him strolling about looking for him was right jokes.

He looked across the smoke-filled room at the tiny mini-skirted girl sitting in the corner. Dressed like some sket with her tits hanging out, Rashida was a useful thing. When no fit girls were about, she did the business. Disowned by her family because she'd got up the duff, she lived well outside Zayn's endz, out in Wapping.

'You can stay long as you like,' she'd said to Zayn when he'd turned up at her door. Then she'd put the baby with some skank next door so she could suck him off. Zayn wouldn't ever actually fuck a woman until he was married. She'd be pure. Not some old dog like Rashida.

'Can I get you a cup of tea?'

Mumtaz was nervous. Lee wasn't surprised. Ricky Montalban was an intimidating character. Built like a brick shithouse, he had a boxer's nose and long, thin, suspicious eyes. Like a snake. They'd gone to the same school, apparently. But Lee suspected that didn't mean too much to Ricky.

His partner, DC Khan, was another matter. A good-looking boy in his early twenties, he smiled easily and, when Mumtaz asked about tea, he said, 'Oh, that would be lovely, Mrs Hakim, thank you.'

She started to get up until Lee said, 'I'll do it.' Then looking at Montalban he added, 'I imagine you'll want to speak to Mrs Hakim alone.'

'Yeah.'

The older man slotted into Lee's chair without asking permission and with ease. As Lee waited for the kettle to boil he recalled quite a few 'Montalbans' from his days in the job. Local, aggressive, entitled. If things had gone differently, these blokes would have become villains. As it was, they contented themselves with the 'right' side of the law and beating the crap out of the odd nonce from time to time. Or the wife.

Once he'd made tea, Lee went and sat outside on the metal stairs. They needed a bigger office. And they weren't doing bad moneywise. But it still wasn't enough to expand. Not yet. Lee lit a fag and tried not to earwig on the conversation inside the office. He failed.

'Rajiv-ji was always good to us when we were children,' Mumtaz said.

'You and your brothers.'

'Yes,' she said.

'Ali?'

'Of course, Ali,' she said. 'And Asif. Like me, he no longer lives on Brick Lane. But whenever he comes to visit he goes to see Rajiv-ji.'

'I see.' Montalban moved his large body forwards in Lee's office chair. He said, 'We know that Mr Banergee had been having trouble from kids on account of his sexuality.'

'Yes.' Mumtaz looked at Bob Khan. 'Those Briks Boyz.'

'You know anyone called Zayn Chaudhuri, Mrs Hakim?'

'Of course,' she said. 'He's the leader of the Briks Boyz, isn't he?'

'You know anything about any relationship he might have with your brother, Ali?'

This threw her. The Arab boys yes, but did Ali really have a 'relationship' – whatever that meant – with the Boyz?

'No,' she said. 'My brother is a religious man. Why would he have anything to do with drug dealers?'

'The Boyz are religious,' Montalban said.

'They say they are, but they still do drugs,' she said. 'Why do you think that Ali and Zayn have any connection?'

But Montalban didn't answer. Leaning back in Lee's chair now – clearly he was having problems getting comfortable – he said, 'Do you know whether Rajiv Banergee was in a relationship with anyone?'

'What, you mean . . .'

'Did he have a lover?'

'No,' she said. 'Or rather not to my knowledge and certainly not someone local.'

'In case they were spotted?'

'Yes,' she said. 'Rajiv-ji may have been flamboyant but he was far from stupid. If he'd been seeing someone local, don't you think that people like the Boyz would know? If there was anyone, he was a long way from Brick Lane.'

'What about in the past? You know if he had any exes hanging around?'

'I know there was a white guy who used to come round to Rajiv-ji's shop sometimes when I was a child,' Mumtaz said. 'A City type. But they only chatted. Maybe he was just a friend?'

'Do you remember his name?'

'No,' she said. 'All I can remember about him is that he was very thin. Maybe Asif would know? Or Ali?'

And then something popped into her head. It made her feel sick. For a moment she tried to use this sickness to justify saying nothing. But she couldn't.

'Oh, ah . . .'

'Yes?'

Whenever Ricky Montalban looked at her, she felt as if he was staring into her soul. Had he been like that as a child? She couldn't remember.

'Rajiv told me something once . . .'

'About a man?'

'He didn't name him,' she said. 'But he did say that they were in love and that he was a Muslim.'

Did Bob Khan move his chair nearer to her just so he could hear better or because he was anxious to hear her words almost before she'd spoken them?

'When was this?'

'He told me . . . must be about eighteen months ago,' she said.

'Which was when . . .'

'I don't know when the affair took place,' she said. 'I got the impression at the time that it was long ago.'

'Why did he tell you?' Bob asked.

'I was investigating a PO Box address,' Mumtaz said. 'Apparently this man and Rajiv communicated via this address.'

And then Ricky Montalban asked Mumtaz if she knew who had administered that PO Box.

People on the Lane didn't grass, but Rajiv Banergee had been murdered. And so she gave Ricky the name which he, and Bob, both recognised immediately.

When the two detectives left, Mumtaz went with them to go and get some lunch. They watched her walk down Green Street while

Bob had a cigarette and Ricky breathed in the smoke. He'd given up five years ago, but he still loved the smell.

He looked across at Forest Gate Police Station and said, 'We'll go and see if DI Collins is about while we're here. She's proper old school but I think you'll like her and she knows this manor inside out.'

'Guv . . .'

'What?'

'Mrs Hakim,' Bob said. 'Look. Talking to that bloke.'

Ricky looked. 'So?'

'That's Wahid Sheikh,' he said. 'I bet your DI Collins knows him.'

'He related to Rizwan Sheikh?' Ricky asked.

'He's his big brother. Lives in Bangladesh. But he's been over here for about a year now.'

Ricky knew of the Sheikh family but because they operated outside his patch he didn't know much.

'Rizwan bought up a load of ex-council property when it was cheap back in the 1990s,' Bob said.

'Slum landlords.'

'And the rest.' He frowned. 'Mrs Hakim doesn't look too happy about talking to Wahid.'

'Maybe she lives in one of his houses.'

'Mmm.'

It was possible, although Bob doubted it. Baharat-ji, her father, was an honest man. He couldn't see him allowing any of his children to have dealings with gangsters. That said, he clearly wasn't a significant influence on his eldest son, and his daughter, it was said, had married a man who'd been distinctly dodgy. What Bob's dad called the 'old ways', by which he meant children doing what their parents told them, were breaking down all over the East End. There were rich pickings to be had in the streets that had once been slums and people were clawing each other to shreds to get at them.

'Oi! Ricky Montalban! Get out my manor!'

Bob heard his boss laugh.

A skinny, middle-aged woman in a tight dress and high heels ran across the road and punched Montalban playfully on the shoulder.

'Vi!'

'What you doing on Green Street?' she said. Then she looked at Bob. 'Hello.'

'DC Khan,' Ricky said, 'DI Collins.'

'Hello.'

Did she really flutter her false eyelashes at him?

'Well, you're wasted in Limehouse, aren't you darlin'? Fancy a move east?'

Montalban shook his head. 'Put him down, Vi. We're here about the death of a cross-dresser on Brick Lane.'

DI Collins looked away from Bob.

'I heard about that,' she said. 'So what you doing here?'

'Came to see one of the victim's old friends,' Montalban said.

'Anyone I know?'

'Couldn't possibly say.'

Vi laughed. It was like listening to sandpaper on rough ground.

'So you gonna ask us over to your gaff for a cuppa then, Vi?'

Then the laughter stopped. 'Nah,' she said. 'Sorry boys, bit busy at the moment.'

Bob would have seen this exchange as just another example of senior officer dick swinging about who was the busiest, if he hadn't noticed where Vi Collins was looking. It was straight at Mumtaz Hakim and Wahid Sheikh.

Shereen didn't like it when her husband worked from home. He used it as an opportunity to drink in the day. When she was home herself, it was doubly unsettling. She had a .75 contract which meant that she worked four days a week. What she didn't need on her one day off was Abbas rattling around the house bewailing his fate into a whisky bottle.

'Why have we not heard from Lee Arnold?' he said.

He was turning the Tooth of Jonah over and over in his hands. Maybe he felt that handling the artefact brought him closer to Fayyad? Shereen knew it had that effect on her. Whether it was an actual tooth from the actual whale that ate the Prophet Jonah was immaterial. It was something that Fayyad had loved and it was something from home.

'We have to just let him get on with it,' Shereen said. 'That's what we agreed.'

'He could be doing nothing for all we know.'

Shereen put the crochet work she had been trying to finish down. 'You know that's not the case, Abbas,' she said. 'Lee is our friend. He would like to involve the police—'

'So maybe he has!'

'No, he hasn't! He promised you. Remember?' She stood up. She didn't want to be in the room with him if he was going to be like this. 'We leave him to it! He will get back to us when he thinks fit.'

'Yes, but . . .'

'When? I don't know,' Shereen said. 'He's helping us for just expenses, remember? Lee is a good man but I'm sure that he and Mrs Hakim have to make a living. I know I do!'

'What's that supposed to mean?'

She picked up her crochet hook and her wool. 'I don't know, Abbas,' she said. 'Or rather I do, but I don't want to discuss it. I'm tired of the subject.'

'You know why I drink,' he said. 'You know that I have to.'

Shereen shook her head with impatience. She'd heard it all before. What Abbas sometimes seemed to forget was that the whole family had been through the trauma of Iraq's dissolution. They'd lost their home, their faith, their past and, sometimes Shereen felt, even their dignity.

'I don't want to talk about it,' she said.

Abbas poured himself a very large whisky. 'You don't want to talk about anything,' he growled. 'One of your sons is a terrorist, our daughter Djamila spends her time with a freak.'

'Fazil isn't a freak. He's a nice young man.'

'He has no job,' Abbas said.

'He's looking. Jobs are hard to come by these days.' She tried to look into her husband's eyes, but he avoided her gaze. 'You don't like him because he's a Turk.'

Abbas tossed whisky down his throat. 'Don't be ridiculous. I am a socialist. I'm not a racist.'

'Yes, you are,' she said. 'I've seen you looking at him with distaste. What is it? That his father is a carpet dealer? That he has a London accent?'

Abbas didn't answer.

'Admittedly his hair is a little strange,' Shereen said. 'I don't understand why a young man with nice hair would choose to shave it all off. But it's Fazil's choice. He's a nice young man and he's nice to our daughter.' She went to leave the room and then turned back. 'Oh, and he's not a religious lunatic. And for that alone, we must thank God – or whoever.'

Shereen walked into the kitchen.

Once she had gone, her husband poured himself another drink and then muttered. 'Don't you be so sure, Shereen.'

'When does this man find time to fight jihad?' Mumtaz said.

Abu Imad had sent her so many messages it was impossible to read them all.

Lee got up and looked at her screen. Most of the messages were questions. These ranged from did she find him attractive to who was her favourite West Ham player and why. Where he wasn't questioning, he was berating.

Mishal, are you there? Answer me.

I am making time for you, please make time for me.

Sometimes he whined.

I so want to see your lovely face, hear your voice. Please send me your Skype address.

'Would a teenage girl be flattered by this?' Lee asked.

'Some would,' Mumtaz said.

'Would Mishal?'

Mumtaz thought about Wahid Sheikh. No young girl, however obedient, would want to marry a man like that. Old and odious. He'd get his hands on her Shazia over her dead body. And yet old men were what some, so-called religious families, expected their girls to marry. Sometimes even quite secular families, like Mishal's, entered into such arrangements, particularly if it was financially advantageous. If only she hadn't had to speak to Wahid Sheikh. But if she'd made a scene, DI Montalban and his young constable might have come over. And that would have been awkward. The old man had delighted in telling her how he was planning to treat her daughter like a whore.

'Mumtaz?'

'Sorry.' She didn't want to tell him about it. Not yet. 'She probably would,' she said.

'Although neither of them have spoken much about what he does yet, have they?'

'I've avoided it. Not wanting to be too keen.'

'What about him?'

'Well, it's acknowledged that there are similarities between paedophile grooming and extremist grooming. The former proceeds slowly, gradually gaining a child's trust and affection. Only towards the end of the process does sex come into the equation.'

'By which time the kid's hooked.'

'The child will have become dependent on the relationship. The thought of disappointing their new friend is very uncomfortable, particularly if they think that friend is their own age. So they do take naked selfies, and worse, and they do worry about their parents finding out. But all the time their, what's known as latitude of acceptance, is being pushed ever outwards by their abuser.'

Lee sat down behind his desk. 'So, do you think it's time to give Mishal's Skype address to Abu Imad?'

As well as being repellent, Mumtaz had found the few conversations she'd had with extremists in the past very boring. They were monomaniacal, never listened and didn't know what they were talking about. They also defamed the religion she loved and that made her skin crawl. She never knew whether to laugh or scream at their ravings.

'If Fayyad is trying to use Mishal to get to the West, we have to help him,' Lee said.

'And if he's not?'

'Then we drop him,' Lee said. 'If he really wants to get out, he will find a way to get to us. If Abbas is right, he's been to Amsterdam already.'

He was right. The whole point of what they were doing was based on an assumption that Fayyad was lying as well.

Mumtaz stood. 'I'd better go and buy a niqab, then,' she said.

TEN

Zafar Bhatti's electrical shop rarely closed. When the old man couldn't be in there himself his son, Jabbar, took over. The 'boy' – he was forty – was cross-eyed and so his father treated him like an idiot. But he wasn't. He was just bored. Both Ricky Montalban and Bob Khan had known the old man and his son all their lives. Walking in to Bhatti's shop was like getting into a time machine back to the 1970s. Despite advertising itself as an 'electronic' shop, there were no computers or in fact any actual electrical devices on sale. Bhatti's was all about individual plug sockets, cable, boxes and boxes of light bulbs and, if you asked Zafar himself and he liked you, the odd dodgy electricity meter.

Ricky saw the old man before he saw him. This was fortunate. Just before he had retired, old DI Kev Thorpe had felt Bhatti's collar about his PO Box business. That had involved the shifting of money gained by blackmail. Lee Arnold had worked that case on behalf of the victim who had been Chief Super at Newham nick. He was long gone, but Bhatti, like the dirt in Brick Lane's gutters, remained.

When he did clock Ricky, the copper saw him jump.

'Hello, Mr Bhatti,' he said.

'DI Montalban!' He straightened his spine against the back of his chair. 'Oh, what now?'

Ricky, like most locals, knew that Bhatti was a villain, but he was also physically harmless and was likeable inasmuch as he represented the old-style 'dodgy' bloke, often beloved of East Enders.

'Don't worry, you're not in bother,' Ricky said. 'Unless you've something to tell me . . .'

He sat down next to the old man in what was usually cross-eyed Jabbar's seat. It smelt a bit animal-y for some reason.

'No, no, no,' Bhatti said. 'Life is as life is. My son is still unmarried, which breaks my heart. But, thanks be to God, we are all still living even if putting food on the table takes more and more effort every day. Giving up the PO Box business did me no good, DI Montalban. Even though, of course, it was quite the right thing to do.'

'Well, it's that I've come to talk to you about,' Ricky said.

The old man's face paled. 'Oh, but I told you that is finished now!' he said. 'I swear that is in the past! Why would I lie? DI Montalban, if you saw my bank statements now, you would weep. Truly. I make nothing now because I do the right thing. And I do it with a good heart, you know.'

'You're a model citizen Zafar-ji,' Ricky said. 'And there's no suggestion you've done anything wrong. I'm here about secrets, not wrongdoing. Nothing criminal.'

'Secrets? What secrets? I don't know any secrets!'

'Ah, but I think you do,' Ricky said. 'Not, as I say, criminal stuff. But when you run a PO Box service it's not easy to ignore who is passing messages to who. Now I know you know that we've had a murder on the Lane . . .'

'Rajiv-ji,' he said. 'A terrible incident!'

104

'Yeah.'

'And who would do such a thing! Such a kind man, he was. Strange, but kind. You know it makes my old heart bleed the way these young people these days behave! So the man is a homosexual! This is Britain, he can be a homosexual. You might not like it, but provided he doesn't make others homosexuals too . . .'

'We don't know who killed Rajiv-ji,' Ricky said. 'Not yet. We're still looking into who he had contact with.'

'Those gangster boys abused him,' Bhatti said. 'You know that boy who is their leader? His father is a drug addict—'

'Rajiv-ji used your PO Box service, didn't he?'

Ricky needed to cut Bhatti's youth-blaming crap. He didn't like the Briks Boyz or indeed any of the other kids on the Lane. Moaning about them was his thing.

'I've solid intel that he used your service,' Ricky said. 'So don't deny it.'

The old man shrugged. Then he said, 'What can I say? It was a long time ago. The poor, unnatural man needed a friend. I made that possible for him.'

'For a consideration.'

'DI Montalban, we all have to make a crust. Rajiv-ji knew this. He was grateful to me.'

'And in your debt.'

'No!' He shook his head. 'He made a friend. That's all! What good would it do to me to break his trust?'

'His "friend" was a Muslim.'

Bhatti blanched. 'Who tells you that?'

'Never mind. I know,' Ricky said. 'And they weren't just friends. You know that, Zafar-ji.'

'I do not! It was a friendship. Between men. Normal and honourable.'

'Oh, don't give me that!' Ricky said. 'Why the PO Box bloody subterfuge if they was just friends? Don't treat me like a fucking idiot.'

Flustered, Bhatti shook his head. 'I swear I didn't know of anything sexy . . .'

'Zafar-ji, Rajiv-ji is dead,' Ricky said. 'Someone smashed him up and then stabbed him until he looked like something out of a splatter film. And I know you used to peddle them too. But what the fuck. We have to catch whoever killed Rajiv before they kill someone else. To do that I have to know everyone in Rajiv's life. Now how long ago, exactly, did he have this PO Box?'

Bhatti looked down at his hands. 'Last time, three years ago.'

'You sure?'

He pointed to his head. 'It's all up here, DI Montalban,' he said. 'I remember everything. People say I should have been a secret agent. Like James Bond.'

'Don't think you've got the body for it, but I see what you mean,' Ricky said. 'Now I want a name.'

Bhatti frowned. 'Oooh.' He shook his head.

'Oh God.'

'Now that would be betraying a confidence, DI Montalban,' he said. 'Rajiv-ji is dead, but his friend is not. My business, though defunct, was all about confidences. What would people think—'

'Who the fuck do you think you are? A priest? A bleeding psychiatrist?'

'Well . . .'

'Bhatti, we can do this the easy way, which is what I'm attempting to do now, or the hard way, which means I get a warrant to tear your property apart so I can get that name,' Ricky said. 'And that would also involve my doing you for obstructing my investigation. Now what's it to be?'

* * *

106

One of the things that had attracted Mumtaz to her late husband, Ahmet, was the fact that he didn't have a beard. A lot of Muslim men did, but she didn't like them. She wasn't surprised that Abu Imad had a particularly straggly example. Militants did. But, sartorially, it did him no favours.

'I wish I could see your beautiful face,' he said.

Mumtaz was glad that he couldn't. She had never considered wearing a niqab and probably never would, but at that moment it made her feel safe.

'But I respect your covering,' he continued. 'If only all women knew how beautiful modesty can be.'

'I would love to cover all the time,' Mumtaz said. 'But my parents say that they are afraid for me if I do it.'

'They think you'll be looked at as what people call a "militant", yes?'

'Yes.'

'Well, they're right but they're wrong to stop you,' he said. 'There is nothing "militant" about covering. And anyway, who and what is a militant?'

'My dad says it's people who do jihad.'

'Jihad is a religious duty,' he said. 'Is your dad a Muslim?'

'Yes.'

'Then he should know this. Don't listen to him, Mishal.'

'Aren't we supposed to obey our parents?'

'Not if they lead us away from the path of Islam,' he said. 'However much we love them, we have to oppose them if they try to stop us on our journey towards a World Caliphate. That's stifling our Islamic destiny. My parents were the same.'

'Do you speak to them?'

'Not now,' he said. 'Even your closest family can't get in your way if you want to come to support the Caliphate with all your heart. Do you want to do that, Mishal?'

'I don't know,' she said.

'You must've been looking for something when you found my video,' he said.

'I have been praying,' she said. 'I want to be useful. To the umma. So many Muslims have taken on these values of the West, like disrespecting motherhood and just thinking the whole meaning of life is about shopping . . .'

'Totally!'

His eyes were so bright and so wide, they looked as if they were about to pop out of his head. The rings of kohl underneath them, to deflect the sunlight, further accentuated their size.

Where he was, exactly, Abu Imad wouldn't say. She had to be content with 'in the Caliphate' for now. His surroundings looked hot and desert-like. Every so often a Kalashnikov-carrying, sand-stained 'brother' would walk behind him as he sat on the saddle of a motorbike. The image he was clearly going for was hard, handsome and cool. And without the beard, he was handsome, to Mumtaz. With it, he was very appealing to Mishal. She had to remember that.

'And you say you support the Hammers!' he continued. 'A girl who realises that materialism is wrong, who covers and who is also a Hammer! Man, you are just the perfect woman, Mishal!'

In spite of her niqab, she lowered her head. Was he goading her or did he mean it?

'And, of course, Palestine,' she said. 'Something has to be done.'

'And ISIS is the outfit to do it!' he said. 'World Caliphate means no more Jews!'

'Send them to America!'

'No, Mishal, kill them,' he said. 'Or make them slaves. There's no place in the World Caliphate for unbelievers!'

'Yeah, but isn't killing, like, a sin?'

'Only if you kill a Muslim brother or sister. Don't you know that?' He laughed. 'Oh poor little Mishal, you're such an innocent. You must've seen ISIS videos on telly or online. Who do you think those people we're beheading and burning are?'

'I . . . er, I saw the Jordanian pilot in the cage . . .'

Back in January 2015 a Jordanian Airforce pilot called Muath al-Kasasbeh had been burnt alive in a cage by ISIS. He had been, according to his family, a devout Muslim.

'He wasn't a real Muslim, Mishal,' he said. 'He came to destroy the Caliphate. There are millions of false Muslims out there. We can't show them no mercy. If we do, they'll try to destroy us. They won't, but they'll try.'

She could hear the nervousness behind the bluster and the overcompensation. In spite of the motorbike, the camouflage gear and a very large pistol in a holster at his hip, Abu Imad was shitting himself. But was this because he was trying to use her as an excuse to get away? Only time would tell. But for the moment, just this short conversation had exhausted Mumtaz. She said, 'I'll have to go in a minute.'

'No! Why?'

He looked genuinely hurt.

'Why?'

But her mind had gone blank. Trying not to look at Lee across the other side of the office, she said the first thing that came into her head.

'I've got a dance class,' she said.

Out of the corner of her eye, she saw Lee grimace.

'A dance class! Oh, Mishal, you shouldn't be doing such things! Dancing is haram, you must know that?'

Had she said 'dance class' because that was what she had done when she was a teenager?

'My mum and dad make me do it,' she said. 'I broke my leg when

I was little and the doctor suggested I do dance to strengthen it.'

He shook his head. 'Your leg was beautiful as it was,' he said. 'It was broken at Allah's behest and it would have been fixed by His grace too. Why do you make it ugly in this way?'

She didn't know what to say. She knew that extremists thought like this. She'd heard them ranting on Brick Lane for years. But to actually have to confront it herself was a new experience. It was one that both alarmed and exhausted her.

'Mum's coming!' she said.

'Mishal—'

She cut the connection. Then she switched the laptop off.

Lee said, 'Jesus!'

Mumtaz put a hand up to her head. 'That,' she said, 'was horrifying.'

The shop was closed for the day and so they went to his house. Bob and a couple of uniforms round the back, Ricky plus two other woodentops, knocking the front door.

'Yes?'

'Mr Ali Huq?'

'You know it's me, DI Montalban, what do you want?' Ali said.

'I've a few questions,' Ricky said. 'About the late Mr Rajiv Banergee.'

Ricky examined Huq's face for signs of nervousness. Nothing.

'What about him?' Ali said.

'I'd like you to come down the station and answer a few questions, please.'

'About Rajiv? Why? I don't know anything about him!'

'Come voluntarily or come under caution,' Ricky said. 'It's up to you, sir.'

* * *

110

Lee put a mug of strong tea on the desk in front of Mumtaz and then sat down.

'I'm drained,' she said.

'I'm not surprised.'

'I wanted to argue him to oblivion when we were talking about my leg!'

'Did you break it?'

'When I was seven, yes,' she said. 'And I did end up going to dance classes. My friend Amy used to do ballet and tap and her mum suggested to my mum that I go too. I'm sure I don't walk with a limp now because of those exercises. But of course, according to the ultra-conservatives, I should. Fate or qadar is something one has to accept as a gift from Allah. And I do accept this. But it depends how far you choose to take it.

'There are people who believe that we shouldn't intervene in what fate hands out to us at all. Therefore, if you break your leg, you should leave it broken. But this is all very well until it happens to you.'

Lee smiled.

'When it's you, of course you get it fixed. Just like whenever you can't get reception on your mobile, you move until you can. So there's a lot of hypocrisy. Much of it is played out by extremists, like Abu Imad. If we try to help ourselves as mere mortals, we are in sin. Except if we do just sit back and do nothing we risk the sin of starving ourselves to death. They use the concept of qadar selectively.' Then she said, 'Lee, this idea about luring Abu Imad to Europe . . .'

'Yeah?'

'We know he's been here because the tooth was posted in Amsterdam. If we assume he posted it himself.'

'Nothing else makes a lot of sense.'

'It's common knowledge that ISIS fighters come in and out of Europe all the time,' she said. 'But everything I've heard about the women who join them seems to involve a journey out to Syria. I wonder if it's some sort of test for prospective brides?'

'I guess we'll find out.'

'We don't know that Fayyad wants to leave ISIS, do we?'

'No. But he was saying something when he sent the tooth to his parents.'

'Or was he? Maybe he rescued the tooth from the mosque as a sort of reflex. Perhaps it caused him to think about his parents affectionately one last time. What if that feeling is now out of his system?'

'He took a risk sending that parcel to his family,' Lee said. 'ISIS don't do relics, just like they don't do people's parents.'

'Unless it was ISIS who told him to send it,' she said.

He sighed. 'You think I've not thought of that?' he said. 'But why would they do that? To draw family members to them? Fayyad would know his father would be watching his brother and sisters like a hawk.'

'Maybe they want Abbas?'

'Why? Abbas was a translator. That was it. He wasn't a member of the Baa'th Party, he didn't have anything to do with Saddam. Alright, he's a Shi'a and ISIS don't like them, but why him?'

'I don't know,' she said. 'I needed to say it.'

'I understand your anxieties, Mumtaz. And like I've said, you can stop this whenever you want.' He shook his head. 'Don't know why I've gone along with something so hooky meself. If DI Collins found out, neither of us would ever work in this business again. I s'pose I feel I still owe Abbas something.'

'Because he saved your life? I'm sure Abbas doesn't think about it like that,' she said.

'Ya think?' He shook his head. 'I invaded his country.'

'In a legitimate war to liberate Kuwait,' Mumtaz said. 'Lee, it wasn't like the second Iraq War. We didn't get involved on the say-so of liars. There was no choice.'

'But Iraq got worse after we went in,' he said. 'We should've finished Saddam off then. But we pulled back and so lots of people were just left to their fate. Abbas and Shereen never wanted to be exiled. And now this thing with Fayyad . . .' He shook his head. 'You know, Mishal should bring up the subject of photography again. Might take his mind off the evils of dancing.'

'Mmm.' Mumtaz turned her head away. 'A bit technical for me . . .'

'I think Shereen gave you a bit too much info.'

'Yes,' she said. 'I'll be honest, Lee, I have for the most part avoided it.'

'You know that Bhatti lies, don't you?' Ali said.

'And you know that he's an old crook with an eye towards the main chance,' Ricky replied.

Ali Huq's lawyer, a man called Maurice Glass, also one-time resident of the Lane, said, 'Do you have any evidence for this alleged relationship between Mr Huq and Mr Banergee, besides word of mouth, DI Montalban?'

Ricky had been both shocked and pissed off that Ali Huq had called his solicitor. He'd just wanted a quiet chat. But he could see where this could go. Glass doing him for harassment. Except that, under the circumstances, he probably wouldn't. He held up his phone which displayed the photograph Zafar Bhatti had sent him.

'What's this?'

'That,' Ricky said, 'is you and Mr Banergee on a day out to the Tower of London.'

They were holding hands, smiling and looking into each other's eyes. It was a nice picture. What a pity they'd been too wrapped up in each other to notice they were being snapped. Bhatti had said, 'I

113

only took it because I thought they looked so happy and I thought I might give it to them later.'

But he hadn't. Taking that photograph had had a much darker purpose. Not that Ricky could prove anything of the sort.

What had Bhatti been doing at the Tower? Had he followed the couple and, if so, from where?

'Is that you?' Ricky asked. 'On the left?'

It was so obviously him if he denied it he'd be a bigger fool than Ricky already thought he was. Now he'd seen the photograph and spoken to Bhatti, it made sense. Ali Huq had always been a stranger in his own skin. Even as a kid he'd always set himself a bit apart from others, even his own siblings. And this religious stuff was too intense. According to the odious Bhatti it had come upon Ali suddenly. In his opinion, it had happened when Ali and Rajiv Banergee had finished their affair four years before.

'Rajiv-ji just cried all the time,' the old electrical shop man had told Ricky. 'I quite feared for his sanity. But Ali-ji . . . Well, he had to keep it to himself, didn't he?'

Ali said, 'Did that come from Bhatti?'

'Is it you?' Ricky said.

Glass said, 'You don't have to say anything.'

But Ali ignored him. 'Yes.'

The lawyer looked at Ricky and shrugged. Glass's dad, Norman, had rented a room to Baharat Huq when he'd first arrived in London with one battered suitcase and a saucepan.

'Ali—'

'Maurice, it's OK,' Ali said. He looked at Ricky. 'I suppose you want to know whether I killed Rajiv?'

'Believe me, I've no interest in exposing your sexual preferences to the world . . .'

'I don't like being me. I am a sin.'

Neither Ricky nor Glass knew how to respond to this. Eventually it was Ali who spoke.

'For a man to love another man, in a sexual way, is a sin,' he said. 'In order to mitigate that sin I have to either be punished or I have to abstain from that activity. I failed.'

'You, your brother and your sister used to go round Rajiv Banergee's shop when you were children,' Ricky said. 'Your brother Asif particularly liked being with him.'

'I don't know how you know that. Do you remember?' Ricky didn't answer. 'Rajiv gave us sweets and tea and spoke to us as if we were grown-ups,' Ali continued. 'My brother was a normal little boy who saw nothing wrong with playing with a much older man who gave him treats. But then Asif is normal, why would he? I knew I had to keep my distance, not because of Rajiv-ji, but because of myself. He never behaved in a sexual way towards any of us. But I knew instinctively what he was. And when I grew up it was not Rajiv who initiated our affair, but me.'

'Did you finish it too?'

'We always met away from the Lane. We'd make arrangements using Bhatti's PO Box. Old-fashioned, but how can anyone use a mobile phone with any degree of privacy now? People just pick phones up and look at them, email is not secure. And yes I was, and am, paranoid.'

'You must've known Bhatti would always be a weak link?'

'He's also venal. I knew I could control him with money. When I finished it with Rajiv I gave Bhatti a thousand pounds.'

'What for?'

'For nothing.'

'To buy his silence?'

'I guess. He never asked about us and we never told him anything but of course he knew. I thought that if I could just finish it I could

115

wipe my sin away somehow. But God isn't bought off, is he?'

'I don't know,' Ricky said. 'I don't do all that. Where were you the night Rajiv was murdered?'

'At home.'

'Anyone corroborate that?'

'No.'

Glass put a hand on Ali's shoulder. 'You need to stop now and we need to talk.'

Ali smiled. 'No, Maurice,' he said. 'That photo can't be unseen. If I'd known about it, I would never have called you.' He looked at Ricky. 'I was alone.'

'Which means that the two young men who are staying with you were out.'

'Yes.'

'Where?'

'I believe at a meeting.'

'What kind of meeting?'

'An Islamic study group, I believe,' he said.

'What did you do?'

'That evening? I read and then went to bed.'

'Read what?'

'The Holy Koran,' he said. 'I read little else.'

'What about online?'

'I don't have a computer at home, only at work.'

'What about your boys?'

'Yes, they have computers. They're young. Young people can't manage without computers.' Then suddenly awash with tears he broke down. 'I didn't kill Rajiv!' he said. 'I loved him! May I be forgiven, but I loved him more than my life!'

ELEVEN

What was the time difference between the UK and Syria?

She looked at the time registration. Two hours. That meant that Abu Imad had tried to Skype her at just past four in the morning, Syrian time. There were messages on Facebook too.

Where are you Mishal? I need to talk to you.

He'd lived in the UK for years. Where did he think a pious teenage girl had been at 6 a.m.? Did he really imagine she'd been waiting for him to call as soon as she opened her eyes?

Mumtaz ignored it. She had a meeting with a woman in Dagenham who suspected her aged father had fallen under the spell of an Albanian prostitute. The client, a Mrs Carter, was worried that her father had changed his will in favour of this woman.

She closed her laptop and put on her headscarf. Abu Imad would have to wait.

Then her phone rang. For a moment she wondered whether he'd somehow got hold of her number, but when she saw the screen, she realised it was her father. She answered.

'Hi, Abba.'

'Oh, Mumtaz,' he sounded breathless.

Her heart began to race. 'Abba?'

'Your brother Ali's house is being searched by the police!' he said.

'Why?'

'No one will say! Your amma is just crying!'

'Abba!'

'Your brother Asif is coming. You must come!'

'I'm working,' she said.

'This is family!'

'I must go to meet a client,' she said. 'It's too late to cancel. I'll come as soon as I've finished. I will be as quick as I can.'

He went quiet for a moment. Good Bangladeshi girls were supposed to put family first, always. But her father was also a realist and, more significantly, he liked Lee Arnold.

'OK,' he said. 'But please hurry.'

'I will.'

As soon as she finished the call, she contacted Lee who said she could take as much time as she needed. Abu Imad would have to wait even longer.

The house was grim. Not dirty or even messy, just antiquated and scruffy. There was no music, no TV, no books, apart from the Koran, Hadith and learned commentaries on the Holy Book.

Bob Khan remembered Ali Huq when he'd been a handsome young graduate. A little more grave than his peers, he'd been someone that fathers pointed to and said, 'When you grow up maybe you can be like him.' Not knowing who he really was. But then nobody except Rajiv Banergee and Mr Bhatti had known that – as far as they knew. Now Ali Huq sat in his chilly kitchen with his head in his hands.

Montalban was at the nick interviewing the two Syrian boys who had lived in the one room in the house that contained significant amounts of stuff. In contrast to Huq's thin mattress on his bedroom floor, both boys had new, comfortable beds, a TV, fashionable clothes and computers. Those had been taken away for analysis. One of the woodentops had told him that he'd found wank mags under one bed. It figured. Religious or not, Qasim Malouf and Nabil Abdella were young men with sexual needs. Bob wondered whether they would say whether Ali Huq had tried to satisfy those needs. He also wondered who the kids were.

They'd told Montalban that they both had refugee status and that Ali Huq was helping them to find jobs. So far there was no evidence for the latter. Was he screwing the kids in exchange for board and lodging or was the 'holy' act in fact real? If it was, did that mean the boys could be extremists? The police had been aware of Huq and his sometimes extreme, publicly voiced opinions for some time. But was that just a cover for his homosexuality?

His phone rang.

'Khan.'

'Bob.' It was Montalban.

'Sir.'

'Caught a whisper that Zayn Chaudhuri might be in Wapping,' he said.

'Bit upmarket for him, isn't it? Any idea where he might be, guv?'

'He was seen on Prusome Street, round the old council flats,' Montalban said.

'A lot of them have been sold to posh people, haven't they?'

'Yeah, but some of the old tenants are hanging on. Can't think of anyone round there who might give shelter to a gobshite like Zayn. You know Wapping, Bob?'

The Thames-side district of Wapping wasn't a place CID went to all that often. Fiercely gentrified since the late 1980s, Wapping was loft-conversion land with a few council tenants thrown in for extra colour, to make it 'real' for the hipsters. Views of Tower Bridge and quiet streets made it very desirable.

'Not much, guv,' Bob said. 'I haven't got any family down there. Although my brother Najib has in-laws down there.'

'They council tenants?'

'Yeah. Can't remember exactly where they live. I'll call Naj. His mother-in-law is a right Asian Auntie, knows everybody's business, disapproves of most things.'

Montalban laughed. Then he said, 'I'm getting some size twelves on the ground. Maybe Zayn was just passing through, but it's all we've got at the moment. CCTV's a bit thin on the ground in that part of the manor.'

'Why would you have CCTV when you don't have anything?' Bob said.

Mumtaz hadn't seen her brother Asif for months. As usual, he was wearing clothes that made him look even more like a kid than he already did. The youngest Huq sibling, Asif was slim, pale and funny. He kissed his sister on both cheeks and then hugged her.

'How you doing, Philip Marlowe?' he said, referencing Raymond Chandler's legendary Los Angeles PI.

She smiled. 'I'm OK.' Then she looked around to make sure that her mother was out of the room. 'How's Tracey?'

Although welcomed into the Huq family with open arms by their father, Mumtaz and Asif's mother, Sumita, didn't approve of his white, British partner.

'Great,' he said. 'Last check-up went well.'

'Good.'

Tracey was recovering from having a hysterectomy. Another bone of contention with Sumita. Now, unless he moved on to someone else, her youngest son would never be a father.

They both sat down.

'Have you managed to speak to Ali?' Mumtaz asked.

'No. No one has.'

'I drove past his house and so I saw the police cars outside.'

'Dad reckons he's in the house,' Asif said. 'DI Montalban, used to be Ricky Montalban . . .'

'Yes,' she said. 'I know him. He interviewed me about the death of Rajiv Banergee. I assume you know . . .'

'Yes.' He shook his head. 'Poor Rajiv-ji. Where are we getting all these crazies from, eh? I don't know this, OK, but I suspect that Montalban is doing Ali's place because of those kids he's taken in. Maybe he thinks they killed Rajiv.'

'Oh, surely not!'

'Mumtaz, they could be anyone,' Asif said. 'They could even be ISIS. You know how Ali has become! I can't even speak to him these days. He looks at me as if I'm a piece of shit on his shoe. I've given up even trying to communicate.'

'DI Montalban interviewed your brother late yesterday.'

They both started to get up when their father came in.

'Oh, sit, sit,' he continued. He sat. 'To be honest, I have thought for a while that it is only a question of time before your brother gets himself into trouble. He has been mixing with bad people for a long while. Then these boys from Syria. Who are they? Why are they here? They make nuisances of themselves in the name of Allah. Persecuting people. The problem with so many these days is that they don't read the Koran. Read it with your whole mind and you will not find hate, compulsion and all these evil things these people do. They follow false teachers, arrogant men who know neither Allah nor humanity.'

'Abba, is Ali's house being searched because of those boys?' Mumtaz said.

'I don't know,' he said. 'I imagine so.'

Her computer beeped. Another message from Abu Imad. Mumtaz put it in her bag and ignored it. He'd have to wait.

Baharat Huq shook his head. 'Your brother's twisted take on religion has changed him,' he said. 'But I cling to the idea that I have brought up only good children and that he has not hurt anyone. But those two boys . . . They persecuted Rajiv-ji. I think they may even have beaten him. He had black eyes. If I'm asked I will tell DI Montalban.'

'Of course.' Mumtaz took his hand. 'Rajiv-ji was always kind to us when we were children. I'm certain Ali would not have hurt him, however much he might have changed lately.'

'Do you really think so?'

She just smiled. She didn't know. Her brother had changed so much in recent years she had no idea what he might be capable of.

'Abba, do you want me to call DI Montalban?' she said. 'I have his number.'

'Oh, I don't know,' the old man said. 'Will calling make it worse, do you think?'

'Can't see how it can,' Asif said. 'And we are his next of kin. Dad, how did you find out what was going on?'

'From Morrie Glass,' he said. 'He told me that Ali had been taken by DI Montalban and that soon they would be searching his house.'

'So Morrie knows . . .'

'Of course he does! But he is a lawyer and so he cannot give out information!'

'Has Ali been arrested?'

'No.'

Mumtaz's machine beeped again.

'What *is* that?' her father said.

'Nothing,' she said. She only kept the sound on in case it wasn't Abu Imad. But a quick look at her computer screen confirmed that it was. She shoved it behind her.

'Abba, I think that Asif and I should go to Ali's house,' Mumtaz said. 'If he's not been arrested there's no reason why we shouldn't talk to him.'

'If he's in. If he hasn't run away and drowned himself in the canal.'

'Abba, he won't have done that,' Mumtaz said. 'Suicide is haram.'

There was a knock at the door. Asif got up and looked out of the window to see who it was.

'Susi Banergee,' he said. 'What does she want?'

'The poor woman is bereaved!' Baharat said. 'Let her in, my son! We must offer comfort and hospitality. Mumtaz, you must make tea!'

Tommy Moore, Lee's off-the-radar absent father of at least three of his client's seven children, lived in East Ham. It was a dark basement underneath a house of what Tommy called 'Pakis'. Lee told him how lucky he was that the 'Pakis' even allowed a tosser like him to set foot on their premises. Tommy didn't like paying for any of the estimated fifteen kids he'd fathered over his almost sixty years on earth. Unfortunately for him, Lee's client Della Smith had other ideas.

'I'm working my tits off to pay for them kids,' she'd said when she'd engaged Lee's services. 'The other father's dead but I know Tommy's out there somewhere.'

And so he had been. Small and timid, it was impossible to see what a big, beautiful woman like Della had seen in him.

Once he'd finished with Tommy, Lee walked over to Abbas's place, which was in the next street. He was alone save for his daughter Djamila who was cooking.

'I'm glad you came over,' Abbas said. He took Lee into his garden, which was where he'd set up a makeshift bar for himself. 'Any news?'

'I told you I wasn't going to tell you anything until I had to,' Lee said.

'Oh, yes.' He poured himself a vodka and tonic. 'Do you want a cola? Cup of tea?'

'No, ta.'

Lee sat down in one of the garden chairs and lit a fag. 'I wanna ask you some questions,' he said.

'What about?'

'The tooth,' he said. 'Do you know for definite that it came from Fayyad?'

'I've told you, yes.'

'How?'

'It's his handwriting . . .'

'Do you still have the envelope it came in?'

'Yes.'

'I want it,' Lee said.

'Why?'

'Never mind why, I want it. I'm laying myself on the line for you, Abbas. I'm trying to manipulate a known terrorist to get him back into the UK. If I didn't feel the weight of guilt on my shoulders over the whole Iraq mess, I wouldn't be doing it. And you can fucking knock the booze on the head if you want me to carry on, too. I'm sick of seeing you fucked out of your head. We all need to be on our game and that includes you.'

Abbas said nothing.

'Fayyad is alive,' Lee said. 'That's all I'm telling you. But I don't know where he is or what he's up to. I need proof that he sent that tooth.'

'I told you, it's his handwriting!'

'So you say. But I need to analyse it.'

'How?'

'Never mind.'

Abbas put his glass down. He'd aged since his son had left. He said, 'Alright. I will get it.'

'Good.'

'Is there anything else?'

'Yes,' Lee said. 'I want you to tell me about Fayyad and girls.'

'And girls?'

'Hi, Lee!'

Djamila waved from the back doorstep and Lee waved back. She was a lovely, smiling, curvaceous girl. A real contrast to the thin, terrified little child she had been back in Iraq.

'Hiya, kiddo,' he said. 'How's it going?'

'Fine,' she said. 'Just making some dolma.'

'Mmm. Love stuffed vine leaves,' he said.

'Not for you, I'm afraid,' Djamila said. Then she laughed.

'Cheeky!'

When Djamila went back inside the house, Abbas said, 'Her boyfriend is dining with us tonight.'

'Oh. Sweet.'

'Not so much,' he said. 'He is a jobless Turk.'

'Oh, so now you're a racist . . .'

'That's what Shereen said.' He shook his head. 'But I am not. The boy's father is a carpet dealer.'

'So money—'

'Oh, yes, the father has money,' Abbas said. 'And I have no issue with him. Mr Dorman is a very personable man. His wife is a charming woman and so is their daughter. But Fazil . . . I don't know. It's not just that he doesn't work. There's something about him that I cannot warm to. I feel as if he is holding something back.'

'Like what?'

'I don't know.'

Lee knew there was no point saying that Abbas should just 'forget about it'. Hunches like this had kept them both alive in Iraq. But Lee also knew that Djamila was not the sort of girl to saddle herself with a loser. She was a smart cookie.

'But look,' he said. 'I have to go soon. Mumtaz can't be in the office today. Fayyad and girls, give me the low-down. What kind of girls did he go for?'

Abbas reached for his vodka.

Much as she'd always loved Rajiv, the few times she'd met his sister, Susi, Mumtaz had always felt an intense dislike for her. Arrogant and high-handed, Susi Banergee had always seemed like a caricature of the Asian woman 'done good'. She was married to a doctor who had lots of money, she didn't have to work and she could afford every beauty treatment under the sun. She was the kind of woman Asian aunties both disapproved of and envied. To marry so 'well' had to be every girl's dream, but to strut about in gold and silver saris flashing diamond rings at everyone was tasteless, if understandable.

At first when Susi arrived, Mumtaz and Asif went off to see whether they could speak to Ali. But they were told that he didn't want to see them.

Why not? They only wanted to help. Mumtaz felt hurt and, when they got back to Hanbury Street, she went up to her old bedroom to have a bit of time on her own. Her dad didn't understand. Bangladeshis hated being alone. Even her distressed mother had put aside her headache to come down and be with her family when Susi Banergee arrived. To be away from the family when guests arrived was bad form. Only Asif knew where Mumtaz was coming from.

As she dragged herself upstairs, she heard her brother say, 'Leave her be. Mumtaz deals with things in her own way. We're all in shock.'

'Which is why she needs her family!'

'Leave her, Abba!'

There had never been locks on any of the Huqs' doors. Mumtaz did what she'd done as a child, and wedged a chair under the handle. Then she opened her computer.

Where are you?
Where are you?
Where are you?

There were so many she couldn't count them. It was a wonder Facebook hadn't blown up. Another message arrived as she was looking at the screen.

She had agreed not to contact Abu Imad if Lee wasn't present. But she had no idea when she'd be seeing him. She'd even told Shazia to come to Spitalfields after college. Who knew when or if they'd be able to speak to Ali? Or even find out what was going on? Was she at risk of losing Abu Imad if she just ignored him?

She constructed her message and read it three times. She had to avoid saying anything inflammatory, sexual, mildly critical or even just cheerful. How could one be cheerful when so many nations were controlled by unbelievers?

She wrote: *Hello. Sorry I've been offline for so long. I got up late and then I had a full day at college. I have to get good A levels if I want to go to uni. But I'm here now!*

The hiatus between her reply and his was over an hour. Mumtaz lay down on her old bed and remembered her life before her husband. She'd always felt safe with her parents and her brothers. Back then, no one had threatened her, tried to undermine or hurt her. Even being with Lee, who was the kindest man outside of her family and Rajiv Banergee she had ever met, wasn't the same. By the time she had met him, the world had changed for Mumtaz. Much of what had happened had been her own fault . . .

The computer beeped. She looked at his message with horror.

Mishal. I am surprised at you. Uni? What you want to go to uni for? Uni won't teach you anything you need to be a good Muslim. Uni's just full of people drinking and having sex when they're not married and other things that are haram. And everyone will see your face! I don't like it. I thought we were close, but now I wonder. What do you want, Mishal? Do you want uni or do you want the Caliphate?

Weren't bookish girls meant to be good girls? Wasn't it good for the 'cause' for girls to be educated so that they could enhance the work of the 'new order'? Abba had told her that Ali only read the Koran, Hadith and learned Muslim commentaries. Thinking about her brother again made her feel cold. What had he done? And why?

Another beep and Abu Imad continued his tirade.

First dancing and now this. What are you doing, Mishal? You think I can afford to waste my time with a girl who doesn't know her own mind? I thought that we had something. I didn't say because I didn't want to frighten you. But you force my hand, Mishal. I have not slept since we spoke. Even though I haven't seen your face I look into your eyes and I know that you are for me. I don't say this lightly. I am a great fighter, I've battled overwhelming odds for the Caliphate. Any number of girls would be honoured to be my wife. But I only want you. Maybe it's because, in spite of being beautiful, young and clever, you are new in the religious life. I can help you! Together we can be the ultimate couple! Married people are given everything here. A flat with all furniture and appliances, we have some of the best doctors in the world, alhamdulillah! And if you want to develop your mind, you can do. Of course, looking after me will be your main job. But you will have servants to help you. When we capture unbelievers we make them our slaves.

Or kill them, Mumtaz thought.

You will have slaves, Mishal. They will do everything you don't want to do. And they will give us time together as husband and wife. Tell me if you feel the same way, Mishal. If you don't, then I will withdraw my proposal of marriage and mend my heart eventually. But if you do, please put me out of my misery and tell me.

Mumtaz wanted to throw up. The 'time together as husband and wife' clearly alluded to sex, while the 'broken heart' image was playing into every teenage sob story of doomed passion. And just to ice the cake he'd asked her to give him an answer to his proposal. What did she do now?

She began to type. But then she stopped. She should talk to Lee. But then would he know what Mishal would say next?

TWELVE

'You what?'

It had been past midnight when Abu Imad had got back to her. He'd been out 'on patrol' looking for enemies of the caliphate. He said he'd found two. And killed them. Getting her answer on top of that had made his day. Now she was in the office, telling Lee.

'I told him what he wanted to hear,' she said.

'That you'd marry him.'

'Yes. He wants me to go out to him. He's arranging it now. He says he will come and get me.'

'Where?'

'He doesn't know yet.'

She knew what Lee was thinking. That it had all moved too fast. It was a speed that was alien to him.

'Lee, a lot of people marry very quickly in his culture and in mine,' she said. 'In some communities the fact that he's seen my photograph is enough.'

He raised his eyebrows.

'And when men are in organisations like ISIS it's all the more likely,' she said.

He had two small plastic bags in his hands. One contained the envelope the Tooth of Jonah had been sent in while the other was a small notebook from Fayyad al'Barri's bedroom. He'd been telling her how he intended to get the handwriting analysed by an old mate who owed him a favour when she'd come out with this.

'Mishal said she'd Skype him this evening,' Mumtaz said. 'He really wanted her to. I won't do it without you. Not on Skype. Lee, he was going to run away. I had to stop him.'

She'd shown him everything.

Lee shook his head. 'We'll have to get a move on, then,' he said. He looked at the plastic bags. 'Have to drop these off to Harry today. You must try and persuade Abu Imad to come and get you from the UK, ideally.'

'Did Abbas know anything about Fayyad's girlfriends?' she asked.

'Only one as far as he knows. She was white British. Met her at uni. Didn't last long.' Then he said, 'Has Mishal ever been abroad?'

'Only with her family to see her grandparents in Pakistan.'

'Is that common?'

'Very,' she said. 'I went to France with the school when I was thirteen but I was lucky. My dad wanted us all to take every opportunity we could to expand our horizons. But I knew many, many girls like me who were not even allowed to leave their streets, except to go to school. Mishal comes from a liberal background but she's no traveller.'

'Mmm. We'll need to plan your next encounter. Have all Mishal's answers down pat.'

'Yes.'

He was angry but he was also out of his comfort zone and he knew it. She had to guide him and he had to follow. She knew there were no 'pat' answers . . .

'What about your brother?'

And now he was changing the subject.

'Why'd the coppers search his house?'

'They're questioning those two boys he has lodging with him,' she said. 'It's about that murder we had in the Lane. The one DI Montalban spoke to me about. But I didn't see Ali. None of us did.'

'Why was that?'

'First he wouldn't see us, then when they finished searching his house, the police took him away for further questioning,' she said. She began to feel tears fill her eyes. 'I know he didn't hurt Rajiv-ji. He wouldn't.'

She saw him make as if to rise, maybe to come over to her, and then sit down again.

'I feel so guilty,' she said.

'Why?'

'Because when I found out that the police knew about those boys Ali had staying with him, I knew that the Sheikhs no longer had that particular hold over me any more. But I didn't anticipate this.'

Lee didn't speak for a moment and then he said, 'Look, I don't know if I can find out any details for you. I don't really know Ricky Montalban. But Vi does. I can give it a go.'

She looked up at him.

'Please.'

Fucking aunties everywhere! Zayn had thought that Wapping was posh, but it was just more of the same. Asian aunties poking their noses, white scumbags yelling 'Paki' and that skank always on his balls. He didn't mind Rashida going down on him, but he didn't want to fuck her. Everyone had been inside her. Saggy old dog. And when she begged him, it was just uncool.

'Have some fucking respect for yourself and for me,' he told her whenever she tried to get him to. 'Why I want your old pregnancy body, eh?'

It was getting tiresome. But where to go next? If he went back to his old man's the feds'd take him in and he didn't want that. Zayn opened Rashida's front door.

'Get me some fags, yeah?' he heard her call from the bedroom. He ignored her.

Outside on the walkway he saw one of the fat old aunties who lived next door hanging out washing. Fucking women! He'd get a face full of sari and old women's wet bloomers. He pushed past. The old girl said something in Urdu that he didn't understand. And then suddenly there was a man.

A young, clean-cut Asian. And he wasn't alone. He had a load of white blokes with him. What the fuck?

'Hello Zayn,' Bob Khan said. 'Your neighbours got a bit fed up with your sex noises.'

He tried to run, but when he went back through the washing the auntie had gone, only to be replaced by more coppers.

It took him a while to work out what the old man was looking for. Or rather who. He'd started coming into the shop about a month ago. Aftab Huq had never seen him before, although he knew he looked like someone. Then his old mate Sid in the fish and chip shop had told him.

'That's Wahid Sheikh,' he'd said over chips and a fag out the back of Aftab's convenience store. 'That old crook Rizwan's brother over from Pakistan.'

'Really?'

'Come to take over the family business now Rizwan's gone funny in the head. Can't get over that favourite son of his dying. Well, that's what me missus told me.'

Sid's wife was half Pakistani and enjoyed gossip in both the white and Asian worlds.

Sid knew that Aftab's family had an issue with the Sheikhs, which was something to do with his cousin Mumtaz, but he didn't know the whole story. Mumtaz's stepdaughter Shazia had been present when some unknown man had stabbed Rizwan Sheikh's son Naz to death. But she'd never been able to identify the assailant. After that, the Sheikhs had stopped coming into his shop – until now.

The old man came in for daft stuff that no one could ever really need. Jaffa cakes, chocolate bars, gummy bears and bottles of Fanta. It always took him a long time to locate what he wanted and Aftab had assumed he was a bit demented. But then he'd seen him looking at Shazia. She worked in the shop three evenings a week and Wahid was clearly getting used to her shifts because he always seemed to be around at those times.

What did the old git want? Revenge? The Sheikhs blamed the kid for Naz's death even though the police had proved she'd had nothing to do with it. But then the Sheikhs were a bunch of psychos.

Aftab had considered talking to Mumtaz about it after he'd spoken to Sid, but then he'd put it from his mind. Now, however, he felt he really ought to. Not that it was going to be easy. Mumtaz's brother Ali was in some sort of trouble with the police and the whole family was in uproar. But if Shazia was in danger, he had to. But then, did Shazia already know? Whenever Wahid Sheikh came into the shop, she became very pale . . .

Baharat Huq stared at the floor. He's rarely seen his eldest child cry. Certainly not since he'd become a man.

Ali had come to the house after being released by the police. The two boys he'd given shelter to were still in custody. Sumita

134

had cried with joy when her son had hugged her. Now she was out with Asif buying food for a celebratory feast. Baharat was glad.

'You should have come to me,' Baharat said once Ali's sobs had abated. 'I would have counselled you. It is what fathers do.'

'How could I? It's a sin!'

Baharat closed his eyes. Ali was right. For a man to lie with another man was a sin. But it had always happened. There had even been men in his old village who had . . . One of them had been his Auntie Fatima's son Ghalib. He'd always shimmied about in his mother's perfume, but nobody ever said anything. Nobody ever stoned anyone or threw men off buildings like those ISIS people did. They just left such men alone.

'I tried to stop it,' Ali said. 'I tried to think about girls. Do you remember when I was seventeen? I asked you to find me a wife?'

'You were too young,' Baharat said.

'I was desperate to be normal!'

'And you think that taking a bride would have changed you?'

'I don't know.'

Baharat looked up. 'Rajiv-ji, did he . . .'

'I came on to him.'

The two men looked at each other. Baharat had to see the truth in his son's eyes for his own sanity.

'I swear to you!' Ali said.

After a moment Baharat said, 'I know. I can see that in your face.' Then he said, 'Have you always . . .'

'Yes. Yes. I don't know why. I have never wanted a woman. I have tried to.'

'You have been with a woman?'

'Once. It was awful. I-I paid . . .'

'Ah. Then maybe that was the problem. Such women are . . .'

'Abba, I can't bear it,' Ali said. 'Women's bodies are . . . They

135

don't make me feel anything. I can't. I can't do anything.'

The old man sighed.

'I started it with Rajiv, because I had always loved him,' Ali said. 'Even when I was a boy.'

'When did this between you start?'

'Eight years ago. It lasted four years and then . . .' He trailed off. 'I have not . . . With no one else.'

'Why did you stop?'

'Because it was a sin! I couldn't live with myself!'

'And Rajiv?'

'What do you mean? Could he live with himself?'

'Well, of course he could! Rajiv-ji was always himself! No! What did he do when you finished with him? Was he upset? Was he angry? What?' He was getting angry and he knew it wasn't helping. He said, 'I'm sorry, my son, do please go on.'

Ali sighed, then he said, 'Rajiv was heartbroken. He even said he'd sell the Leather Bungalow and we'd go and live far away from London where no one would know us. He would have given up everything for me. But I just couldn't.'

'Why not?'

He put his head down. 'My family, my religion. When it came down to it, I just couldn't. I broke Rajiv's heart and my own.'

'And so you became a fanatic.'

'I became an observant man, Abba,' he said.

'No, no, you became a fanatic. What are those boys in your house if not fanatics? Abusing the man you had loved in the street. What is that? Is that religion? I think not. Islam is a religion of peace and of intellect. You have exhibited neither in recent years.'

'I did what I had to in order to stop my thoughts!' He stood up. 'Thinking about what I had with Rajiv every day! I purged everything except Islam! All I allowed myself to think about was my religion and the fight against the rising tide of Islamophobia that is taking over the world. My desire to help people in Syria is genuine! I want to help. I do.'

'And you think it helps that you criticise the way your sister's daughter chooses to dress? I have puzzled at the bitterness that comes out of you, Ali. I have tried to force myself to live with it. Now I know its cause . . .' he shrugged.

'Abba, don't reject me because of this, please!'

Ali began to cry again.

'Because of what?'

'Because of my sin!'

'The feelings you cannot crush? In spite of yourself? No,' the old man said. 'I will not reject you for that, my son. What I will find hard to forgive are your lies. Those you told me and those you have told yourself. Because now this dishonesty, this moving in circles that can only bring us harm, has put this family at risk. It has brought the police to our door.'

'I didn't kill Rajiv, Abba! I didn't!'

He sank to the floor and put his head in his hands. His father stroked his head, gently.

'I know you didn't, Ali,' he said. 'I know.'

'Can men see a girl's face if they're engaged?' Lee asked.

'These days we all see each other's faces before we marry,' Mumtaz replied. 'Unless of course you're a . . .'

'Nutter like Abu Imad.' Lee shook his head. 'Not that I should be using the word "nutter". He has his point of view.'

'No, he is a nutter,' Mumtaz said. 'And his point of view stinks. I'll wear the niqab for the Skype session and let's see what happens. I won't offer to take it off. I'm still not sure he'll buy me as an eighteen-year-old.'

'He liked your photograph.'

'Taken by a very talented photographer.'

They both fell silent for a moment. Now that Mishal was 'engaged' they had moved more quickly than either of them could have anticipated towards some sort of conclusion.

Lee said, 'You know we have to draw him as close to the UK as we can.'

'Yes, Lee,' Mumtaz said. 'You've spoken of little else today.'

'I was at home with me old man. Aks him!'

Ricky Montalban had a particular hatred for anyone who wasn't Afro-Caribbean talking as if they were.

'You mean "ask" him.'

'Yeah, aks, like I say.'

Ricky shook his head. 'So why did you bugger off down to Miss Ahmadi's flat in Wapping when you knew, because your dad must've told you, that we wanted to talk to you?'

Zayn shrugged. 'Everyone goes down Rashida's one time or another. I wanted a little bit lollipop action, you get me?'

'You what?'

'She sucks cock better'n anyone. Trust me.'

Ricky looked down at his paperwork. 'So she gave you a blow job that lasted two days? Impressive.'

'Nah! I just spend some time wit the girl.'

'So you didn't have to talk to me?'

'Nah.'

'I think the word you're struggling for is "yes" but let's see where we are, shall we?' Montalban said. 'Your dad says he's not sure whether you were with him or not on the night that Rajiv Banergee was murdered on Brick Lane.'

Zayn sucked his teeth.

'On account of being off his face,' Montalban said. 'By his own admission. As for your "Boyz", they were all apparently tucked up in bed, with the exception of Sultan Ibrahim. He says he was out and about that night, with you.'

'He's lying.'

'Is he?'

'Yeah. Sultan's a pussy, he'll say anything. He's frightened of you feds, innit.'

'Sultan's frightened of everyone,' Montalban said. 'But he's mostly frightened of you, you being such a stickler for good behaviour in the Lane.'

'Don't want no skanks on the Lane, no perverts. This is where Sharia is king, you get me.'

'Yeah,' Montalban said. 'So zero tolerance on gay people.'

'They ain't gay, they unnatural. Our religion don't allow that, man.'

'The Muslims I know accept gay people.'

'Pussies.'

The gangsta language wrapped around a poor understanding of a religion Zayn claimed to love was unnerving.

'Where were you on the night Rajiv Banergee was murdered?' Montalban asked.

'I told you. I was at me dad's.'

'No you weren't. Where were you?'

'Me dad never told you I was out.'

'How'd you know that, Zayn? Were you there when I asked him?'

'No. Why'd you think that? Course I weren't.'

Montalban was fast coming to the conclusion that somehow they'd missed Zayn when they'd searched Suleiman's flat.

'Sultan says you were with him,' Montalban said. 'So put that together with your dad saying you were out . . .'

139

He let that information hang. Zayn was stupid in many ways, but not when it came to his own personal safety.

'If I say I was out you'll fucking charge me.'

'Not necessarily. Depends what you were doing.'

Zayn looked down at the floor.

'Sultan reckons you were on patrol,' Montalban said.

The boy remained silent.

'I asked him what he meant and do you know what he said?'

Zayn shrugged.

'He told me you look for drunks, or should I say people who've had a drink,' Montalban said. 'Looking for drunks was my job last time I looked, but you and your mates watch out for people who've had a few jars. You like, according to Sultan, to catch hold of people of Asian heritage particularly. Like Rajiv Banergee . . .'

'I never even saw the old pooftah!'

'Oh, but you were out?'

He mumbled. 'Yeah.'

'So you lied to me.'

'You wouldn't understand.'

'No? I think I understand very well,' Montalban said. 'You go out and force your will on other people so you can feel powerful. Nothing to do with religion. Everything to do with you and your pathetic little gang. I get it, Zayn, I do! I grew up on the Lane watching all the bankers come down from their glass towers to gawp at us all through curry house windows. Being treated like something subhuman by fucking tits with pink hair and trust funds. It fucking stinks. But if you want it to change, roughing up pissheads ain't the way. Now I'm gonna have to take your DNA . . .'

'Man!'

'What do you want me to do, Zayn? You can tell me you didn't kill Mr Banergee until the cows come home, but I have to prove you didn't.'

'Well, you wanna DNA them boys what live in the house of Ali Huq, then,' he said.

Montalban had interviewed both lads who, unlike their landlord Ali Huq, told him they had been in all night. The issue with them, at present, was the triumphalist jihadi images on their computers.

'Why?' he asked.

'Because they're into ISIS and all that, innit.'

'Yeah. So are you, aren't you?'

Zayn shook his head. 'Ain't the same, man!' he said. 'And, anyway, them two boys were out the night Rajiv died. I saw them. So did Sultan. Aks him if you don't believe me.'

THIRTEEN

'You must come now.'

'How?'

'You get a flight to Istanbul and then a bus to a place called Gaziantep where I'll meet you. Lots of Sisters have made that journey.'

Mumtaz had to force herself not to look at Lee. It was difficult to maintain eye contact with Abu Imad. Whenever she did so for any length of time, she felt violated. She didn't know why. He had not, so far, been sexually suggestive to her.

'But I've got no money,' Mumtaz said.

For a moment he looked as if he might get angry. But he just sighed. Then he said, 'Look, Mishal, you really want to come and be with me, right?'

'More than anything!'

Mumtaz felt her skin crawl underneath her scalp.

'Well, then you're gonna have to trust what I say,' he said. 'Trust that it's right. Because it is, Mishal. That you come here to the Caliphate and be part of Allah's plan is the most important thing that you will ever do. We will raise our children to be pure warriors here. That's impossible where you are, in the land of the kaffir.'

'I know, but—'

'Listen!' he raised a commanding finger. 'Sacrifices have to be made, yeah? And one of those is your family. I know it's hard to hear, Mishal, but they are infidels. You're not telling them about your plans for a very good reason. I mean, why aren't you asking them to give you money for your flights?'

'Because they wouldn't approve,' she said.

'Right. And they won't approve because they're living in darkness. They're infidels! I'm sorry, Mishal, they are. Anyone who isn't with us, is against us. If you don't come, you'll be against us and I would hate that.'

'Me too!'

'Because what we have here is the pure land Muslims have always deserved,' he said. 'If your parents can't see it, that's their problem. What you have to do is get over your feelings for them so that you can reach your full potential. They will only hold you back!'

'Yes, but—'

'Does your mother have a bank card?'

His eyes shone as he spoke. He looked through her.

'Yes . . .'

'So buy your ticket online with it,' he said.

'Steal it?'

'Borrow it. A flight to Istanbul is a hundred and fifty pounds. Nothing! And when you get to Istanbul the bus to Gaziantep is pennies. Then we'll be together!'

She paused. This was a momentous decision for Mishal. She said, 'I've never been anywhere on my own before . . .'

'No. But I will be at the end of your journey, waiting for you. Think of that, Mishal! Hold onto that!'

Did he really believe what he was saying? Could anyone be that arrogant?

'I will.' She lowered her eyes.

'But you know that it is permissible for me to see your face before I become your husband,' he said. 'Provided we are betrothed. And we are, aren't we, Mishal? I have arranged for us to marry as soon as possible.'

'Oh.'

He smiled. 'I knew that would make you happy. Now you make me happy, eh? You take off your niqab and show me your beautiful face.'

'Do you know where this meeting your lodgers attended was held?' Montalban asked.

'Not exactly. South London somewhere,' Ali said. 'Nabil and Qasim attend a lot of religious meetings.'

Ricky Montalban leant back in his chair. It was strange for him to think of straight-laced good-boy Ali Huq as homosexual.

'How'd you come to take the boys in?'

'There are many refugees from Syria at the moment,' Ali said. 'We do what we can.'

'We?'

'There are many organisations dedicated to assisting displaced Muslim children from Syria.'

'So which one did Nabil and Qasim come from?'

'Mr Aziz Shah runs a small local charity . . .'

'Aziz the tailor.'

'Yes.'

Another 'person of interest'.

'You have their computers and you've questioned them,' Ali said. 'What's the problem?'

'The problem,' Montalban said, 'is that they were seen in the

144

vicinity of Arnold Circus on the night that Rajiv Banergee was murdered.'

'Well, that's quite possible. They were probably coming back from their meeting.'

'Their meeting, Mr Huq, was, according to you, in south London. Arnold Circus isn't on any route back to your place that I can see from round there.'

'Have you spoken to them?'

'I'm just about to,' Montalban said. 'Do you want to tell me anything before I do?'

Mumtaz had never felt so exposed. On reflex her eyes quickly flashed towards Lee.

He saw it.

'What are you looking at?'

'Oh, er, I'm just a bit nervous,' she said. 'My mum's downstairs.'

'OK.'

He was so volatile. His mood could change in a second.

He smiled. 'You're so beautiful,' he said. 'Better than your photograph.'

She'd put on more make-up than she usually did. Young girls tended to wear more than she had when she'd been a teenager. But did she really look eighteen?

'Thank you,' she said.

Maybe the background of Shazia's bedroom helped? Soft toys, flamingo lights and posters.

'Man, I can't wait until we can be together,' he said. 'It will be soon, inshallah!'

'Inshallah.'

She felt as if she'd just blasphemed. Using the Sacred Name to one who had killed.

'A lot of men here like to have converts for wives, white girls,' he said. 'But a girl born and bred a Muslim is a real jewel.'

'Thank you.'

'You know what a warrior needs, by instinct.'

What did that mean? Mumtaz felt her stomach turn when she remembered her husband who had said something similar once.

'We must plan for our wedding immediately,' he said. 'I'll fix everything this end. You must get those tickets booked as soon as you can.'

She hesitated for a second. Just a second. But he noticed.

'What's the problem?'

'The problem?'

'You seem hesitant,' he said. 'Don't you want to come to me? Don't you want to be my wife? You know those convert girls I told you about? They'd all be my wives if I wanted them to be. But I've been waiting for a real Muslim girl. I've been saving myself. Don't disappoint me, Mishal.'

His voice was calm but there was menace behind it. She would have to reassure him somehow if she didn't want to lose him.

She said, 'I'm afraid.'

'Afraid? What's to be afraid of? I'll be waiting for you. I won't let anything bad happen to you! I will be your champion, Mishal. Like one of Saladin's warriors, I will stand between you and the Crusaders unto death!'

'Yes, but—'

'I'm offering you paradise and you say, "yes, but". . . What is this Mishal? Are you just playing with me?'

'No!'

'Then why are you scared? You know I will care for you. Take your mum's card and book that flight! Believe me, if I could come to the UK and get you, I would. But if I set foot in that hellhole, they will arrest me because I would be a big catch for them.'

'Taking money from my mum . . .'

'She won't notice if it's on her card!'

She had to think fast.

'She won't, but my dad will,' she said. 'He checks their joint bank account every day. If over a hundred pounds goes out, he'll ask questions and then they'll find out and go mental.'

He blinked, but didn't speak. Mumtaz suspected that he was boiling inside.

Then her phone rang.

Aftab Huq put his phone in his pocket and walked out the back of the shop to where old George was having a smoke over by the disreputable shack Aftab described as his warehouse. George had worked for Aftab ever since he'd 'retired' fifteen years ago.

Aftab said, 'Got a fag?'

George gave him a cigarette. 'Shazia on the counter?'

'Yeah.' Aftab lit up. 'Been trying to talk to her mum about Wahid Sheikh,' he said. 'But she ain't picking up.'

'Ah.'

George knew all about the Sheikhs and their involvement with Aftab's family. He said, 'You want me to walk Shazia home tonight?'

'Yeah. That'd be good,' Aftab said.

'No worries.'

In his youth, George had been a boxer and so in spite of his advanced age, Aftab knew that Shazia would be in safe hands.

'Who was that on the phone?'

Mumtaz had ignored it. She'd not even looked.

'I don't know.'

'Well, look!' he said. 'And then show me.'

It was Aftab. Probably something about Shazia. She held her phone up to the computer screen.

'Aftab? Who is he?'

'He's my cousin,' she said.

'Not your boyfriend?'

'You are my boyfriend.' She lowered her eyes.

'Are you sure? Because I'm not,' he said. 'I ask you to do one small thing for me and you disobey.'

'I've looked at flights to Paris and Amsterdam,' she said. 'They are really cheap. If someone could meet me there . . .'

'Who? Who would meet you there, Mishal?'

His face was red now.

'I-I don't . . . If Dad sees that Mum has spent more than a hundred pounds he will question it,' she said. 'I—'

'So, take a friend's card!' he said. 'I don't care how you get here, just get here! All the better if you have a friend who is a kaffir. You know it's permissible to take from them, don't you? Mishal, I am so anxious to be your husband. I am also' – here he lowered his voice – 'I am so hot for you.'

Mumtaz was stunned, and appalled.

'I-I'll do what I can,' she stuttered.

She was shaking. His sudden foray into sexualised language had made her feel cold with dread. She had to end this conversation – now.

'Oh, I can hear my mum,' she said.

'Mishal—'

She cut the connection.

For a moment she buried her head in her hands and then she looked up. Lee's face was white.

She said, 'I'm sorry, I—'

148

'You're not doing this any more,' he said.

'Lee—'

'It's like listening to a paedophile grooming!'

'We can't stop now!'

'I don't care what Abbas says, Fayyad isn't trying to leave! The bastard wants a child-bride!'

'Then why send the tooth to his parents?' Mumtaz said.

'I don't know!'

He took his cigarette packet out of his pocket.

'Go out and have a fag,' she said.

Lee was going through the door when she got the message via Facebook. It said:

I'm sorry I was angry. I just want to be with you so much!!!!! If you can get to Amsterdam we have people there who can help us. If my duties allow, I will come myself to Amsterdam and escort you to our new home. I love you.

The lights were on and the door was open.

Baharat Huq wasn't happy about going in to the Leather Bungalow on his own but he felt he had to. If someone was inside who shouldn't be he couldn't just walk past without doing anything. He put his head round the door.

'Hello?' he said.

For a moment there was nothing and then a female voice said, 'Who's there?'

'Susi? Is that you?'

She walked out of what had been Rajiv's office. She had a small laptop computer in her hands.

'Oh, Baharat-ji,' she said. 'Hello. Is anything the matter?'

'Oh, no,' he said. 'I just saw the door open. And knowing the situation . . .'

'Oh, how kind,' she said. 'Come in.'

It was strange to see the shop without Rajiv. It looked lifeless – and that wasn't just because all the coloured lights he used to have around the doors and windows had been taken down. Rajiv had always imbued his shop with an energy that no one else could ever replicate.

Baharat walked inside. The rails were empty too. Piles of coats, trousers and skirts lay on big sheets on the floor.

'I'm trying to make sense of my brother's accounts,' Susi said. 'He wasn't all that meticulous, you know.'

It was sad that the poor woman was having to do this on her own. As far as Baharat knew, Rajiv was still to be cremated. Where was her husband? Surely he should be helping her at this time?

'So much to do,' he said.

'Tell me about it!'

He had to say something. 'Do you need help?'

'That's kind, but no,' Susi said. 'My brother's lawyer has everything in hand. I am simply seeing what is here. What I will have to deal with.'

'You?'

'I am Rajiv's sole beneficiary,' she said. 'I think that some members of my family thought that they would be named too, but it seems that isn't to be. I must manage alone.'

Had her marriage ended? Overcome with curiosity, Baharat said, 'Your husband—'

'Oh, Dilip is far too busy to get involved,' she said.

'Oh.'

'I can't bother him with this.'

Maybe Susi's husband had disapproved of her brother? It was difficult to know. Susi had left the Lane so long ago. But then surely her husband had to be interested in the money that would eventually come to his wife from the sale of the building – if she sold it. The shop with the flat above had to be worth at least two million pounds. But Baharat also knew that Rajiv had not liked his brother-in-law. He'd always sneered when he'd talked about him, calling him 'Mr Dr Surgeon-ji'.

'I was just checking that all was well,' Baharat said.

'Everything is fine,' she said.

She was oddly upbeat. But then that happened sometimes with grief. There was a period of elation when plans had been made and official business taken care of. But in light of how Rajiv had died this did seem odd.

'I will sell the property,' Susi said.

Baharat had wanted to ask but had felt that might be rude. 'You grew up here,' he blurted.

'I know.' For a moment she looked sad. 'But one must move with the times, Baharat-ji,' she said. 'The past is another country in which we are not welcome.'

But he wondered. Susi Banergee had left the Lane long ago and had rarely visited. Was this now her final goodbye?

'Hi Lee.'

'Oh, hello princess.'

It was almost midnight. What was Lee doing at their flat? Shazia said goodnight to George who Cousin Aftab had insisted walk her home, and went inside.

'What's going on?' she asked Lee.

'Your mum and me had some work to finish up,' he said.

Mumtaz came out of the kitchen. 'Hello, sweetheart,' she said. 'How did it go?'

'Oh, usual,' Shazia said. 'Lots of boys trying to buy booze, some Eastern European man trying to find some sort of food we'd never heard of.'

Working in the convenience store in the evenings was often tiring but it was rarely boring. Sometimes when groups of underage boys were refused alcohol it was positively vibrant.

'Well, I'm off,' Lee said.

'See you in the morning,' Mumtaz replied.

When he'd gone, Shazia said, 'It's not like you to work at home, Amma.'

'We've a lot on.'

'Oh.'

Was her amma blushing or was it Shazia's imagination? She knew that Lee had gone through a period when he'd had feelings for Amma, which she suspected her stepmother shared. She had always hoped that she did. Like her, Amma had suffered under the 'regime' that had been imposed upon them both by her father. If anyone deserved a little happiness it was Amma. She decided to carry on keeping old Wahid Sheikh's appearance in her life to herself. Now was not the time to bother Amma with that.

FOURTEEN

The little shits were clamming up tighter than a gnat's arse.

'Tell 'em if they don't tell us where they were, we'll have to arrest them,' Bob said.

The Arabic interpreter relayed this information to Qasim Malouf and Nabil Abdella even though Bob and Ricky Montalban knew they had to speak English to some extent. By his own admission, Ali Huq's Arabic was basic at best and so they'd had to communicate somehow. They certainly knew the word 'faggot', which they'd shouted at Rajiv Banergee whenever they felt like it.

The interpreter said, 'They told you they went to a meeting in south London. It was an Islamic prayer meeting.'

'Yeah, but only when they realised Mr Huq had dobbed them in. Where exactly did it take place, this meeting, and who was there?' Bob said. 'They don't have an alibi from their landlord, so they must give us one from someone else. Can anyone at this meeting vouch for them?'

The translator did his stuff. Then he said, 'Yes.'

'Who?'

But they wouldn't say. That was, the boys said, their own business.

Bob saw Montalban look at the boys' brief.

'I'm gonna have to arrest them,' he said.

The interpreter rattled something in Arabic.

For a moment both boys were silent and then the oldest of the pair, Nabil, made a speech that went on and on. Bob just wanted to close his eyes and go to sleep. He'd been up all night, first finding the boys, then bringing them in, then organising an interpreter, then organising the interview along with Montalban.

The interpreter nodded as Nabil spoke, then he asked a question, which the other boy, Qasim, answered.

Montalban, who was just as tired as Bob said, 'Mr Saqqai, what is going on?'

The interpreter asked the boys one more question and then he said, 'Nabil and Qasim say that Mr Huq is lying. They say they were lying too because they are ashamed.'

'Ashamed? Why?'

'Because,' the interpreter said, 'they say that Mr Huq forced them into doing sex with him.'

Bob felt his skin prickle. Could this be true? Ali Huq had been very clearly wrestling with his conscience when he told the police about his affair with Rajiv Banergee. He'd also said that he had been celibate ever since. But had that been a lie?

Montalban said, 'Tell Nabil and Qasim that they were seen at the top of Brick Lane the night that Rajiv Banergee died by independent witnesses.'

The distinctly dodgy Zayn Chaudhuri and Sultan Ibrahim.

Another Arabic confab happened. This time it was heated.

'Mr Saqqai . . .'

'They say that is a lie,' the interpreter said.

'Well, with respect, they would,' Montalban said. He

154

looked at Bob. 'Bring in Aziz Shah, the tailor. According to Huq, he brought these two into the country.'

Mumtaz spent the morning answering the questions and bowing to the demands of her 'betrothed'. She'd told him she wasn't free to speak but he could send her private messages, which he did. Fitting him in around what should have been a morning of writing up reports for clients wasn't easy. Lee was out trying to serve divorce papers for a second time to a man in Wanstead and so she was effectively alone with Abu Imad.

Get a pay-as-you-go mobile just before you leave and give me the number. Throw it away when you arrive at Schiphol.

The office phone rang.

'Arnold Agency.'

'Mumtaz, it's Aftab. I tried to call you last night but you never picked up. Everything alright?'

'Yes,' she said. 'Sorry. I was working and didn't hear it. What did you want?'

It was about Wahid Sheikh. He was going into the convenience store, looking at Shazia. She wasn't surprised, but she was alarmed. She was also very tired. Mumtaz said, 'Thanks for letting me know, Aftab. I'll sort it out.'

'If you want any help . . .'

'Thanks, but no,' she said. She put the phone down. Did the old man know that his hold over her had weakened? The Sheikhs were all over East London so surely Wahid Sheikh had to know that Ali Huq's house had been searched by the police. If he didn't, then she needed to tell him.

I want to give you a list of things I need. Is that OK?

Resisting the urge to quote his own contention that they had 'everything' in the caliphate back at him, she asked him what he wanted. A besotted teenager, even if she had detected inconsistencies in her beloved's argument, would be too timid to actually say so.

I need nice cologne. It's very hot here and I want to smell good for you. I also need new sunglasses and some cool T-shirts. There may be other things. Have you booked flights? Remember to get a return, it's less suspicious.

Mumtaz looked at flights to Amsterdam from Stansted, Heathrow and Gatwick. The last thing he'd written to her the previous night was that she should come soon. But he hadn't said when.

Mumtaz wrote, *Give me a date when you'll be there. I really, really, really, REALLY want you to meet me in Holland.*

There was a long pause before he answered. She began to wonder whether he was going to answer. But then:

Next week. Inshallah I will be in Amsterdam on Tuesday. Come quickly. I do not want to be in the kaffir lands longer than I have to. I will send you a detailed shopping list.

It was Friday. She had three days. Mumtaz sat down and breathed.

They were questioning the boys again and, rumour had it, Aziz the tailor was 'helping' the police as well. Ali Huq had always assumed Aziz Shah acted in good faith. But had he been fooling himself? Of course he had. Aziz had only one interest and that was money. Everyone knew that. He and his associates preyed upon anxious parents who paid to have their kids brought to a safe place. Poor Syrians who didn't know that their sons had already been well on the way to becoming radicalised before they even left Damascus. But they prayed and they fasted and so what was Ali to do? He had to atone for his sins somehow and if that meant supporting the caliphate then that was how it had to be. Anything rather than burn in hell, anything.

Only his father knew about his sin. He'd said that provided Ali never again went with a man it would be alright. If he didn't do that and if the police investigation ended, there would never be any need for his mother or anyone else to know. But Qasim and Nabil were being questioned again and Aziz the tailor . . .

Ali had occasionally wondered why Aziz had chosen him to host asylum seekers from Syria. He was so unlike the other hosts he knew. They were all, like Aziz, elderly men who had been brought up on stories of early Islamist movements, like the Muslim Brotherhood in Egypt. Much as he'd wanted to, Ali had not been able to delight in the resurgence of that movement during the Arab Spring of 2011. He'd wanted to approve. As a Muslim he should have been delighted at the prospect of Sharia Law being established in Egypt. But his upbringing screamed against it. As well as drumming the virtues of religion into all his children, Baharat Huq had also taught them that to be successful, countries had to be ruled by national laws. Deep down, in spite of his outward appearance, Ali Huq still believed this.

At the beginning, Aziz had said that he valued Ali because he knew he came from a 'kaffir' background and he admired him because he had turned away from all that. But was that the truth? Had Aziz picked him because he knew about Rajiv? Had he thought that if he had that information he could blackmail Ali if he didn't want to do something or stepped out of line? The Lane was a village. Everyone knew everyone.

Aziz was bringing kids in for money and for something else too. They went to 'meetings', which agitated them, they did things that people found offensive, they were becoming less themselves every day. They were being prepared. By whom and for what . . .

Oh, he had a good idea. But as long as he wasn't sinning with men, that was alright. That had to be alright and it had to be enough. But it wasn't.

Much as he'd tried to concentrate on his accounts, he couldn't. Old Adnan-ji from the Rajput restaurant had been in the shop for over an hour, poking about amongst the shalwar khameez, waiting to pick up some gossip. Everyone knew that Ali's house had been searched by the police.

The front door opened. Another pair of flapping ears? Ali looked up – and his heart raced. It was DC Khan.

'Mr Huq,' he began, 'I'd like you to come . . .'

What had the boys said? What had Aziz?

Ali stood up, pushed his chair over and he ran.

'Leonard?' Mumtaz said. In spite of the gravity of the situation, she stifled a laugh.

Lee dropped his passport down on her desk.

'Why do you think I call meself Lee?' he said. 'Leonard's an old geezer in a greasy mac who drinks pale ale.'

'Is it a family name?' Mumtaz asked.

'No. But as I've told you before, my old man was a bastard,' Lee said. 'He never liked me or me brother or even Mum very much.'

Mumtaz knew that Lee's father had been an alcoholic with a bad temper. What she hadn't known until Lee had shown her his passport was that his father, back in the so-called 'swinging' 60s, had given his son an old man's name.

'But the name's useful when I travel,' Lee said. 'That's why I've never changed it. Should Fayyad find his way to a passenger list for that flight, he won't find Lee Arnold.'

'Leonard Reginald Arnold,' Mumtaz read.

'Yes, it gets worse,' Lee said. He picked up his passport. 'I think my old man wanted me to be a member of the British National

Party. It's that sort of name. He was a twat.' He sighed. 'I need a fag.'

He left the office and went outside. His smoking place was on the metal stairs that led down to the street. As usual he took his phone when he left and closed the door behind him.

Mumtaz looked at the list of luxury goods Abu Imad had sent her. He'd even costed them.

RayBan Wayfarer Sunglasses – £161
Bentley Infinite Rush male fragrance – £60
Alexander McQueen Ribcage T-shirt x 3 – £195 each

Mishal had asked him how he thought she could pay for such expensive items and he'd told her to use her mother's credit card. The couple had an argument. He'd written:

Take her card and use it the day before you come.

Mishal had said that there was a risk her dad would check on transactions and she was afraid. She told him her mum had almost gone mad looking for her bank card when she'd taken it to buy her air ticket. How could she now take a credit card? She told him she was shaking.

He said, *Well, don't! If you think he's about to check up then take your ticket and leave. If I have to go without my presents then that is what I will have to do. Stop being a baby. You're about to become the wife of an ISIS fighter, behave with dignity!*

Mumtaz had expected Abu Imad to go quiet then. He'd done so before when she had 'disappointed' him. But oddly he came straight back, seemingly in an entirely different mood.

Mishal, I am sorry for my harsh words. I know that this is hard for you. But you must show courage and resolve now. I am doing my part. I am taking a huge risk by coming to Europe to get you.

But I love you so much I can't risk you not being able to be my wife because you are afraid. Once we are in the Caliphate, all will be well. But in the meantime, take a deep breath and take your mother's credit card. You managed to get her bank card because you've booked your flight. And I can't believe your father checks on her credit spending every day. I think that maybe he tells her that in order to control her.

Mumtaz would have laughed if his messages didn't remind her so much of the early days of her marriage. Ahmet had manipulated in just the same way. Telling her that he loved her 'so much' while at the same time getting her to do things to which she objected. He too had pointed the finger at how other men controlled their wives.

Lee was still not back from his smoke. But then if she listened hard, she could hear that he was speaking on the phone. She couldn't hear what he was saying.

They'd booked flights from Stansted Airport at 16.50 on the Tuesday afternoon. Abu Imad had been delighted.

Allah has surely chosen to bless His humble servant.

If only there were anything humble about him.

Maybe Lee was speaking to Abbas and Shereen? He'd told them right at the start that he'd not be giving them updates but now that they were going to Amsterdam, and the possibility of meeting Fayyad was real, perhaps he'd wanted to put them in the picture.

A message arrived.

Suggest you get all my presents at the same place as it will save you time. Harrods is a good bet.

Did the irony of sending her to buy luxury goods from a shop that was the epitome of Western materialism occur to him, she wondered? That was, of course, assuming that Abu Imad/Fayyad was not faking his true purpose anyway. They were counting on

160

the idea that he was. That was what his parents thought.

Another message.

I know that places like Harrods are evil but we exploit them, yeah?

Yeah. Right.

And do not travel in your niqab or even cover your head. Covered Sisters get hassled by security at Western airports. We're all terrorists to them! LOL.

Mumtaz pulled a face. Very funny – not – in the words of a youth both she and Abu Imad had left behind.

The office door opened and Lee came in, smiling.

'Good smoke?' she asked.

'Brill,' he said.

In common with everyone else on the planet, Ricky Montalban had watched the destruction of the Twin Towers of the World Trade Centre in New York in 2001 with ice running down his spine. What kind of people would do such a thing? And why had the CIA not stopped them? At the time it had felt as if al-Qaeda and its sympathisers were unstoppable. Ditto, more recently, ISIS. But most of the time they were stopped, in spite of occasional high-profile events across Europe. And if the tailor Aziz Shah was anything to go by, they had a lot of weak links.

'They told me the children were just refugees,' he told Ricky. 'I believed them. I did what I did in good faith, Inspector Montalban. They said they would provide religion classes for them and who wouldn't want that for young children alone in a new and unfamiliar city? Religion is something familiar to them. It is civilising and moral.'

'They' were, apparently, an organisation called 'Light of True Belief'.

'They are a registered charity,' Aziz said.

'No they're not,' Ricky said. 'But that's beside the point. Why'd you get Ali Huq to help you?'

'Oh, Mr Huq is a very good man!'

Last Ricky had heard, Bob Khan and a squad of woodentops were still looking for Huq who'd done a runner.

'So this "Light of True Belief" mob get kids from Syria, how?'

'It's all legal . . .'

'How'd you know? There are mobs like this all over the place at the moment. Some kosher, some not . . .'

'Oh, they are good people, they say—'

'They can say anything, don't mean it's true.'

He nodded his head to one side as if wanting to agree and disagree simultaneously.

'The children have been granted asylum.'

'Yeah, I know. But how'd they get into the country?'

'Didn't they tell you?'

'I want you to tell me.'

The boys had owned up to coming in illegally. They claimed not to have known who had got them in. Their parents had paid a man in Syria, so they said.

'I don't know!'

'So how did the boys come to you?'

'From "Light of True Belief", I told you.'

'And they are?'

'Ah, you see I know them through my brother-in-law, Mr Vakeel Uddin,' he said. 'He knows many, many Syrians. It's all above board, totally legal.'

Which sent all sorts of alarm bells ringing in Ricky's head.

'You know the two lads are being questioned in relation to the murder of Rajiv Banergee?' he said.

'Oh, no! No they can't have done that, no! They're good boys, well behaved and pious . . .'

'With jihadi recruitment videos on their laptops.'

'Laptops? They must have been given those. Qasim and Nabil are not those kinds of boys. Ali-ji must have given them those computers, ask him.'

'What, the "good" man, Ali Huq?'

Mr Shah shrugged as if to say 'who can tell?'

'So this "Light of True Belief" mob,' Ricky said, 'where are they?'

'Where?'

'Yeah. I know they exist but I can't find them,' Ricky said. 'Where'd they operate out of?'

'All over.'

'All over where? All over London?'

'Yes. Yes, they do much good work . . .'

'Mr Shah you're not listening,' Ricky said. 'Where are they based? If, as you claim, they're a charity, they must have an office somewhere.'

The tailor went quiet.

'Well?'

He shrugged. 'All I can tell you, DI Montalban, is where my brother-in-law lives. My wife's young brother, you understand. A solicitor. We're not close. He's a clever boy, whereas I . . .'

'Where's he live?'

'Forest Gate,' the tailor said. 'His house faces on to Wanstead Flats.'

Why had he run away? It had been stupid then and it wasn't getting any less stupid now.

Once he'd managed to lose Bob Khan, Ali had headed for

Christ Church. When they'd been kids, he and his siblings had played in the graveyard – much against their parents' wishes. The dead were unclean. But he'd always comforted himself with the knowledge that they'd never, ever been into the crypt. There, it was said, loads of bodies were stored in open coffins in what had once been something called a 'charnel' house. But in recent years the crypt had been turned into a cafe. Neither hungry nor thirsty, Ali nevertheless bought himself a coffee and sat behind a vast stone pillar in order to think.

One of those guides who took people on 'Jack the Ripper' tours around the area had once told him that Christ Church had been built by a man called Nicholas Hawksmoor. A pupil of Christopher Wren, who'd built St Paul's, it was said that this Hawksmoor was also a magician, that he raised the dead and spoke to demons. Some people even, apparently, called him the Devil's Architect. What a place for a good Muslim man to end up!

Except he wasn't a good Muslim and, by running away from the police, he was stating that to the world. But what else could he do? If the police already had Aziz Shah then they'd know about the 'charity'. The tailor was stupid. He had no idea who he was dealing with. His brother-in-law, who was the kind of man whose grievances regarding the status of Muslims were genuine and heartfelt, had allowed himself to be used by both Aziz, who made money from the operation, and his contacts in Iraq and Syria. Ali had only once met one of those. He'd tried to feel, as well as speak his approval, but he couldn't. The man had been evil.

Why did coffee have to have an identity these days? he thought. He'd asked for coffee and been given too many options. He'd reiterated that he just wanted coffee. This had turned out to be something the girl behind the counter had called an 'Americano'.

What was that? Apparently okay coffee with milk. He lifted the cup with a shaking hand.

What now? If he'd ever had a plan for what would happen after he ran out of his shop, he'd forgotten it.

'Mr Huq?'

And then there was DC Khan together with three uniformed officers, framed by two ecclesiastical arches, the light pouring in behind them like faintly yellowed water.

Ali stood. There was nowhere to run this time. It was only then that he remembered something from his primary school days. The John Cass School had been and remained an institution administered by the state religion, the Church of England. And as such, that church had special historical privileges. He hoped they still applied.

As Khan walked towards him he said, 'DC Khan I must tell you that I'm here because I am claiming sanctuary.'

FIFTEEN

Mumtaz couldn't relate to the deceased Princess Diana or her lover, Dodi Fayed, but she was at one with the albatross they appeared to be clinging on to. She looked up at the staggeringly ugly statue between two escalators and felt yet another urge to cry. But she stopped herself. Harrods Department Store, which had its own dress code (no uniforms, no scruffs) probably didn't allow crying. She leant up against a vast marble wall and tried to collect her thoughts.

Ali, her brother, had claimed sanctuary in Christ Church. She had a dim memory that such a thing existed but she didn't know that anyone actually did it any more. Charged though not arrested, he'd been in the crypt all night. Her father had told her it was not anything to do with Rajiv Banergee's death but was related to an accusation of male rape. Those boys he'd given shelter to had accused him of abusing them. Specifically they'd accused him of abusing them on the night Rajiv had been murdered. They'd either killed Rajiv themselves or they knew who had. Although when she'd told Lee, he had said it was too early to jump to any sort of conclusion. She disagreed. Her brother wasn't gay! Her brother, now she came to think about it, wasn't anything.

* * *

Lee looked into Abbas al'Barri's bloodshot eyes and said, 'You're going to have to trust me.'

Abbas tipped what remained of his whisky down his throat. 'He's my son,' he said. 'The jewel in my crown. How can I do that?'

'Because it's me,' Lee said. 'Because, if you like, you saved my miserable life for a reason. This is that reason. I don't know, Abbas. But you've got to do it.'

Shereen touched her husband's arm. 'Lee is right, Abbas,' she said.

'Can't you tell me where you're going?' Abbas asked. 'Is it Istanbul?'

'I'm not telling you,' Lee said. 'Don't ask me.'

'Why not?'

'I've told you why not.'

Lee watched his friend turn the Tooth of Jonah over and over in his hands.

'To send this to us has to mean something,' he said.

'I hope so,' Lee replied.

'You get no sense, from talking to him that . . .'

'I won't know what his motives are until I get there,' Lee said. 'We know he's in the caliphate and we also know that while he's there he will be watched. If he does want to get away he has to pretend that he doesn't. That's why we can't rely on anything he says or does while he's there. If he does want out then he's going to have to keep that well hidden until he gets away.'

'You must be going to Istanbul.'

Abbas looked into Lee's eyes, searching for clues. He found none.

'What day are you leaving?'

'Abbas,' Shereen said, 'Lee can't tell us.'

Abbas handed the tooth to Lee. Then he poured himself another drink and went back into the house.

When he was out of earshot, Lee said, 'You know I'm not going into this with no plan, don't you, Shereen?'

'Of course not.' She lit a cigarette.

'I've got bases covered,' he said. 'I take risks, but I don't take stupid ones.'

'No.'

He put the Tooth of Jonah in his pocket.

'When you show him the tooth, tell him we love him, won't you?' Shereen asked.

'Course.'

Lee leant back against the big cushion Shereen had put on the deckchair for him and closed his eyes. Last time he'd spoken to her, Mumtaz had been in a right state about her brother. He hoped she was OK on her shopping trip to Harrods.

Not even his mother's cooking had been able to tempt his son to eat. Ali had just stared at it while his father and the vicar, the Reverend Reid, tried to make him see sense. Why had he claimed that sanctuary nonsense? What was even more frustrating for Baharat was that his son hadn't even known what DC Khan had been coming to arrest him for. He had assumed that it concerned Rajiv Banergee. But it didn't. It was about those damned boys who lived in his house, making accusations.

What Ali was doing made him look guilty. He wouldn't have it, but that was the truth. And now his claim to sanctuary was all over the area. Everyone thought it was to do with Rajiv. Except Baharat and his family. And the police, who were furious with him. DC Khan had first laughed and then lost his temper when Ali had made his strange, archaic claim for sanctuary. It was only when he had contacted his superior, DI Montalban, that he'd calmed down. Montalban, so the Reverend Rcid had told him, had instructed Khan to let Ali's claim stand. Why?

Sumita had cried. She'd not really stopped ever since Ali had been questioned by police the first time. Asif claimed that he'd always known his brother was 'in the closet' as he put it and Mumtaz had gone quiet. What was more, she was going away to work on Tuesday. Abroad somewhere. That had never happened before. Shazia was going to come and stay, which was nice. Although not his own blood, the girl was about as close as Baharat had to a granddaughter – or may ever have. Asif's girlfriend had just had her womb removed, poor woman. And now that Ali was gay . . .

The world was beyond Baharat at such times. He'd told the vicar, who had said that it was beyond him too. That hadn't helped.

It had been a while since Baharat had wandered down Folgate Street. Years ago he'd known the American, Dennis Severs, whose house had become a sort of monument to Spitalfields past. He'd been an interesting, if eccentric man, who had lived the last years of his life in his four-storey Huguenot house in Folgate Street, turning his dreams of the past into some sort of alternate reality. An unusual city attraction, number 18 Folgate Street was just one of many Huguenot houses on Folgate, now overshadowed by an ever-increasing number of glass and steel tower blocks. The seemingly endless demand for city office space had to be addressed. Dennis would have been horrified.

Baharat looked around more as a form of meditation than anything else. Maybe walking and thinking about the past would ease his mind in some way? Then he saw a familiar face. Coming out of that house he knew to be rather like the Severs place, but a hotel, was Susi Banergee.

Baharat knew that she'd stayed at a local hotel when her brother had first been found dead. But surely she wanted to be in her own home now?

Paying over a hundred pounds for a pair of sunglasses was mad, paying nearly six hundred pounds for three T-shirts was absurd. Mumtaz could see that the material was good quality but she couldn't really understand why the young woman serving her was wrapping each garment so reverentially. Something, she imagined, to do with the Alexander McQueen designer 'magic'.

'That will be five hundred and eighty-five pounds please, madam,' the shop assistant said.

Mumtaz handed over her credit card. Lee had already put enough into her bank account to cover all these purchases, although whether Abbas al'Barri was going to ultimately pay off everything, she didn't know. She hoped so.

Was the whole scheme crazy? What if Abu Imad became violent? He could. And why hadn't she considered Shazia more carefully? If she was killed or kidnapped, what would happen to her?

'Is everything alright, madam?'

She looked up at the assistant and smiled. 'Yes, I'm sorry, I'm just a bit tired.'

The assistant smiled. She was a pretty young woman with wonderful, slanted green eyes.

'If you'd like to put your PIN into the machine.'

Mumtaz typed her number. The assistant tore off her sales receipt and put it in the bag with the T-shirts.

'Have a nice day, madam.'

'Thank you.'

* * *

Chief Superintendent Vine closed the newspaper on his desk.

'Does Mr Huq know about this?' he said.

'He knows what he's charged with but not about the media coverage, sir,' Ricky Montalban said. 'At least I don't think so. We've shut the crypt and we're limiting Mr Huq's access to media of all kinds.'

'Does he have a phone?'

'No.'

'Thank Christ for that. What about the family?'

'DC Iqbal has been appointed FLO,' he said. 'She's over there now.'

'Good.' He looked at the newspaper again. 'How did this get out, DI Montalban?

'No idea.'

'There'll have to be an investigation.'

'I know. But we also mustn't lose sight of the bigger picture. Aziz Shah has fingered his brother-in-law in connection with this hooky "Light of True Belief" mob . . .'

'Who passed the two boys who lodged with Huq onto him?'

'Yeah. Well, this brother-in-law, Vakeel Uddin, lives in Forest Gate,' Montalban said. 'He's a local solicitor and he's also a person of interest up at Forest Gate nick. Associates with known Islamist radicals, although nothing concrete on him, so far. Has his law practice on Green Street where he specialises in asylum and immigration. Course all of this is unofficial until you've spoken to the Super in Newham . . .'

'Superintendent May is one month into the job, should be interesting.'

May's predecessor, Superintendent Venus, had left Newham amid accusations of consorting with criminals and fraud. Eric May, his permanent replacement, was still struggling to get up to speed with the complications involved in running a large, inner-city police force.

'Who did you tap up in Newham?' Vine asked. 'Just between us.'

171

Montalban trusted him. 'DI Collins,' he said without hesitation.

Vine smiled. 'Vi,' he said. 'Straight down the line copper.'

'Which is why I tapped her.'

Vine looked at the newspaper again. He read the headline.

'"Brick Lane Trader's Dirty Sex Secret". Talks about Christ Church! Says the "source" is close to the investigation.'

'Which seems to imply an insider, but may not,' Montalban said.

'Of course, not helped by Huq's strange request for asylum and your, quite frankly, bizarre decision to allow him to do that,' Vine said. 'Everyone knows he'd holed up in Christ Church!' His anger got the better of him. 'What were you thinking, man?'

Ricky had already been through this once, but he did it again. 'Sir, with the way things are round Brick Lane at the moment, I thought the sight of police officers dragging a Muslim man out of a church might not play well for us, for community cohesion or for Huq. I've got serious doubts about his guilt and at least like this we know where he is.'

'We'd also know where he is if he were banged up!' Vine shook his head. Then he sighed. 'So what does DI Collins make of this Vakeel Uddin?'

'Seems he's in contact with members of the local Syrian community, amongst others. Most of 'em are just ordinary folks going about their business in a foreign country. Don't want no trouble. But, according to Vi, there are exceptions,' Montalban said.

'Names.'

'Not yet. Mr May'd have to sign off on names.'

'Yes, but knowing DI Collins . . .'

'Uddin regularly communicates with a bloke in the caliphate,' Montalban said. 'She wouldn't say who. I don't know she even knows.'

Vine looked back at the newspaper and scratched his head.

* * *

'Do you want me to call your daughter?'

'No . . .'

'Abba, she will have to know,' Asif said. He looked up at DC Iqbal. 'I'll phone my sister, thank you.'

'No!' Baharat shook his head. 'Your sister must go away on business next week! I don't want her to worry.'

'So you want Mumtaz to find out by accident?'

The old man slumped. 'Go home, Asif,' he said. 'Look after Tracey, she needs you.'

'It was Tracey who told me to come,' Asif said. 'Her mum's with her. She's fine.'

DC Shamima Iqbal had been assigned as Family Liaison Officer that morning. She'd walked into a house where the mother had locked herself in her bedroom and was crying and Baharat Huq and his son had been sitting in stunned silence.

'Ali told me he had stopped the homosexual acts when he finished his relationship with Rajiv-ji,' the old man said. 'And I believe him. Who would say such things about my son?'

'The allegations come from the two boys who lodged with him,' Shamima said. 'But they are unproven, at the moment. We've no idea who leaked the story to the press, Mr Huq.'

'Bastard!'

'What we need to concentrate on now is getting Ali to leave the church voluntarily and, most importantly, quietly,' she said. 'It's calling way too much attention to the story.'

'He ran because he was frightened.'

'I know. But it's not helping. Reverend Reid and Imam Yusuf are both with him.'

'I want to see my son!'

'You've seen him.'

'Not since this newspaper vileness!'

173

'He doesn't know about that, Mr Huq,' Shamima said. 'And we want to keep it that way.'

'Why?'

'We want Ali to be calm,' she said. 'He knows what the two boys have alleged and that they have been examined by a doctor. They will be questioned again. Your son's business premises is being searched.'

'For what?'

'For evidence,' she said.

'Evidence of what?'

'I don't know, Mr Huq,' she said. 'But for the moment there's nothing we can do. We just have to wait.'

The old man lit a cigarette.

'Abba . . .'

'Oh don't lecture me about smoking, Asif!' he shouted.

'You gave up five years ago.'

'Yes. And now I have started again. Leave me be!' He looked at Shamima. 'What has happened to Brick Lane, eh? Suddenly we have murderers, perverts and terrorists!'

Shamima said nothing. The Lane and its environs had always been volatile. But of course all the old man could see was how things had been so much better in the past.

Asif stood up. 'I'm going to call Mumtaz,' he said.

Baharat Huq slumped. 'If you must.' Then he said to Shamima, 'When will we have peace, eh? Not even Rajiv-ji's bereaved sister can take up her life. He is not cremated and she remains away from her home.'

'I'm sure that the funeral will happen soon,' Shamima said. 'I'm not part of that investigation, Mr Huq.'

Ricky Montalban parked his car on Fournier Street, to the side of Christ Church. When he walked round to the main entrance, he clocked the woodentops either side of the front door. What a fucking waste of manpower. Ali Huq must have been totally off his head with fear when he claimed sanctuary. Now he had to tell him that the medicals on the boys were inconclusive. Both of them had taken part in anal sex. Both were damaged. But the kids were refugees and so who knew what they'd had to do to get out of Syria and across Europe? People traffickers took what they wanted from their 'customers' in any form that suited them. But the kids were still sticking to their stories about Ali Huq in spite of testimony from Zayn Chaudhuri and his mate Sultan to the contrary. They still claimed to have seen them the night Rajiv died. Perhaps they were both right? Maybe Huq had fucked them and then they'd gone out and killed Rajiv Banergee? Sort of a proof of their own straight manhood thing?

Ricky walked into the church and down into the crypt. Shamima Iqbal reckoned Ali's parents weren't coping well but luckily the other brother, Asif, was remaining calm. He was going to tell Ali's sister, Mumtaz Hakim. That name brought Newham to Ricky's mind.

His phone had rung as soon as he'd got in the car to come out to Christ Church. The Super had told him that Vakeel Uddin, the solicitor from Forest Gate, was not to be touched. Newham had him in their sights and the last thing they needed was intervention from Tower Hamlets. Not that Ricky really needed more to do. But he had hoped to follow the trail Aziz the tailor had begun.

Ali Huq and the Reverend Reid were having coffee. Sitting together, talking quietly, they looked almost relaxed. The vicar cracked a smile. 'Ah, DI Montalban,' he said. 'I expect you'd like to talk to Ali on your own.'

He didn't especially. He had nothing to tell him except that the tests on the boys were inconclusive. For a moment he wondered whether Aziz had told the press. Why would he?

'No, it's alright, Reverend,' he said.

Ali Huq didn't react when Ricky told him about the medical reports on the two boys. The vicar made them all more coffee, which struck Ricky as a really 'vicary' thing to do. Then Ricky said, 'Look, Ali, both of those boys are over sixteen and so whatever may or may not have happened to them while they've been in your care, we are not talking about the abuse of minors here.'

'I didn't—'

'Forget all that,' Ricky said. 'What really interests me is Rajiv Banergee's murder. Now we've got two witnesses who claim to have seen your two lads out and about around Arnold Circus the night Rajiv died. Now you, Mr Huq, say you thought the boys were out at a meeting. Did you see them go?'

'No. But the house was quiet that night and they told me later on that they'd been to a meeting in south London.'

'OK, that's fine.' He quickly looked at the vicar and then back at Ali. 'Mr Huq, we don't, as yet, have any evidence those boys killed Mr Banergee. But we do have anecdotal evidence that they were indeed out. So it's like this: did you have sex with those boys early that evening . . .'

'No!'

'I'm sure you understand the notion of consensual sex . . .'

'I did not have sex with those boys!' he said. 'They're lying. I've had sex with no one since Rajiv! I promised and I have kept that promise!'

Ricky scratched his head. Bob Khan had found the magazines within seconds of searching Huq's shop.

'Mr Huq,' he said. 'We found certain magazines at your shop.'

It seemed that Ali would never speak. Ricky felt like a bastard. There'd been three copies of a magazine aimed at the Gay community in a drawer in Ali's desk. Bob had told him that it contained a few photos of men in mildly suggestive poses. But these were basically news and views mags, keeping people in touch with the wider gay world.

'We found them easily in an unlocked drawer,' Ricky said. 'While I've been wondering how the boys found out about your sexuality . . .'

'They know nothing,' he said.

'What if they saw your magazines?'

Ali lowered his head.

'Because they could've done, couldn't they, Mr Huq?' Ricky swallowed. 'You've been charged, accept we have to clear this up and come quietly. Being in here is not doing your case any good at all.'

'No,' Ali said. 'Why should I? You've already made up your mind that I'm guilty.'

'That's not true,' Ricky said. 'No one's made their mind up about anything.'

Maybe, Ricky thought, allowing Huq to claim sanctuary had been the wrong thing to do.

Running a shop was sometimes a dangerous business. If you didn't please your customers, you could go bankrupt, stock could fall on your head and kill you and gangsters wanted to 'protect' you from time to time. Running a convenience store was not a game for sissies and Aftab Huq was in no way a sissy. But he'd had trouble with the Sheikh family before and so approaching Wahid Sheikh wasn't easy.

He came to the shop to buy things, like a regular customer. But unlike a regular customer, straightforward purchase was not his principal aim. When he'd first started coming he'd just looked at

Shazia, but now he'd begun to leer. Even George, whose eyesight wasn't what it had once been, had noticed.

Unless you looked into his eyes there was a lot of the 'dear old man' about Wahid Sheikh. He was polite, courteous, he shuffled a little as if his feet hurt . . .

'I'd be obliged if you didn't bother the young lady.'

Wahid Sheikh looked up. 'Bother?' he said. 'What do you mean?'

Shazia, who had been stacking toilet rolls, went outside to the back of the shop.

'I mean standing so close it makes her feel uncomfortable,' Aftab said. 'And talking to her. She's a good girl . . .'

'If she's a good girl, then why doesn't she cover herself?'

'Because, as you well know, Mr Sheikh, covering is a choice. Or it should be,' Aftab said. 'The girl's said nothing to me, just to be clear, but I've noticed she's nervous when you're around. Come into my shop, you are welcome. But I'd ask you, respectfully, not to make my staff uncomfortable.'

He smiled. 'Mr Huq,' he said, 'and just to clarify what we both know, my late nephew had trouble with you and with that girl. My nephew who died in most strange circumstances, in the presence of that girl.'

Aftab didn't know how Shazia had come to be with a dying Naz Sheikh in a deserted house in Forest Gate. She'd told the police a man she didn't know had come in and stabbed him and they had believed her. Naz Sheikh had died before he could say anything. Aftab had never asked Shazia or Mumtaz about those events. All he did know was that the Sheikhs had issues with his cousin that had once led them to threaten him and his business.

'You're leering,' Aftab blurted.

'Leering?' he laughed. 'That's what you think?'

178

'Yeah.'

He moved towards him. Aftab backed up.

'I am not leering, my dear man. Oh no. I am merely fascinated by the sight of such a young girl simply getting on with her life while my nephew rots in his grave.'

'She never touched him!'

'Ach. So some people think.'

'The police.'

He shrugged.

'Look, just leave her alone, right?' Aftab said.

'Mmm.' The old man turned away.

As he left the shop Aftab heard him say, 'For now.'

When he went out the back to see Shazia, Aftab found her crying on old George's shoulder. As soon as she was able to talk, she said, 'Will I ever be free of those people?'

SIXTEEN

The computer kept beeping to attract her attention. It was him.

Under her breath, Mumtaz said, 'Fuck off.'

Abu Imad with more instructions, more demands, more pointless, childish declarations of love. He'd even sent her a video clip. A vile thing featuring women being beaten by other, completely covered women, for so-called 'hijab-violation'. This was the al-Khansaa Brigade, which Abu Imad suggested she might like to join. Bastard. Her life was in free fall and yet still she was getting ready to go on this hare-brained mission. What had she, and more significantly, Lee been thinking?

Asif had told her about Ali the night before. She hadn't slept. How could Ali be those things? A murderer? A rapist? His views had become rigid and sometimes extreme in recent years, but she felt his relationship with Rajiv-ji went some way towards providing an explanation. Why had she never realised that Ali was gay? Rajiv had even told her he had been involved with a Muslim. Had Rajiv wanted to tell her everything?

Now Ali was hiding from the storm that was raging around him in Christ Church and the world apparently knew what he was supposed to have done. Someone had told the press. Her dad said he thought it was Mr Bhatti in the electrical shop. But he didn't want to confront him. He didn't want to go out.

Then there was Shazia.

In spite of her efforts, Wahid Sheikh had continued to hang around Aftab's shop, unnerving the girl. Would she have to call the old man again?

Mumtaz slipped her passport into the side of her rucksack. She'd have to remember to put it away as soon as she cleared immigration. Abu Imad couldn't see it. Once she was with him, Lee would follow. Only if/when she was alone with this man would she broach the subject of the tooth. With Lee, figuratively, at her back, she could be pulled out of the situation. This was all assuming, of course, that Abu Imad turned up at the airport . . .

What if he didn't?

Mumtaz put a packet of aspirin in her bag. She knew the flight to Amsterdam only took an hour but her father had always been paranoid about deep-vein thrombosis – a fear which had rubbed off on her. Lee would probably laugh at her. Maybe she deserved to be ridiculed?

Suddenly weary, Mumtaz sat on her bed. The computer beeped again and again she ignored it. She'd need to go shopping. 'Mishal' wouldn't wear the white shirts and black trousers that, for Mumtaz, were almost a uniform. Even pious teenagers dressed more interestingly than that. She would need to go to Stratford and visit the massive Primark in the Westfield Shopping Centre. Most of their stuff was aimed at teenagers and it was cheap. Shazia went there with her friends all the time.

It was Sunday, but Westfield was open. It was open every day. She had to go to the office on Monday, same as usual. So she could only go shopping now. But then once it was over she'd have to go and see

181

her parents. Even the thought of it filled her with dread. How were they going to be? When Asif had phoned her she hadn't even heard them wittering on in the background, like they usually did.

He was distracted and he knew she knew it. It was pretty bloody obvious.

'If you say "it's not you, it's me", I'll lamp you,' Vi said as she pulled her jeans back on and rearranged her T-shirt. Thin but muscular, she had a good body for a woman in her late fifties even if she herself described her own face as 'a dried apricot'. Forty years of smoking would do that.

But, as well as being good in bed, Vi was a mate. In his own way Lee loved her. Just not on this occasion, it seemed.

'Sorry.'

She lit a fag. 'Don't worry about it,' she said. 'If you think this has never happened to me before, you're wrong.'

He smiled. But he didn't know why he'd been unable to perform. He'd called her, after all. Maybe it was anticipation of the flight? He'd never liked flying. He'd been sick for most of the journey when he'd gone out to his first tour in Iraq. But then maybe that wasn't it. Maybe it had more to do with what was going to happen once he and Mumtaz got to the Netherlands. Would Fayyad even be there? And even if he was, what was his agenda?

'So when you and Mumtaz coming back from your little trip, then?' Vi asked.

'Thursday,' he said.

He'd booked two nights at the Ibis Hotel, Schiphol. He hoped he didn't need them.

'First time you'll've been away with a woman for a long time.'

Vi had the idea that, if he could, Lee would have an affair with Mumtaz. She was right except that an affair was not what he

182

wanted. He desired much more. But he also knew that, due to the differences in their backgrounds, that was all but impossible. He tried not to think about it.

'What's the job?' Vi asked.

'None of your business.'

'Oooh, confidentiality.'

She laughed. She always found the notion of confidentiality in private investigation amusing. A lot of coppers felt that way. PIs were just 'plastic plods' following people about and serving divorce documents. And even though Vi knew that Lee was much more than that, she liked to tease him.

'I'd have to kill you,' Lee said.

'Fair enough.' She sat on his bed. 'But do be careful, yeah?'

'Yeah.' He stroked her face. 'Yeah.'

She stood up. 'It's a rough world out there,' she said.

'I know.'

'Well, don't forget it.'

She left soon afterwards. Would she have taken off so quickly if they'd had sex?

Lee wasn't sure. She'd had the look of a woman on a mission.

Whatever he said, they'd made their minds up. And Ali didn't care what Ricky Montalban said.

What the boys were saying was that he'd had sex with them and then gone out. Then he'd killed Rajiv. Ali assumed his motive was supposed to be self-disgust. But 'owning up' to the sexual abuse wasn't going to absolve him of Rajiv's murder. So why hold his hands up to rape? It hadn't happened any more than his killing Rajiv had happened. And the boys had gone out that night, not him!

Ricky had been tight-lipped on whether the police had any

183

forensic evidence. Maybe what they had found hadn't yet been analysed. As far as he could tell the real world of forensic investigation wasn't like those CSI programmes his mother watched on the TV. Real life moved at a much slower pace.

Reverend Reid had set him up a bed in the corner of the cafe, which was kind. But he'd not slept since he'd been in the church. The previous night he'd heard kids mucking around outside. He'd heard them shouting and throwing stuff about. He'd heard the word 'nonce' used. Had word got out about him and his supposed 'crimes'?

And if it had, how was he ever going to be able to leave the church without getting lynched?

'Guv.'

'Bob.'

Montalban didn't usually take calls on a Sunday. But with Ali Huq still squatting in Christ Church he felt he had to. He walked out of the living room and into his small garden. As usual, he'd taken his mum to Mass in the morning and then she'd cooked him lunch. Now she was asleep in a chair in front of the telly.

'The lab have got back with results on Rajiv Banergee.'

At fucking last!

'Good.'

'Well, good and bad,' Bob said. 'There were two sets of DNA found on the corpse. Both came from bloodstains.'

'Matches?'

'Yeah.'

'Rock 'n' roll.'

Maybe now those two little Syrian oiks would tell the truth.

'One's to a possession of class A . . .'

'Which was?'

184

'Coke,' Bob said. 'Two thousand and fourteen. Perps name is Amir Charleston, twenty-eight at the time and living with his parents in Holland Park. Worked or maybe still works for a merchant bank.'

'Posh boy.'

'Seems like it. Got fined, community service, slap on the wrist. Daddy's a QC.'

Montalban rolled his eyes. 'And the other one?'

'Ah, well that's where things get a bit weird, guv.'

'In what way?'

'Well, that DNA reveals a familial relationship to the victim.'

'Oh.'

'Yeah.'

'So no Syrian kids? No Ali Huq?'

'No.'

Ricky sighed. 'Got an address for this Charleston bloke?' he said.

'Yes and, of course, we've an address for Mrs Chopra, the victim's sister,' Bob said.

'I'd better make my excuses to Mum, then,' Montalban said.

'Sorry, guv.'

Heidi sat on her front doorstep like she usually did when the weather was warm. Her husband, George, was working in the convenience store as he usually did on a Sunday and so Heidi was alone.

She'd lived with George in their two-bedroom flat on Avondale Road, Canning Town all her married life but she knew none of her neighbours any more. They'd all moved out to Essex. Now almost all the flats were owned by private landlords who rented them out to a shifting population of mainly young people. Her cousin Glad had told her that flats in Heidi's block were selling for a quarter of a million quid! How fucking mad was that? Heidi and George were still council tenants.

Two young white boys walking along the balcony wasn't an unusual sight. Heidi stubbed her fag out on the ground and smiled at them.

The taller of the two, a smartly dressed kid with blonde hair smiled back. 'You Heidi?' he asked her.

'Yes, love,' Heidi said. 'Can I help you?'

'Can I have a word?'

'What about?'

'Your husband,' he said.

Heidi felt her face drain.

'My George? What—'

'Oh, it's OK,' the young man said. 'He's fine. Can I come in? Just for a minute?'

Heidi was anxious to know what this young man had to say about George. She was too anxious. George was always saying how they shouldn't let anyone they didn't know into the flat.

'Yeah,' she said.

She got slowly to her feet. The tall young man followed her, while his mate stayed outside. Heidi led him down the corridor and into her kitchen.

'Well, love,' she said.

He punched her so hard, Heidi heard her nose break. Then she was on the floor.

Standing over her, he said, 'You can tell George that's from Mr Sheikh. Next time his boss, Aftab Huq, wants to try and humiliate Mr Sheikh in public again, you'll think a broken nose is a birthday present.'

Heidi was speechless. Who the fucking hell was this Mr Sheikh? She'd never heard of him.

'Ditto calling the police,' the young man said as he rubbed the knuckles of his left hand on his T-shirt. 'Don't do it. Not unless you want to hurt really badly.'

And then he left. Only after he'd disappeared completely, or so it seemed, did the pain begin. And the shaking. But Heidi was determined she wasn't going to cry. Broken nose or no broken nose, a little shit like that wasn't going to make her break down.

As soon as she felt able to do so, she stood up and walked down the hall to where the phone was plugged in. She called George on his mobile.

'Some fucking little bleeder's just punched me in the mush!' she said.

Amir Charleston no longer lived in Holland Park. No doubt chasing a 'cool' urban vibe, he'd got himself a flat in an old mansion block equidistant from the tech hub that is Old Street, Liverpool Street Station and Shoreditch High Street. It got no funkier. But then he was in banking.

Montalban asked him to come with them. Charleston, who was an attractive, fit-looking man, said, 'I've not touched drugs since my conviction.'

But later, Bob Khan claimed to have watched him sweat as he made himself ready to go to Limehouse. Now in a large and rather cold interview room he was shivering. His solicitor, some high-flier from a big City of London firm, sat by Charleston's side.

'I was out running.'

'All evening?' Montalban asked.

'No.'

'So give me times.'

He sighed. Entitlement written all over him. He also had the remnants of a black eye.

'I left the office at around six. Jogged across to Commercial Street then down to the river and back again.'

'Back to where?'

'Spitalfields.'

'What for?

'I belong to a gym. In Hanbury Street?'

Montalban frowned. 'I don't know of a gym in Hanbury Street.' He looked at Bob. 'You?'

'No, guv.'

'Well, it's not actually a gym . . .'

'So what is it?'

'Well, it's a sort of a . . . A friend has some friends around to his flat and we, well, we box.'

'A private boxing club. Where?'

'I told you, Hanbury . . .'

'What number?'

Charleston looked at his solicitor and then said, 'I'd rather not say. My friends don't have anything to do with this. They no more know this Banergee chap than I do.'

'Says you.'

'Says me, yes,' he said. 'I don't know this man. I've no idea how my blood came to be on his clothing. Maybe I passed him in the street? As you can see, my latest bouts did my face some damage.'

Montalban nodded. 'How'd you get home after your "bouts" that night?'

He thought for a moment. 'Probably got a cab.'

'You don't know?'

'It's been over a week. In the meantime I've been to our office in Frankfurt for two days.'

How the other half lived.

'Well, had you walked you would have gone through Arnold

188

Circus to get to your flat, unless you decided for some reason to go another way, which I am open to.'

'I really don't remember,' Charleston said.

Montalban had looked up Charleston's father, the QC. He was the most English-looking man Montalban thought he'd ever seen. Amir had to be more like his Pakistani mother, dark and aquiline.

'Maybe I did walk through Arnold Circus but I don't remember doing so. Don't you have CCTV footage?'

Montalban ignored him. There was no footage of the attack on Banergee. Like all too many street cameras, those on Arnold Circus had been inoperable. 'We have to know who you were with that night . . .'

'That's impossible!'

The solicitor put a hand on Charleston's arm.

'Because if you don't have an alibi, given what we've found, you could be royally fucked, Mr Charleston,' Montalban said.

SEVENTEEN

The convenience store had never been shut on a Monday morning before. But Aftab could hardly ask George to man the barricades after what had happened to Heidi. Just thinking about what the poor woman had endured made him cringe with guilt.

Going to see Wahid Sheikh in his no doubt very ostentatious house in Chigwell was all Aftab could do. Throw himself on the old cunt's mercy. If he had any. He certainly wasn't going to tell Mumtaz or Shazia about Heidi – that side of the family had enough problems with his cousin Ali.

And yes, Wahid-ji's house was like a cross between a Disney film set and a municipal building from the nineteen sixties. Inside was even worse. The old man showed him into a vast living room that contained three huge, gold-coloured sofas and the biggest television he'd ever seen. On the floor was what, the old man told him, was a real tiger skin.

'My father shot it in 1935,' he said.

But Aftab hadn't come to discuss endangered wildlife.

'Wahid-ji,' he said, 'I believe I owe you an apology.'

'Do you?'

He smiled.

'Well, it seems so,' Aftab said. 'Because if I don't, then I can't really fathom why the wife of one of my employees got punched in the face by one of your men yesterday.'

'One of . . .'

'With respect, Wahid-ji, you know it,' Aftab said.

A young man with blonde hair came into the room and sat down next to the old man.

'Ah, this is Hasan, my niece's husband . . .'

'With great respect again, Wahid-ji, I don't care,' Aftab said. 'I've come to give you my apology for making you uncomfortable in my shop.'

He frowned. 'Uncomfortable in your shop?'

'Over the girl,' Aftab said.

The old git was deliberately not understanding.

'Ah. The bride,' he said. 'Yes, I was a little peeved.'

The bride? Aftab said, 'Shazia Hakim.'

'Oh, yes, well that's very decent of you, but I assure you on my mother's life that I had nothing to do with any attack upon your employee's wife.'

Aftab didn't know what to say. The bride?

'Although I'm sure she doesn't know it yet, the young lady is to be my wife when she finishes her examinations.'

The blonde man beside Wahid Sheikh smiled. Heidi said the man who'd punched her had been a blond, white guy. Aftab felt cold to his bones.

'And you are not to tell her Aftab-ji,' the old man said. 'I want it to be a nice surprise for the young lady.'

It was DC Shamima Iqbal who had told them that Susi Chopra was staying in a hotel. Bob had been to her marital home only to be told by her husband that Susi was staying at the Weavers Hotel on Folgate Street. Apparently, it was where she always stayed when she was unfaithful to him. He had already started divorce proceedings.

When she managed to stop crying, Susi said, 'I didn't kill my brother.'

'But you did assault him,' Bob said.

'He wouldn't listen!'

Every time she moved, her jewellery jangled and tinkled.

'Rajiv was always moaning about his business! I gave him a chance to realise the capital in that building. With the flat above the shop plus the outbuildings at the back it's worth four million pounds. Even splitting the money two ways, he could have retired.'

'And you could have continued to live in comfort when your husband divorced you.'

'Dilip is ridiculous!' she said. 'He threatens me! He says, *you're not getting a penny when we divorce!* And so I say, *but we bought this house together!* He says, *you have never worked. I have kept you all your life.* I say, *but I have supported you in the home so that you can pursue your career.* Then he says, *ah, but you couldn't give me children, could you?* And then I realised . . .'

'Realised what?'

'That because we have no children I do not have a very firm claim.'

'Because you committed adultery?'

'Ach.' She nodded her head. 'My husband did too. Admittedly long ago. But I have no proof.'

'But he has?'

'Photographs,' she said. 'He hired a detective.' She leant forward in her chair. 'DC Khan,' she said, 'I went to see Rajiv in the shop the night he died, but when I left him he was alive. We argued and I ended up hitting him. As I hit him one of my rings cut his cheek and also damaged my finger. We were both crying by then. He let me staunch the blood from my finger on his shirt. He was sorry and I was sorry. But he still wouldn't move on selling the shop. I left.'

'What time?'

'Around nine. I went home. Dilip, my husband was away on business.'

'Where?'

'I've no idea,' she said. 'We haven't talked for weeks. I didn't go out again that night. I certainly went nowhere near Arnold Circus. When I discovered that Rajiv had been killed the next day, I was distraught. I came to Brick Lane, booked into my usual hotel on Folgate Street and tried to make sense of everything.'

'You stay in Tower Hamlets a lot?'

'Since my husband rejected me, yes. And that happened a long time ago, DC Khan.' All her animation deserted her. 'I couldn't have children. When Dilip realised that . . . Well, he organised separate rooms. I didn't cheat on my husband from choice. Not to start with.'

'Why didn't you tell us all this when we first contacted you, Mrs Chopra? You must know how this looks now.'

She sighed. 'Of course I do,' she said. 'But I was afraid and for the most shallow reason.' She shook her head. 'I knew I had left my brother alive. Your officers told me that Rajiv had been murdered outside. I didn't kill him. But I worried that if I told the whole story it might affect my inheritance.'

'How?'

'I don't know. But I knew I didn't want to speak to our family solicitor. Mr Patel is disturbed enough by my divorce. I am sure it is the same in Muslim families but in Hindu society everyone looks at everyone else when things like this happen. They judge. But at the same time they rub their hands in case there is something in it for them.'

193

Bob Khan couldn't help smiling. 'I'm sure that's true of all families whatever their religion, Mrs Chopra,' he said.

Lee was outside a hotel somewhere in Earls Court in his car. He was tracking the movements of the husband of a local actress who had been inside the hotel with a young girl for over half an hour. So far.

Mumtaz was finding it hard being Mishal on Skype.

'So, my darling, are you looking forward to seeing me in person tomorrow?' Abu Imad said.

'Oh, yes.'

It didn't look as if he was still in Iraq. He certainly wasn't strutting around inside a tent carrying an AK47 over his shoulder. His surroundings looked like a nondescript office.

'Now, when you arrive in Amsterdam,' he said, 'you must go to McDonalds and order a Big Mac meal. Stay in McDonalds until you are met.'

'By you?'

He hesitated.

She said, 'You are coming to meet me, aren't you?'

He tipped his head to one side. 'Maybe.'

'Yes, but you said—'

'Don't question me, Mishal!' He held up a hand. 'I am a wanted man. Places like airports are really dangerous for me. Maybe, maybe not. But someone will meet you and we will be together.'

'In Holland?'

'Inshallah,' he said.

Mumtaz had to work hard to keep control. What if he didn't turn up? There was no way she could go to him. Putting up with his bullshit would all have been for nothing. It was also time she could have spent with her hard-pressed family. Her mother hadn't eaten

194

since that story about Ali had appeared in the local newspaper. Mumtaz really feared for her, and for Ali.

'Inshallah.'

He smiled. 'That's my girl!' he said. 'Soon we'll be together in the Caliphate, which you are just going to love. And remember, my darling, if you don't always feel like doing everything for me yourself, we will have slaves. I mean, when I say I'm a big man in the Caliphate, I mean I am a BIG man!'

Slaves. Little Yazidi or Christian girls she imagined. Tiny little workhorses who were also expected to fulfil their 'master's' baser sexual needs.

'So look, time is short,' he said. 'I have to go.'

'Where?'

He frowned. 'You know, Mishal, you mustn't question me like this. Out, OK. Just out.'

She lowered her head. 'Sorry.'

His smiles came as quickly as his frowns. 'It's alright,' he said. 'But look, travelling tomorrow, you don't wear hijab or even a scarf, yeah?'

He'd said this before.

'Yes.'

'People will give you grief. And don't read your Koran on the plane.'

'No.'

'And if a man comes and sits beside you, you'll just have to put up with it. Don't ask to move, it will call attention to you.'

Mumtaz had never even considered it.

'I know you only ever want to be beside me now, my darling, but we all have to make sacrifices if we are to bring about the World Caliphate.'

'Yes.'

He smiled again. 'I kiss your eyes, little Mishal,' he said. 'My brave girl. When we are together, I will never so much as look at another woman ever again.'

Mishal hugged herself with pleasure. Mumtaz on the other hand, thought, liar! You'll be off with your slave girls within a week! Bastard.

'It's only a question of time before I find your gym buddies,' Montalban said. 'If I want to I can close Hanbury Street and go into every house and flat.'

The solicitor, Mr Dugdale said, 'I don't think so, DI Montalban.'

'Oh, yeah?'

He was an arrogant prick. All Savile Row suit and hair gel. Probably north of five hundred quid an hour. Why would someone like Charleston go to some bloke's flat in the East End to box? Sounded like fucking *Fight Club*. . .

'You need an alibi, Mr Charleston,' Montalban said. 'At the moment you don't have one. You're not co-operating, which is against your own interests. I don't understand this. What is this "gym"?'

'It's a gym.'

'So why not give me the names of the people who go there? They're your only hope at the moment. If they vouch for your presence with them at the time of the murder, you have a defence. If not, you don't.'

He took a piece of paper out of his pocket.

'This was handed to me this morning,' he said. 'It's some brief notes from my officers who have been searching your flat. One of your T-shirts has come up positive for bloodstains using a luminol test. Do you know what that means?'

The solicitor said, 'Luminol is a chemiluminescence agent that can detect blood even if objects or clothes have been washed.'

'That's right,' Montalban said. 'And when one of your T-shirts was subjected to testing it lit up like a fairground.'

Montalban saw the solicitor look at his client in, what seemed to him, a different way.

Mr Dugdale said, 'DI Montalban, may I have a moment alone with my client, please?'

'Lee!'

It was Shereen al'Barri. What was she doing on Green Street? Wasn't she supposed to be at work?

'It's the school holidays,' she said when he asked.

'Oh, right.'

He had photographs of the actress's husband kissing a girl young enough to be his daughter inside the entrance to the hotel in Earls Court. It hadn't been a bad day's work.

'Lee, you are going away,' Shereen said.

'Soon.'

'When?'

'Don't you think it's best you don't know?' he said.

She began to cry. He put his arm around her shoulders.

'I can't bear not knowing!' she said.

'Come on up to the office,' he said. 'Let's get you a cuppa.'

Mumtaz was up there but she wouldn't say anything.

The police had a lead on Rajiv's murder. A rumour was going around that he'd been killed by his sister. But Baharat Huq couldn't believe that. Susi Banergee had always been a strange woman, and very, very acquisitive, but murder? No!

DI Montalban would neither confirm nor deny Susi as a suspect. But then the police were always cagey about these things. He had also been very clear that he didn't want Ali to know. Not yet. Baharat felt this keenly. Surely his son had to know something was happening? Or maybe Montalban was keeping him in the dark on purpose. Perhaps he felt that Ali would soon tire of being disconnected from the world and leave the church of his own volition. Why the DI wasn't just dragging him out and taking him to the police station was beyond Baharat. There had to be a reason. The Reverend Reid had called Baharat that morning to report that Ali was as well as could be expected. But the vicar was worried about some of the graffiti that had appeared on the building overnight. He didn't specify exactly what it said, but Baharat took it to mean that some believed his son to be a paedophile. He knew that he wasn't and it seemed possible that soon his son would be exonerated – at least of Rajiv's murder. But he feared the mud would stick. Accusations of sexual abuse did, whether the person was guilty or not. That was at least how it seemed from reading the newspapers.

At least Sumita was eating again and he'd finally managed to persuade Asif to go home to Tracey. Mumtaz was going away on business and so he felt he should talk to her, but he really didn't feel up to it. If Ricky Montalban called to say that he had arrested someone for Rajiv's murder, then he might. But that still left the problem of the two Syrian boys and their accusation against his son.

Did the police really have Susi Banergee in custody? He hadn't seen her, but then he'd hardly left the house.

DC Iqbal had gone out to buy tea and cigarettes. Baharat had drunk so much tea he'd feared he might wet himself. As for the cigarettes? It had been really stupid to start smoking again, but what else could he do? He'd never felt so helpless.

The flat, which was in an old council block called Casson House, was owned and apparently occupied by a man called Taha Mirza. This was probably the man Charleston had known as

'Grasshopper'. Christ, it was all so bloody James fucking Bond! Charleston caved in at the end – he had no choice. But it was obvious he was afraid of this character.

Mirza didn't have a record but had been a professional boxer in his twenties. Now forty, he worked as a bouncer at a nightclub in the West End. Charleston claimed to have met him at a fun run around Victoria Park in Hackney. They'd bonded over fitness and Mirza had invited Charleston to his home boxing gym.

When he'd gone along to the first training session, Charleston had met other men. But he wasn't going to say who they were. Mirza, he said, would vouch for his presence at the gym at the time of the murder. Apparently he thought that once he had an alibi that would be that.

Ricky knocked on the door of the ground-floor flat and waited. When nothing had happened for over a minute he knocked again. A bleary-eyed Asian man came to the door wearing nothing but a pair of boxer shorts.

'Taha Mirza?' Ricky asked.

'Yeah. What is it?'

'Police.'

The door slammed in Ricky's face and he cursed himself for not wedging it open with his foot. But it didn't matter too much. He had the back of the flat covered. And so five minutes later, he saw Taha Mirza again; this time he was being escorted by a uniformed constable.

The other thing that was known about Taha Mirza, which Mr Charleston did or didn't realise, was that back in his boxing days, he'd gained a bit of a reputation for being a religious zealot. Although not obviously allied to organisations that supported terrorism, Taha Mirza the boxer hadn't liked 'queers' attending his matches and had been very vocal in his opposition to women's boxing. 'Sisters,' he had once claimed, 'have their husbands to fight for them.'

'Hello, Mr Mirza,' Ricky said. 'I'm DI Montalban. We want to talk to you about your boxing gym.'

He looked as if he'd been struck by something.

'A friend of yours, a Mr Charleston, says he was with you and some other men at this property on the night of the 5th April.'

Mirza just silently stared.

Ricky looked at the uniform beside Mirza and said, 'I think we need to continue this conversation inside Mr Mirza's flat.'

'No!'

'No?'

'No!' Mirza repeated.

And if he hadn't said that then maybe Taha Mirza could have got himself out of trouble.

Ricky smiled. 'Take him inside Constable Erikson, will you?'

'Yes, sir.'

Mumtaz, though champing at the bit to tell Lee about Abu Imad's possible change of plan, nevertheless made the tea. Shereen al'Barri was not a guest she had expected.

Lee had brought her in. They'd met on Green Street and, during a conversation about her son, Shereen had burst into tears. Once he'd settled her in the office, Lee joined Mumtaz in the small kitchen area and said, 'She wants to know when we're going to meet Fayyad.'

'You didn't tell her, did you?'

'Course not!' he whispered. 'But then she started crying and I couldn't just leave her in the street.'

'No.'

He started to return to the office when Mumtaz said, 'Oh Lee I heard from Fayyad – Abu Imad. I must remember to call him by his jihadi name.'

'Right. And?'

'He's not sure he's going to be able to meet me in person at the airport. He's such a wanted man it might be too great a risk.'

'Christ,' Lee rubbed his face.

'I'm to meet him or whoever at McDonalds at Schiphol. I've to order a Big Mac meal and wait.'

'For?'

'Who knows?' she said.

'I'll speak to you later.'

He went back into the office and asked. 'Do you want sugar in your tea, Shereen?'

Ricky Montalban had once had a mate who'd lived in the Casson flats. Taha Mirza must have had to take down the wall between the lounge and one of the bedrooms to make way for his boxing ring. It was a good job they were decent-sized rooms. It was an even better job that there was no flat underneath.

As well as the boxing ring there was also a three-piece black leather suite and a large flat-screen TV. When they first walked in, Ricky thought that Mirza had a war film on. And so it was. But it hadn't been made by Hollywood.

A group of terrified men were being herded to the edge of a rooftop by hooded characters dressed in black who pushed them to their deaths on the ground below. This was accompanied by a hysterical commentary by a man speaking what Ricky imagined was Arabic.

He looked at Taha Mirza. 'Into this, are you?' he asked.

He said nothing.

Ricky took his phone out of his pocket. 'I s'pose I'd better get a warrant to search this place,' he said.

EIGHTEEN

Aftab hadn't slept. He'd gone to bed but he'd just laid down and looked at the ceiling, seething. Had Mumtaz really agreed to marry Shazia to that vile old man? Had she really not told the girl? His cousin had always been a caring person, how could she do such a thing?

He managed to stop himself phoning her until 8 a.m. and then he rang. Shazia had told him she was going into college early to do some reading in the library. She'd said she was getting the 7.30 bus. He hoped she'd made it.

And, luckily, Mumtaz was alone. Aftab didn't mince his words. 'Are you marrying Shazia off to Wahid Sheikh?'

There were a few seconds of silence, then she said, 'How do you know about that?'

'Because I had to go and see the old bastard and he told me!'

'Why did you have to go and see him?' Mumtaz said.

But Aftab didn't want to talk about George and Heidi. He also wanted Mumtaz to stick to the point.

'You've not answered my question,' he said. 'Do you intend to marry—'

'No!' she said. 'Of course not!'

'Well, Wahid Sheikh thinks you are!'

'Wahid Sheikh is wrong,' she said. 'Listen, Aftab, I know this is going to be difficult, but there are things you don't know . . .'

'Bloody right!'

'I mean things that mean that my daughter will not even get close to marrying Wahid Sheikh.'

'He knows that, does he?'

'No.'

'Oh, well it's gonna be fun for all the family when he does find out!' Aftab said.

'Everything will be alright!' she said. 'You have to trust me!'

'You think? Mumtaz, if you're planning some sort of revenge . . .'

'I'm not!'

'Your mum and dad can't take no more,' he said. 'All this business with Ali . . . The whole family's up in arms. I can't believe he'd hurt anyone but nobody cares what I think . . .'

'Look, Aftab,' she said, 'I can't tell you why, but you have to trust me. Shazia will not marry that old man.'

'Bloody right she won't,' he said. 'I'll go and take her away from him myself!'

'It will work out,' she said. 'And also, Aftab, know that he can't touch her until she's finished her exams. Again, I can't explain. But that is a fact.'

Aftab shook his head. 'This is all fucking beyond me,' he said.

'I know. I'm sorry.'

He put the phone down. Could he trust Mumtaz? The idea of not trusting her was more to the point, and so he had to ignore that. But he didn't feel good about it.

'My client doesn't know anything about ISIS.'

Montalban stared. Amir Charleston's face was a classic

depiction of guilt. Taha Mirza had given him the names of the two other men who attended his 'gym' without a murmur. Both highly paid City whizz-kids, both white, they'd shaken with terror when they'd been dragged from their beds and brought to Limehouse the previous night. One of them, some sort of analyst, had bleated on about 'meaning'. Ricky hadn't understood. The geezer lived in a fucking mansion in Blackheath and drove a Ferrari, how much more 'meaning' did he need?

'So what was your client doing hanging around with someone like Taha Mirza?' Ricky asked.

'Mr Mirza runs boxing sessions . . .'

'Yes. He also has more radical material on his computer than most terror suspects we've arrested and put away.'

'Mr Charleston has no knowledge of that.'

'Really? That's not what his boxing mate Mr Lewis says.'

'What does Mr Lewis say?'

'Mr Lewis says that Mr Mirza is training fighters for Syria. He also says that he, Mr Charleston and Mr Cranmer were put in touch with Mr Mirza when they joined an Islamic study group in south London. All young and fit and apparently sold on the idea of fighting for something. I didn't get the impression from Mr Lewis that what they were fighting for mattered too much.'

'DI Montalban, you're going off the point,' Mr Dugdale said. 'How does this relate to the accusation of murder that has been levelled at my client?'

'Oh, I think that Mr Charleston knows the answer to that,' Ricky said. 'Don't you? You didn't meet Mirza on no fun run did you?'

Charleston turned away.

'But seeing as he's been struck dumb, I'll tell you,' Ricky said. 'The aim was always to train for something. Religion was the hook, but it wasn't the reason. Some stressed-out City lads need some sort of physical outlet, that's not unusual. What is unusual is to find City lads being trained by a bouncer with dodgy views about women and gay people. But then, for reasons I'm sure we'll find out in the end, Lewis, Cranmer and your client were attracted to Mirza and his gym. How am I doing, Mr Charleston? Right so far?'

Mumtaz walked through the door of her parents' house and into her mother's arms.

'Do you have to go away now?' Sumita asked.

Mumtaz put Shazia's suitcase on the floor and said, 'I'm sorry, Amma.'

Her father came into the hall from the living room.

'Oh course you do,' he said. He kissed her. 'But come and sit with me, just for a moment.'

Mumtaz didn't really have time for small talk with her father, but she followed him into the living room. Her mother said, 'I'll make tea.'

Mumtaz knew that was more for her mother's benefit than for her. Bengali milk tea took at least ten minutes to brew. She'd have to be on her way back home by that time.

But she sat down with her father.

'How is Ali?'

She felt guilty for not going to see her brother, even though Asif had told her that Ali wanted no visitors.

Baharat Huq lit a cigarette. Mumtaz hadn't seen her father smoke for years, it saddened her, but she ignored it. He was dealing with a terrible situation in his own way, she had no right to criticise.

'I am told he is managing,' Baharat said. 'Maurice Glass is

visiting him. But I have also been told, by the police, that they have another suspect for the murder of Rajiv-ji.'

'Who?'

'They will not say. There are rumours that Susi Banergee was taken to Limehouse Police Station and, yesterday, a flat was raided in Casson House.'

'Down the road?'

'Yes. I don't know if it was connected to Ali, but I hope,' he said.

'I'm sorry I've not been around to help,' Mumtaz said.

'Ah, you mustn't worry!'

'I do!'

He held her hand. 'You have a heavy burden, what with the girl and having to work . . . You should have been cared for by your husband . . .'

Would he ever stop feeling guilty for arranging her marriage to Ahmet Hakim? Mumtaz knew that nothing she could say to reassure him would ever make it better. She changed the subject.

'Abba, we know that Ali is innocent but even so, now everyone knows about his sexuality . . .'

'That was Bhatti from the electrical shop!' he said. 'He told the papers. Knowing him, for money!'

'Do you know for sure it was Bhatti?'

'I know in my soul,' he said. Which meant he had no proof. Even though Mr Bhatti had known about Ali and Rajiv all along. Whoever had leaked the story, the damage was done.

'Abba, how will Ali live here, as a gay man?'

Her father visibly shuddered when she used the word. Then he said, 'Well, he won't.'

Mumtaz didn't understand. 'He won't . . .'

Baharat shook his head. 'I have thought and thought and I

come to no conclusion but that he will have to go,' he said.

'Where?'

'I do not know. There are good people here, Mumtaz, people who do not judge, but . . . Rajiv-ji could do the gay thing because he was different, always. His father wore women's clothes. His family came here from India a long time before we Pakistanis and Bangladeshis arrived. He was accepted. Ali will not be.'

Mumtaz knew that was possible, but she said, 'If he goes, those people will have won.'

'And if he stays he will be beaten up, maybe killed,' Baharat said. 'You know there are people here who will not let others live in peace, Mumtaz. There always have been. When you were a child it was the BNP . . .'

'UKIP are still around.'

'Yes, I know, but there are also people within our community,' he said. 'You know . . .'

She nodded.

'I don't know what will happen when this is all over,' he said. 'Inshallah we will all survive.'

Mumtaz said, 'Inshallah.' Because, as far as she knew, the outcome could only be as God willed.

'Mrs Chopra is staying at her hotel,' Bob said. 'She knows she's not to leave.'

He'd joined Montalban for lunch in the canteen. What they had both chosen contained far too many chips.

'She didn't kill her brother,' Montalban said. 'I mean, she's always been pretty terrifying, I remember Susi Banergee when I was a kid, but that story she told you rings true to me.'

'And me,' Bob said. 'What about your bloke, guv?'

'Charleston? He did something. I can see it on his face,'

Montalban said. 'Also the other gym bunnies are, probably unintentionally, fingering him.'

'How?'

'Lewis and Cranmer say when they left the gym, Charleston was still there. Mirza says Charleston left after midnight, on foot, which means he could have been at the top of Brick Lane at the same time as Rajiv was being murdered. Mind you, Mirza could be lying. The search of his gaff brought up some very unsavoury contacts.'

'And what does Charleston say?'

'Sweet FA. Mr Dugdale, the solicitor his daddy's bought for him, does all the talking so far. Fucking pissed off with it.'

Bob didn't say anything. Even with forensic evidence it wasn't always straightforward to obtain a conviction. Charleston's blood on Rajiv's shirt didn't prove that he killed him. Although Bob knew that Montalban had hopes about the faint stains that had been detected on Charleston's T-shirt. If that blood proved to be Rajiv's, that could be enough.

'Next step's going back to those kids who lived with Ali Huq and getting Charleston in an ID parade,' he said. 'Whether Huq had sex with them or not, they were out that night. A bit of persuasion might just tease the truth from the little sods.'

'Where are they now?'

'In care,' Montalban said.

'I didn't think we did ID parades any more.'

'We don't, not often. But I think I'd like to see Charleston on one. Think it might make him sweat even more than he already is.'

'Does Mr Huq know we've got someone?' Bob asked.

'No. I want to be sure of Charleston before I let him know. I've told his father it's on the cards. Bit frightened old Baharat-ji might go into cardiac arrest. But Ali's safe where he is for the time being. If I release him anything could happen.'

'I've never heard of anyone being held in a church before,' Bob said. 'When he claimed sanctuary I had to ask him what it meant.'

'Ancient privilege, sanctuary,' Montalban said. 'Course people don't normally use it these days. I'll be honest, I've used it for me own purposes. Keeps Ali out the way, no protests outside the nick either for or against the prisoner, and with the imam going in, no hassle for the church either. Couldn't have planned it better.'

Bob looked down at his chips. 'I suppose every community has people who're intolerant.'

'Yeah,' said Montalban. 'Shit innit.'

Stansted Airport in Essex is forty miles outside London. It can be reached by road or rail in an hour to an hour and a half.

Lee chose to drive. He'd booked a parking space at the airport and his journey took two hours, mainly because of traffic build-up on the North Circular. Mumtaz went by train from London Liverpool Street. Lee arrived first at 2 p.m. while Mumtaz made it by 2.30.

Although their plane didn't take off until 4.50, all passengers for international flights were advised to arrive a good two hours before. Not even the check-in desks were open when Lee arrived and so he drifted about occasionally looking at the odd book in Smiths. It was while he was perusing Andy McNab's latest that he saw Mumtaz. She wasn't wearing her headscarf, as instructed, and her eye make-up was very thick. She looked amazing.

Imam Yusuf was his own age. He was different from any imam, Ali had ever met before.

'There are Muslim groups who do not discriminate on the grounds of gender or sexuality,' he'd said. 'I know them.'

Ali had said, 'People like me should be killed.'

209

The imam, who was an astute man had said, 'And what would your death achieve?'

Ali hadn't answered. Now, alone except for the policeman outside the cafe door, he knew the answer to that question. It would stop the pain. It would also mean that his family's honour would be restored. His parents and his siblings would be able to walk the streets with their heads held high again. And, selfishly, he wouldn't have to face either prison or a future hiding in the shadows. In prison, if no one would believe his innocence, he would be killed. That was what happened to nonces.

If he didn't go to prison, he didn't want to go to some group of 'queer' Muslims! What kind of freaky people would they be? How could they even call themselves Muslims? How could he?

Montalban still hadn't got back to him and the Reverend Reid had gone to see one of his parishioners. He felt as if he was on the edge of the world. The crypt's windows were high up and small, which meant that he could only see people's feet. He had no TV, no phone, no newspapers. He had no idea what was going on in the world. Not for the first time, he wondered whether this was by design. What did the police not want him to know?

There were books but he had no patience to sit and read and so he just thought. It would have hurt Rajiv so much to see him like this. At one time they'd even talked about leaving the Lane and starting up as a couple somewhere new. But Ali had realised that wherever they went, he could not escape his guilt. That was why he had ended it. Rajiv had cried. They'd made love one last time and then they'd both cried. But Ali had stuck to his guns. He'd seen Rajiv countless times in his shop or in the street. They'd even spoken, from time to time. But always in an atmosphere of bitterness.

What a way to live. But then it wasn't living, was it?

He went to the lavatory with the intention of simply relieving his bladder but then, while he was washing his hands, a thought occurred to him. Then something else happened.

It was stuffy in the airport and so Mumtaz treated herself to a cold drink with which to take her precautionary aspirin, and sat down to wait for the check-in desk to open. She hadn't seen Lee but she was sure he had to have arrived. By reflex she took out her phone. As soon as she saw it she remembered that it was just a pay-as-you-go thing. It wasn't her real phone. She couldn't speak to Shazia or Abba on it. Lee had the number and Abu Imad and that was it. But if she phoned Lee, Abu Imad would know. He was that kind of man. Or was he?

She put the phone back in her bag. Who was Abu Imad/Fayyad al'Barri? On the face of it he was a totally radicalised terrorist who had, by his own admission, killed people. He was arrogant, sexist, dictatorial and materialistic – in spite of his adherence to the 'caliphate'. But was that really who he was? Or rather was that someone he had become and now no longer wanted to be? If he was playing a game in order to leave ISIS, he was playing it very well. Maybe too well. Maybe that was him.

The only evidence to the contrary that existed was the Tooth of Jonah. A star of the religious relic world, a bright, shiny thing that all Fayyad's parents' hopes centred on. Lee had known from the start that it could just be delusion. But Mumtaz knew that his motivation for helping the al'Barris went deeper than just finding Fayyad. Abbas had saved his life. Lee had to try and make that up to him. Also there was his guilt over being part of an invasion force that had wrecked Iraq. It didn't matter what the intentions of the British government may have been, that was what had happened.

Mumtaz drank her very expensive orange juice and looked

up at the boards for gates checking in. Amsterdam was still not showing.

Then something occurred to her that she hadn't thought about before. What if Mishal, her teenager alter ego, was actually a radical? If Fayyad really wanted to return to the UK, how could he know that this girl would help him? She might not. But then maybe he was relying on his sex appeal to make her do whatever he wanted?

'Mishal?'

It was a woman's voice and, for a moment, Mumtaz didn't know where it was coming from. She looked around, but saw no one.

'Hello? Mishal?'

She was standing behind her. A column of black material, only her eyes visible.

'I bring greetings from Abu Imad,' the woman said.

Mumtaz forced a smile.

'There's been a change of plan.'

Mumtaz felt as if someone had put a large, cold stone in her stomach.

NINETEEN

In the short time they'd been away from Ali Huq's house the boys, Qasim and Nabil, had changed. They looked genuinely nervous.

Ricky Montalban instructed their translator to give them very specific instructions. This was their last chance to tell the truth. He was implying that in the past they'd lied and that was quite deliberate. He wanted them to know. He also believed, sincerely, that they had lied.

Amir Charleston stood in a line of random men, some of whom were Asian and some not, behind one-way glass. He'd started sweating heavily even before the sergeant in charge of the line-up told them all to be quiet and keep still.

Qasim and Nabil, fascinated by the fact that they could see while not being seen, walked up and down getting used to the idea. Ricky feared they could do that all day. He asked them to stop, to concentrate and to tell him if they recognised any of the men on the line. If they did, then from where and when did they recognise them?

The boys walked up and down more slowly. Their translator followed. From time to time one or other kid spoke.

Eventually Ricky said to the translator, 'What they saying?'

His eyes moved in that way that was sometimes described as 'shifty'.

'Well?'

They were standing in front of Charleston but not looking at him.

Eventually the translator said, 'They think they know this man.'

'Number 3?'

'Yes.'

'How?'

He spoke to the kids who now, for some reason, whispered.

When he'd finished the translator said, 'They know him as a good Muslim.'

'Oh? Really?'

'That is what they say.'

Like his Pakistani mother, Charleston was a Muslim. He also exercised a lot, which modern 'good' Muslims did seem to do. But he had also mixed with people like Taha Mirza whose choice of home entertainment had little to do with caring and compassionate religion.

'Where'd they know him from?' Ricky asked.

The boys said they'd seen him running on Brick Lane. He asked them the man's name, but they didn't know.

'So how can you tell he's a good Muslim?'

The translator asked and, this time, the boys clammed up.

They knew Charleston alright and Ricky would have put money on that having little or nothing to do with running on Brick Lane.

Then he asked them whether they boxed.

There'd been no time to get his car out of the long-stay and so Lee Arnold did what Mumtaz and her burqa'd friend were doing and got a cab.

But as soon as he got in, someone else joined him.

'What the fuck are you doing here?' he asked Abbas al'Barri.

The cabbie said, 'Where to gents?'

Lee pointed to the cab that contained Mumtaz. 'Follow that,' he said. Then he turned his attention on Abbas. 'Why are you here?'

It had been a coincidence. Shereen hadn't planned to go to Lee's office when she'd gone shopping on Green Street. But then someone had left a printout of an e-ticket out on a desk, which she'd seen.

'Doesn't explain why you're here though, does it?' Lee said.

'That is obvious. I want to see my son.'

'So you've a seat on the 16.50 flight?'

'Yes. What is happening? Do you know?'

Lee was furious he had Abbas in tow. He'd been beside himself when he'd watched Mumtaz go off with that woman. Now Abbas complicated everything.

'No, I fucking don't,' he said.

They exited the airport and pulled onto the A120.

'You want me to carry on following?' the cabbie said.

'Yeah. Ta.'

Abbas, his eyes wide with fear or excitement or the wonder of the Essex countryside said, 'Do you know where they're going?'

Lee didn't even bother to dignify that with an answer.

He couldn't do it. Reflex kept pulling his head up and forcing his lungs to fight for breath. Maybe if he smashed his head against the sink? Ali began to cry. He couldn't even do that. When his head was finally pulled away from the sink by someone else, his nose was full of snot.

'Mr Huq!'

She was young and pretty and she had a very strong grip.

215

'I'm DC Iqbal, remember?' she said.

The family liaison woman from the police. He'd seen her once.

'I'm not going to ask you what you think you were doing because I think that's obvious,' she said. She pulled him towards the door. 'Come on. We need to talk.'

Ali didn't want to, but he also didn't fancy the bother of saying 'no'. She gave him a towel to dry his face.

'How did you know where I was?' Ali asked.

'Once I'd looked around the cafe, you could only be in the loo,' she said. 'And I heard you.'

He hung his head.

'If we're talking drowning, you should know that doing it in a sink is probably one of the hardest methods,' she said. 'The temptation to breathe is far too great. But moving on . . .'

They both sat down. Water from his beard dripped down onto his chest and he felt embarrassed.

'I'm here to tell you that DI Montalban is questioning someone about the murder of Rajiv Banergee,' she said.

'Who?'

'Can't tell you,' she said. 'But this person's a strong contender. We're just waiting on the results of one forensic test . . .'

'What?'

'Can't tell you that either,' she said. 'But what I can say is that there's no need to take your own life whatever.'

'Whatever?'

'If the test is positive for what we think, then you are in the clear. If it doesn't you're still in a stronger position than you know.'

'But what about Qasim and Nabil? The allegations of . . . sex . . . ?'

She looked at her hands. 'Can't tell you anything about that,' she said.

'Oh.'

'Not because I'm not allowed to, but because I don't know. What I do know, however, Mr Huq, is that you need to leave here now.'

The woman still hadn't told her her name. Now they were in a taxi with a stranger, she couldn't exactly ask her. The woman for her part, remained silent.

Mumtaz tried to remember where she'd told the driver to go. It had been a weird name. Something about Easter?

The woman didn't make eye contact. She looked out of the window to her left. Mumtaz, too, watched. She had to try and remember where they were going. She'd seen Lee walk out of the queue that had started to form by the check-in desk for their flight. There was a car behind that had followed them from the airport, but she couldn't see any faces.

They exited the A120 and turned into a village.

The driver said, 'Good Easter. Right?'

'Yes,' the woman said. 'Fambridge End.'

So it was 'Easter'. But what was it and where?

Mumtaz looked at the woman's hands. They were smooth and beautifully manicured. Her nails, which had to have been painted professionally, were spectacular. Long and tapered, they were a deep, dark red and they shone. Mumtaz's own nails were a disgrace. Weak and malformed, she kept them short. If she didn't, typing became difficult, as did doing the washing-up. Now, though, she used them as a distraction. She was frightened. Her chest felt tight and she was sweating. So far her heart hadn't begun to palpitate, but it soon would.

The possibilities were mind-boggling. Abu Imad could be at this Good Easter place or not. But if he was there, then how had he got into the country? And if he wasn't, what was waiting for her at this place, which may or may not be a village? She knew that there was a private airfield somewhere near Stansted because one of her old uni friends had taken flying lessons there. Maybe they were going to Amsterdam from that?

She quickly glanced inside her handbag to make sure that she still had her phone.

The trouble with luminol was that it had to be mixed with hydrogen peroxide in order to create a mist that could be sprayed on suspected bloodstains. And while the luminol itself didn't degrade DNA material, the hydrogen peroxide could. This meant that there was a possibility they would never know the profile of the person who had bled onto Amir Charleston's T-shirt.

The lab said they'd call at five or thereabouts. It was way beyond that. Montalban was visibly twitchy. If the sample hadn't degraded and it did come back positive for Rajiv Banergee's blood, Amir Charleston was finished.

The two Syrian kids hadn't said whether they'd seen Charleston the night Rajiv died or not. What they had said was that they'd seen him with Taha Mirza, who they knew to be a Muslim 'brother'. They claimed to like Mirza but had said that their landlord, Ali Huq, did not. Apparently there were a lot of 'brothers' Ali Huq hadn't wanted the boys to be around. So far they hadn't added anything to their sexual abuse charge against Huq. Significantly they hadn't withdrawn it. But now that Huq was out of the church and actually in custody, hopefully they could begin to investigate his side of the story more easily. And if Ricky had his way, Ali Huq would soon be released into the care of his family. Hopefully, being in familiar surroundings would encourage him to open up.

Montalban spoke. 'You heard of "soft" radicalisation?' he asked.

'What does that mean?' Bob said.

'Means radicalising someone through some unconnected interest or activity,' Montalban said. 'Mirza goes to a meeting about Islam and meets a few blokes mildly interested in religion but really into fitness. He's already running his own gym from his house for his mates, so he invites these new geezers along. They're obviously looking for something. He says, according to Lewis and Cranmer, Charleston's sparring partners, that he can train them for action in Syria. And Lewis and Cranmer, at least, liked the sound of that. Not because of religion, but because they both want to be Andy McNab.'

'That's pretty lame.'

'Yeah. But I don't think it applies to Charleston,' he said.

'Mirza's not owned up to training for Syria, guv,' Bob said.

'Lewis and Cranmer disagree, as do the many truly vile bits of film he has in his house.'

'Yeah . . .'

'Did poor old Rajiv flutter his eyelashes at Charleston just after his *Fight Club* session when he was pumped full of testosterone?' Montalban said. 'Or was he just in the wrong place at the wrong time?'

'But if Charleston did kill him, why?'

Montalban shrugged. 'Pumped up? Maybe he really did get the twisted religion of the jihadis? Islam may well mean more to him than the others because his mum's Pakistani.'

'Maybe.'

'Anyway, we'll find out,' Montalban said. 'Because we will hear from the lab any minute . . .' He pointed at the landline on his desk, '. . . now . . .'

Nothing happened.

Bob smiled. 'As a Muslim,' he said, 'I have to say it makes me so sick the way people make up their own Islam. Infidels!' He shook his head. 'They talk about infidels? They're infidels. All different groups! The Boyz . . .'

'Oh come on, with the Boyz, it's just an excuse to beat people up and nick their drugs.'

Bob smiled. 'True. But this Mirza guy and Ali Huq and his network? That's serious stuff, guv.'

'I know.' Montalban pointed at the phone again. 'Now!'

This time the phone rang.

They stopped outside a house that Mumtaz's mother would have described as a 'typical English cottage'. Four-square and white, it stood in the middle of a large, well-tended garden. It even had roses round the door.

The woman paid the cab driver and said to Mumtaz, 'Come inside.'

She opened the front door into a wood-panelled hall. It smelt of pine and rose. Mumtaz stepped over the threshold.

'When can I see Abu Imad?' she asked.

The woman said, 'Soon.'

She led her into a large lounge where the balance of the house, in Mumtaz's opinion, went a bit awry. Large, blood-red leather sofas and ornate gilded tables topped with marble didn't look right. They also reminded her of Wahid Sheikh's tasteless house. Like that place, there were no books, and in a room with ceiling beams that looked strange.

'What's your name?' Mumtaz asked.

'I am Umm Khaled,' the woman said. 'Sit down and be comfortable.'

And then she left the room. Mumtaz heard her lock the door behind her.

She sat down and tried to steady her breathing. She looked at the phone in her handbag and wondered whether she should use it. Umm Khaled would almost certainly hear her if she tried and also she was only supposed to use the phone to call Abu Imad.

Then it rang.

Her nerves already at breaking point, Mumtaz just managed to turn what would have been a scream into a whimper. But it wasn't easy. She took the call.

'Hello?'

'Hello, my darling!' she heard him say. 'Are you comfortable in that beautiful house in the country?'

'Where are you?' she said.

'Close by.' She heard him laugh. 'I'm so sorry you had to go to all the bother of buying an airline ticket, but we had to make sure that nobody knew where you'd be.'

Mumtaz felt cold. 'Really.'

'As I told you, I am a wanted man. Now listen, Umm Khaled will take care of you until I come. So you just relax and prepare for the flight we really are taking.'

'What flight? Where?'

He laughed again. 'Well, not to Amsterdam,' he said.

'So, where?'

'So, I will tell you when I see you,' he said. 'Be patient. All you need to know is that I love you.'

He cut the connection. Mumtaz wiped sweat from her forehead. Stopping herself screaming at him had been tough. Maybe what he'd told her was correct, that he'd organised this change of plan for security reasons. But then it was also possible he'd planned it all along. Maybe he'd known all along, about her . . .

Mumtaz heard noises from outside the door. A woman talking, a man's laughter. Had he already arrived?

* * *

Montalban charged him.

Amir Charleston looked bemused. Eventually he said, 'I didn't do it.'

Later, Ricky took Bob to the Ten Bells on Commercial Street for what he called a 'few lemonades'. In Bob's case that was true. Ricky, on the other hand, was on the lager.

It was a warm evening and so they sat outside on the street watching as tourists went by and pointed at the pub.

'That's the place where Jack the Ripper met his victims!'

It wasn't. It was where Jack met his last victim, but neither Ricky nor Bob could be bothered to correct them. Jack the Ripper was a major industry in Spitalfields. Who were they to disrupt that?

Instead, Ricky raised his glass and proposed a toast.

'To luminol,' he said.

'To luminol.'

Of course it hadn't been the luminol itself that had pointed the finger of guilt at Amir Charleston. That had come about via a DNA test. But it had been the luminol that had shown the way when it exposed bloodstains from Rajiv Banergee on Charleston's T-shirt.

After the toast they sat in companionable silence for a few moments until Bob said, 'You think Taha Mirza knew what Charleston did?'

'No idea,' Ricky said. 'So far, there's nothing to connect him directly to the killing of Rajiv.'

'Yeah, but what about his connection to that dodgy lawyer in Newham? Didn't his computer throw up contact?'

'Yeah, but . . .' Ricky shrugged. 'Dunno. Super says that's a no-go area.'

'I wonder why?'

'Could be anything.'

'Terrorism?'

'Who knows? Vakeel Uddin's a lawyer, maybe it's fraud?' he laughed. Then he became grave. 'Or maybe not. Whatever it is, it's Newham's business, not ours. We don't touch it.'

Behind the house and its garden was farmland. Flat and featureless, there were few places to conceal oneself apart from a half-demolished hay barn. It was, however, a good place from which to observe the house. But it was there that any advantages they might have, stopped.

Lee didn't even want to look at Abbas. Without him, he might stand a chance of finding out what was going on, but just his presence was driving him mad. Why the fuck had he thought that going to Amsterdam was a good idea? What did he think he might do when he got there? Lee didn't bother to ask. What was the point? He was saddled with him in a village with no facilities – not even a shop that he could see – and no car. And Mumtaz was in trouble. What kind of trouble he didn't dare think.

He took pictures of the house on his phone and, when a man walked out of the back door, he snapped him too. Not that there was much to see, just a large figure wearing a greatcoat with the collar pulled up around his face. He was either cold or he was frightened of being recognised.

'Who's that?' Abbas whispered.

'I don't know,' Lee said. 'Left me crystal ball at home.'

'Sarcasm, huh?'

'You got it.'

Abbas moved back into the shadowed interior of the barn, leaving Lee alone with his guilt.

Persuading Mumtaz to take this job had been easy. Just the

thought of people's kids hotfooting it to the caliphate made her shudder. As a Muslim herself she also felt it was her duty to prevent the spread of the ISIS ideology. He couldn't know what that felt like. What he could and did know was how he'd taken advantage of that to help a friend. Not even really a client, a friend. So far, he'd made sweet FA out of the search for Fayyad. In fact he was out of pocket.

'Look!'

Abbas was back, pointing at one of the windows on the ground floor.

'What?'

'Look! Look!' He moved Lee's head into the right position and then said, 'Fayyad!'

Lee squinted. There was a man and he did have a beard. But he couldn't be sure it was Fayyad. From where he was, it could be almost anyone. He said so. But by that time he was speaking to thin air because Abbas was running, keeping low to the ground, towards the house.

TWENTY

His father was visibly relieved to see him. But Ali Huq's mother didn't even look at him.

'She will come round,' Baharat Huq said. 'Inshallah.'

Shamima Iqbal sat down opposite the two men and said, 'DI Montalban will be round to see you in the morning. You know, Ali, he had to pull quite a few strings to allow you to be released into the care of your family.' Then she added, 'I assume it's OK . . .'

'This is my son's home,' the old man said.

'Which you mustn't leave for the time being.'

Ali lowered his head. 'No.'

'That's very important,' Shamima said. 'DI Montalban has charged an individual with the murder of Rajiv Banergee but we're far from out of the woods.'

Baharat frowned. 'What do you mean?'

'The defendant will have to appear in court in order to enter his plea,' she said. 'I have to tell you that we think, at the moment, that he will plead not guilty. But that isn't set in stone. He may change his plea at any time and also, of course, when the case comes to trial, he could lose.'

'Could lose?'

'Nothing is ever certain, Mr Huq,' she said to the old man.

She'd got the call from Ricky Montalban when she'd been in the crypt with Ali Huq. He'd charged the City banker just after the lab had confirmed that the blood on the suspect's T-shirt had belonged to Rajiv Banergee.

They'd had Mr Banergee's sister in earlier, a Mrs Chopra. Shamima didn't know what had gone on, but she'd seen the woman leave. She'd looked furious. Shamima had wondered whether she'd killed her brother but then maybe her expression had more to do with Mrs Chopra's rather fierce personality.

Sadly, Shamima had heard nothing more about the sexual assault charges made by the two boys against Ali Huq. Montalban was convinced they were making it up, but Shamima wasn't so sure. Didn't you always have to make believing child victims your starting point? Also there was something else going on, so she'd heard. Certain connections Montalban had made had led, so it was said, to a situation of stalemate. People had been implicated in the Huq investigation who could not be touched, not yet.

Old embittered officers would sometimes mutter about villains under surveillance, sometimes for years, who were never brought to justice. Shamima didn't like to think about it.

Umm Khaled brought her mango juice.

'Is Abu Imad—'

'He'll come,' the woman said. 'Here. Have a drink.'

Mumtaz took the glass from Umm Khaled's gloved hand. Why was she so completely covered indoors? Then she remembered she'd heard a man's voice. It hadn't sounded like Abu Imad's but she couldn't be sure. Was he already there? And if he was, why hadn't he come to see her?

Umm Khaled left and, again, locked the door behind her.

Mumtaz sat down and sniffed the juice. She was very thirsty but she distrusted it and so she poured it onto the roots of a pot plant. Then she took her phone out. She couldn't hear Umm Khaled any more but she also couldn't see through the keyhole in the door – presumably because the key was still in it. She could be outside, listening.

Mumtaz really wanted to call Lee. She had to trust that he was somewhere nearby. She looked out of the window and saw the taxi they had arrived in. It was parked behind the house. And yet she'd seen it drive away . . .

What was happening?

Then she saw the taxi driver.

Without thinking any more, she punched Lee's mobile number into her phone. He answered after one ring.

'Mumtaz!'

She whispered, 'Lee this is bad.'

'I know!'

'The taxi driver who brought us here is one of them, whoever they are.'

'Christ!'

And then there was a sound of breaking glass, followed by screaming.

'Mumtaz!'

But she'd dropped the phone.

Once Shazia arrived, Sumita Huq left her bedroom.

'How are you, darling?' she asked the girl. 'I hope you'll be happy staying here for a few days.'

Shazia smiled. She didn't much like being in Brick Lane. It was a long journey to college and also her step-grandparents, though kind, rarely left her alone.

'Yes,' she said. 'But I will have to work, didima. I have my A levels . . .'

'Of course. Of course. You can shut yourself in your room and we will all be as quiet as mice.'

But Shazia knew that wouldn't happen. First would come the many little treats her didima would cook for her, then they'd hassle for her to come and watch David Attenborough on the TV. Or something.

Cousin Aftab had driven her to Brick Lane. Just lately he had become extremely protective. This manifested in fears about her walking the streets on her own. It was really sweet, if a bit irritating.

'Now, your Uncle Ali is with us for a little while too,' Sumita said. 'He's not very well.'

'Oh. What's wrong?'

Her didima waved a hand. 'Ah, nothing,' she said. 'He will be in his old room for most of the time. Just know that he isn't ignoring you. He's just not well.'

Shazia went to what had become 'her' room at the top of the house and looked out of the large weaver's window into the street. Long ago the Huq's house had belonged to Huguenots, protestant refugees from France famed for their silk-weaving skills. They had been clever people. British history was littered with Huguenot names like Isambard Kingdom Brunel the engineer and Joseph Bazalgette the man who had designed the London sewerage system. Shazia wondered whether, one day, the name 'Hakim' would join the long list of notable immigrant families in Britain. When she was the first Asian heritage, female Commissioner of the Metropolitan Police, then maybe.

She took her books and her computer out of her bag and lay down on the bed. She knew Uncle Ali wasn't ill. He was implicated in a sex scandal and in the murder of Rajiv-ji. People said they had been lovers.

Shazia could understand that. Uncle Ali, in spite of his outwards piety, had to have a sex life of some sort. Although why fun-loving Rajiv-ji had found that dried-up old stick attractive was beyond her. Shazia had never liked him. But he was her amma's brother and she did worry about what Uncle Ali's antics were doing to her.

A voice from downstairs interrupted her thoughts.

'Shazia, darling! Food!'

At this rate she was going to fail her A levels and then she'd never be Commissioner of the Met. But what could she do?

Shazia called back, 'Coming!'

The door opened and there he was. Abu Imad. Over his shoulder was a man who was either unconscious or dead.

Mumtaz was behind the sofa, but he saw her.

'Ah, Mishal,' he said. First there'd been the sound of breaking glass falling to the ground, then voices, then a dull thudding sound. She stood up.

With what looked like ease, he threw the body down on the floor. Small flecks of blood hit her face. To Mumtaz's horror she recognised it. In spite of the blood that smeared his face and his neck, she could see that it was Abbas al'Barri. He had a great bloody hole in his chest where he'd been shot. What had he been doing in the house?

Mumtaz put her hand in her pocket and checked whether her phone was still on. It seemed to be. When she'd heard the glass break, she'd dropped her phone on the floor. But then she'd picked it up. With any luck Lee was listening. What he'd do, she didn't know. But she felt better in the knowledge that he was there, somewhere.

'Is he dead?' Umm Khaled asked.

'Yes.'

He said it with such lack of emotion, it made Mumtaz gasp. That was his father!

The woman said, 'Good.'

Mumtaz looked at her eyes. They were cold and green and, for a moment, Mumtaz had a feeling she'd seen them before. But then he, Abu Imad, clicked his fingers in front of her face.

'So, my lovely wife,' he said. 'Aren't you pleased to see me?'

She couldn't speak. She needed to, but the words wouldn't come. 'Mishal?'

And now he was smiling and it made her flesh crawl. His own father was dead!

'You know who this is?' he asked.

She just about managed to shake her head.

'No? It's my father,' he said. 'An infidel. What can you do, eh?'

The taxi driver came in from the hall and said, 'You OK?'

Abu Imad said, 'Fine.'

'And you?' he looked at the woman.

'I'm fine too,' she said. 'Why wouldn't I be?'

He shrugged and then he left.

Abu Imad pushed the body of his father out of his way with his foot and sat down.

'So why don't you come to me, Mishal?' he said.

Abbas must have gone mad! He hadn't even tried to be discreet. He'd just smashed his way in. Lee had started to follow him, but boy, could he move! If anything had stayed in his mind from his service in Iraq, apart from the horror, it was the sight of Abbas al'Barri racing low to the ground, moving on his knees like a ninja.

But where was he now? Lee had heard breaking glass followed by shouting but then the house had become silent. Was Abbas dead? Or was he wounded? And where was Mumtaz?

He took his phone out and put it to his ear but it was dead. He'd heard her voice and then the glass and then nothing. So what now?

A man in his early twenties arrived. He was thickset and had a shaved head.

He said, 'We'll need a glazier.'

'Why?'

Abu Imad had his arm around 'Mishal' while his feet rested on his dead father's body. Mumtaz was having trouble breathing.

'Because my dad'll lose his mind if he sees it.'

Abu Imad shrugged. 'I don't know why you're bothered,' he said. 'We're leaving.'

'Yeah. But what if I want to come back?'

'Come back?' He addressed himself to Mumtaz. 'You hear this, sweetheart, Fazil wants to come back! From the Caliphate!'

'If it doesn't work out or—'

'Go into it with that bad attitude and it won't,' Abu Imad said. The woman came into the room.

'Umm Khaled,' Abu Imad said, 'did you know that the man you think is a true sword of Islam is in fact a doubting snake?'

She stood in the doorway, frozen. 'Fazil?'

'No, I'm not!' the young man said. 'I just think that if we leave this place with a broken window and the police are in the area, or the neighbours notice, they might follow us!'

'Or, in case it doesn't "work out", your daddy will be upset with you.'

No one said a word.

He heard a car engine start. He couldn't see where it was but no vehicle had entered the lane in front of the house as far as he could tell. It sounded as if it came from the vicinity of the house. Mumtaz had told him that the taxi she'd ridden in had been driven by 'one of them'. Was the fake taxi driver preparing to take someone somewhere?

Lee looked at his phone. He couldn't go in there on his own. Those inside could have guns and he was unarmed. Abbas or Mumtaz or both could be wounded or even dead. He had no choice.

He began to dial when he felt something hard dig into his back.

As soon as the woman took off her burqa, Mumtaz knew her. It was the young woman she'd bought the T-shirts from in Harrods.

Abu Imad held her tightly against his side. Mumtaz felt sick. If that was the woman from Harrods then she had seen her credit card.

The young man was still standing in the middle of the room, but now he was sweating. He said, 'Look, let's just go, shall we? Murad has brought the car round.'

Abu Imad shrugged. 'OK,' he said. Now he was bright and breezy. In person his unpredictability was even more frightening than it was online.

The woman said 'OK' too. But Mumtaz could see her watching her. Was she imagining it or was there a smirk behind her anodyne smile?

'Fazil,' she said to the young man, 'do you want to go and get my bags?'

'Yes.'

He left the room so fast, he almost ran.

When he'd gone the woman said, 'Is everything ready?'

'Yes,' he said.

'So shall I call Murad in?'

'Yes.'

She left the room.

Mumtaz felt his hot breath on her cheek. He said, 'You

know that we are married now, don't you, my little Mishal?'

That couldn't be. For a nikah ceremony to be lawful she had to consent.

'No . . .'

'Our qadi performed it,' he said. 'A brother from Damascus, a true emir of the Caliphate declared the responses on your behalf.'

That wasn't lawful!

'No!'

He threw his entire weight on top of her, pinning her arms behind her back. Mumtaz knew that it was pointless to scream but she did it anyway. He laughed. Then he put his hand up her shirt and grabbed her breast.

'Nice titties.'

'Leave me!'

'Me? Your husband?' He slapped her face. Mumtaz briefly saw shards of light flash across her field of vision. 'No, you give me pleasure, that's what you do, that is your purpose.'

He pulled her trousers and pants down and got his cock out.

Mumtaz crossed her legs, but he punched her in the chest until she stopped.

'Whore!'

'I thought I was your princess! I thought that you treated your wives with respect!'

'Respect?'

Her resistance was turning him on. He pulled her legs apart and she felt his penis touch her thigh. Then he said, 'Tell me you want me, bitch!'

She heard footsteps. Then she heard the woman say, 'Oh, can't you do that later? Come on, we have to go.'

For a moment, Mumtaz thought that he wasn't going to stop, but then as quickly as he'd come on to her, he stopped. He put his penis back in his shalwar khameez and said to her, 'Make yourself decent, you look like a whore.'

She tried, but her hands were so shaky it was difficult. Also her face and her chest hurt so much she had to really concentrate so that she didn't cry.

'Come on! Come on!'

She saw the woman watching her. She had to know that she wasn't who she claimed to be and yet, as far as Mumtaz could tell, she hadn't told Abu Imad. Why not? Was she some kind of fifth columnist planted by the police? But how?

There were five of them in the room. Abu Imad, Umm Khaled, the young man Fazil and the driver who was called Murad. Only Mumtaz was sitting down. The driver was on his phone.

Afterwards, Mumtaz wasn't sure whether Umm Khaled had looked at Abu Imad briefly first, but some sort of signal passed between them. Because they both started shooting at exactly the same time. She screamed.

'Put this on, there's a good boy,' Vi said.

She handed Lee a Kevlar vest.

He'd just had a couple of seconds to, figuratively, shit himself when he'd been poked in the back by a sub-machine gun. Then Vi had come along, complaining about how the 'fucking countryside' brought her allergies on.

He'd only seen two of the ten SO15 Counter Terrorism Command officers deployed alongside DI Vi Collins. But one of them had stuck a gun in his back and so he felt they, at least, had a bond.

As he put the vest on, Lee said, 'What the fuck is going on, Vi?'

'Could ask you the same thing,' she said.

They were inside the ruined barn in the field behind the house.

Then they heard a scream.

'But don't think we've got time,' Vi said.

When weapons are fired using a silencer, the noises made by those wounded or killed take on an eerie, disconnected quality. What sound like innocuous thuds produce noises of fear and pain and bodies twist in shapes not natural for human beings. Then, as the two men, the young one and the driver, lay on the ground, their attackers advanced upon them and put bullets in their heads. Mumtaz felt tears burst down her bruised cheeks and soak her shirt. Neither Abu Imad nor Umm Khaled showed any kind of emotion. Were they going to kill her too?

The woman, looking at the body of the young, shaven-headed man, said, 'What kind of warrior trusts his girlfriend to buy his airline ticket, eh? Didn't even want to see it. Didn't want to go. He would have been useless to the Caliphate.'

'He served his purpose,' Abu Imad said. 'They both did.'

He shoved his weapon in the waistband of his shalwar khameez while the woman put hers down on top of a magazine on the coffee table. Mumtaz tried not to look at either them or their guns. She also tried hard not to wet herself.

'So,' she heard Abu Imad say, 'what do we do with you now, then, Mumtaz?'

Of course the woman had seen her credit card. If in fact that made any difference. These two knew each other and so it was possible the whole thing had been a set up, right from the start. But to what purpose?

When she found her voice, she said, 'You sent the Tooth of Jonah to your parents.'

'Who got Lee Arnold to try and smoke me out,' he said. 'I knew he'd do something.'

'Which has cost him his life.' Her heart was beating what felt like irregularly. She thought about Shazia – and her parents. What with the business over Ali, they would just fall apart when they were told she'd died.

Abu Imad sighed. 'I'm not going to go into why I'm doing what I'm doing,' he said. 'You know that. More to the point, why is a woman like you working to try and destroy the Caliphate?'

'You're wasting time,' Umm Khaled said to him. 'Just get it over with.'

Heavily armed men converged on the house. They moved quickly, silently and low to the ground. A roadblock had been erected at the entrance to the lane, but no vehicles had approached and the whole area was eerily soundless.

Until Vi spoke into her phone, Lee felt as if he could be in a silent film.

'Thanks, Tone,' she said.

Usually her DS, Tony Bracci, was with her, people said they were joined at the hip. But he was clearly elsewhere.

She spoke into her radio. 'Ally McBeal secure?'

Lee recognised this as code for someone, probably someone with legal connections.

The two SO15 officers in the barn with them began to move out.

Vi's radio crackled. She said, 'Yeah. Thirty-four, IC4, black hair, black trousers, red blouse.'

That was Mumtaz. Had the scream he'd heard been her?

'Vi—'

'They can see her,' Vi said. 'Now we wait.'

'What for?'

Vi said nothing.

Lee felt his mouth go dry.

TWENTY-ONE

They both aimed at her face. Mumtaz had a vision of her father trying to formally identify her body. But she said nothing. Abu Imad and the woman clearly enjoyed provoking terror. She didn't want to give them even the slightest satisfaction. What would be, would be. She just hoped that, some day, her family would be able to forgive her.

Whether Abu Imad's eyes moved in response to a sound or a movement, Mumtaz didn't know. But for just a second he looked away. Then he looked back again.

Umm Khaled kicked the body of the man they'd called Fazil and tutted impatiently.

'Come on,' she said to Abu Imad. 'We agreed, hit them on their home ground. She dies.'

Mumtaz saw him smile. 'OK,' he said. She watched him take the silencer off his weapon. Why? Who knew? Maybe he enjoyed the noise?

Mumtaz closed her eyes.

The sound, when it came, was deafening.

* * *

It all happened at once. Screamed words she couldn't understand. There was smoke, liquid splashed onto her face and there was pain. It was unlike any pain she'd ever felt before. She couldn't even scream. Was this what it was like to be shot? Mumtaz hoped she'd pass out, even die, anything. Only when the smoke cleared did she realise that someone was pinning her to the ground. A body was on top of her and the muzzle of a gun was in her face.

A rough voice yelled, 'Get up!'

She began to say, 'I can't . . .'

But then the body on top of her began to move.

'Hands where I can see them!'

She thought she saw Abu Imad stand over her and raise his arms above his head. But she was in too much pain to be sure of anything.

Lee hadn't seen Fayyad al'Barri in the flesh for five years. He was taller and bigger than he had remembered. The first time he'd ever seen Fayyad he'd been a skinny kid.

Peering through smoke and the barrels of semi-automatic weapons he could see that there was a tangle of bodies on the floor. All were bloodied. None moved. But as his eyes adjusted to the conditions, he recognised Abbas al'Barri. He started to move towards him but Vi held his arm.

'Leave it,' she said.

And then real fear stabbed him. 'Where's Mumtaz?'

Vi pulled him away from the carnage and into the hall.

'You know the score,' she said. 'Leave them to it.'

And yet she'd brought him into that house.

'The bloke standing up, was that Fayyad al'Barri?' she asked.

The face belonged to the man he'd seen on Mumtaz's computer screen. 'Yes . . .'

238

Vi signalled to one of the SO15 officers. Then she took him out of the house and into the garden.

'Mumtaz . . .'

'Let 'em sort it out,' Vi said.

She couldn't sit up. It hurt too much.

'Lee . . .'

She thought she'd heard his voice. But she couldn't see him.

'You alright, love?'

Weirdly, putting the pain to one side, she was. Mumtaz looked up into a pair of blue eyes.

'Am I shot?'

'No, I don't think so. I need to check. I'm gonna touch you. Is that alright?'

He was very young but he was also confident.

'Yes.'

As he touched her, she cringed. It was completely different to the way Abu Imad had touched her but it was still an ordeal.

He said, 'Sorry . . .'

Other officers moved around them. Abu Imad had disappeared.

'It's OK,' she said.

When he'd finished the young officer said, 'I think you've got a couple of cracked ribs. Can't find anything else, but we'll get a doctor to you. Just lay as still as you can.'

'Thank you.'

'You Mrs Hakim?'

'Yes,' she said. 'How do you know my name?'

He smiled. 'You're gonna be OK.'

Maybe. But even with the limited view she had of that room from the floor, Mumtaz knew she was laying amongst the dead. She couldn't hear one groan, not one voice raised in pain or pleading.

Just policemen carefully negotiating a crime scene of corpses.

She couldn't fathom why she wasn't dead. It didn't make sense. Abu Imad and the woman from Harrods had raised their weapons to kill her. What had happened and where was the woman now?

Was she safe?

Vi put her radio back in her pocket. 'Mumtaz is alive but she's got a couple of cracked ribs,' she said.

Lee felt his legs become weak. He sat down on the carefully manicured lawn and hugged himself. Suddenly cold with shock. Vi put her jacket round his shoulders.

'You know someone's gonna have to interview the both of you about this?' she said.

He said nothing.

'Left field even by your standards, Arnold.'

'But you knew,' he said.

'Oh, yeah. I even knew that it was very possible we'd end up here.'

'Which is . . . Where the fuck are we, Vi?'

'Ah,' she said, 'this very nice gaff here is the weekend cottage of a Mr Ibrahim Dorman.'

'Don't know him.'

'Turkish carpet dealer,' she said. 'Very successful. His son, Fazil, has been seeing Djamila al'Barri for almost a year. She radicalised him.'

Lee looked up at her. Djamila al'Barri had been a bright spark ever since she was a little kid. A clubber with a taste for high fashion, Djamila had been a party girl.

'That can't be right.' He shook his head.

'Well, it is.'

'Djamila?'

'And she radicalised her brother too,' Vi said. 'We've had

240

the whole family under surveillance for almost two years.'

Lee had to let that sink in. He found himself wanting to say stupid things like *You never told me. We slept together!* But he knew that was irrelevant. She'd done her job. That was all that mattered, not just to Vi's superiors but to her as well.

When he did finally speak, all Lee managed to say was, 'You could've warned me.'

'And alerted your mate Abbas?'

What of Abbas? Lee had seen him in that room. He'd looked dead.

An ambulance drew up outside the house.

'I want you checked out by a doctor,' Vi said.

Lee looked down at the ground. Fuck that.

'Get Mumtaz sorted,' he said.

'Yeah, and you.'

'No.'

Vi squatted. 'Listen, shitface,' she said. 'I couldn't tell you and I don't even have to explain why. You were in the job yourself. You know nothing else matters.' She lowered her voice. 'So we have some dirty sex from time to time. It's just shagging. I like you but I don't owe you shit.'

She was right, she didn't. He knew how these operations worked. He'd been used. But this was a terrorism investigation. It was totally justified.

Vi stood. 'I've got to go and see how the SO15 gang are getting on,' she said. 'They'll want your phone.'

She left.

Lee pulled her jacket up round his face and hid his eyes.

TWENTY-TWO

When a police car pulled up outside her house, Shereen al'Barri felt her heart rate go up. Were they coming to see her? If they were, why?

She looked at her watch. Abbas had to have been in Amsterdam for over an hour. And yet every time she'd tried to call him his number had been unavailable. Surely if some sort of incident had taken place at either Stansted or Schiphol she would have seen something about it on the TV?

When they knocked Shereen almost screamed. But by the time she got to the front door she had composed herself.

The officer was pleasant enough. A middle-aged white man in plain clothes who was called DS Bracci. He asked her where Abbas was and she told him that he'd gone to visit friends in the Netherlands. It was only partly untrue. Shereen's brother lived in Rotterdam.

DS Bracci asked her to sit down. Then he asked her about the children.

'Djamila's gone away with her boyfriend,' she said. 'Hasan and Layla are in their rooms.'

'Can you get them please, Mrs al'Barri.'

The kids didn't want to leave their computers but they did, reluctantly. As she led them downstairs, Shereen's head began to swim. What had happened? What had gone wrong?

But it would be a while before DS Bracci told Shereen anything. Although not under caution, the family were questioned. Shereen felt sick.

Where had her husband gone? Why? Did she have a contact number for her brother in the Netherlands? Which airport had Abbas travelled from? What had been the purpose of his journey?

The kids only knew the cover story and so they clearly thought nothing of it. They just wanted to get back to their games.

Then DS Bracci said, 'I'm afraid, Mrs al'Barri, that your husband has been involved in an incident . . .'

Lee handed Vi the Tooth of Jonah.

She pulled a face. 'That it? Looks better online.'

'It's been through it a bit,' he said. 'But it means a lot to all the people who come from the Nineveh Plain. When I was there it was still in the mosque that no longer exists.'

She started to leave.

'Vi . . .'

'What?'

'What's going on? What's happened?'

She walked towards him. 'Abbas and Djamila al'Barri are dead,' she said.

Lee felt as if he'd been punched in the stomach. 'How?'

'Not your business,' she said.

This was a version of Vi Collins that Lee had never experienced before.

He pulled her close. 'Since when did you work for counterterrorism?'

She pushed him away. 'I don't.'

243

And maybe she was right. Vi hadn't been in charge of the operation. That had been someone inside that house. Maybe even someone Lee hadn't seen.

Vi said, 'We're at war, Lee. And in war you do anything to win. You use anyone and everyone.'

She walked away.

What was happening didn't appear to make sense. The doctor she'd seen in Accident and Emergency had told her there was no effective treatment for broken ribs except painkillers and rest. But she wasn't going home. Alone except for a plain-clothed policewoman, Mumtaz was locked into a room usually reserved for private patients. She had no phone, her luggage was nowhere to be seen and nobody would talk to her about Lee. There was no point talking to the policewoman because all she did was smile and then go back to her copy of *Bella*.

At least the painkillers took the edge off her physical distress. But they did nothing for what was happening in her mind. Had Abu Imad really killed his own father? Who was the woman who had met her at the airport? Was Abu Imad a terrorist or wasn't he? And where was Lee?

In spite of being in the care of police officers, Mumtaz was afraid. How was her own part in whatever had just happened going to be interpreted?

She heard the door unlock. The policewoman stood up and smoothed her skirt down to her knees. Then a man walked in and closed the door behind him. He smiled.

Probably in his early sixties, he was a tall, slim, smart man with a moustache. He was rather attractive in a grey, slightly grizzled way. He sat down on the chair beside Mumtaz's bed and said, 'So how are you, Mrs Hakim?'

Her first urge was just to say 'fine' but then she thought better of it. She wasn't fine and this man wasn't a doctor.

'Confused,' she said.

'About?'

She noticed that the policewoman had switched on some sort of hand-held device.

'Is that a recorder?' Mumtaz asked.

'What, specifically, are you confused about, Mrs Hakim?' the man said.

She didn't even know his name. 'Who are you?' she said.

'Mrs Hakim, I will need to know what was the precise nature of your relationship with Fayyad al'Barri, also known as Abu Imad.'

It was like talking to a brick wall.

'I know that at the moment you are probably not able to do that,' he said. 'But until you are, you will have to remain here. You will be under medical supervision at all times.'

'Where's here?' she asked.

The ambulance she had travelled in had deposited her at a hospital somewhere. She hadn't been in a position to know where.

'This is Broomfield Hospital in Chelmsford,' he said.

'I have a daughter . . .'

'Who is with your parents in Spitalfields, yes,' he said. 'They believe you are away on business. Your family are safe, Mrs Hakim.'

How did she know that?

'Look,' she said, 'who are you? If I don't know who you are, how can I trust you with my family? How?'

He sniffed. There was a pause and then he said, 'Mrs Hakim, the house you were in with Abu Imad and his associates was raided by SO15 counterterrorism officers. I work for Her Majesty's Government alongside that organisation. My name is of no interest to you but my purpose, which is to debrief you, is. Now, I am aware that you are in

245

pain and I appreciate you remain in a state of anxiety, but I have to know, in your own words, exactly what you experienced today.'

'You have a long history of drug and alcohol abuse.'

'Most people who've served in Iraq have problems,' Lee said.

The woman sitting in front of him in the familiar surroundings of an interview room at Forest Gate nick had appeared less than an hour ago. He hadn't seen her at the house in Good Easter and she hadn't accompanied him in the car back to London. She'd told him her name was Emma. Lee would have put money on the notion that she was telling the truth about that. He'd met a lot of Emmas. Not in the police, but in the upper echelons of the army. Emmas tended to have 'daddies'.

'Why did you become friends with Abbas al'Barri in 1990?'

'He was a translator, he spoke English. I liked him,' Lee said.

'You got drunk together.'

'Yeah.'

'And he saved your life.'

'He did. And now he's dead,' Lee said. 'You obviously know all this. And I don't understand.'

'Why did you break off relations with the al'Barri family?'

'I didn't.'

'Until Abbas al'Barri contacted you about the Tooth of Jonah, you hadn't seen the family for five years,' she said.

'I meant to. I called Abbas when I heard that Fayyad had joined ISIS. We spoke on the phone a lot. I met him once.'

'But you didn't visit?'

'No.'

'Why not?'

He shrugged. 'Life.'

* * *

246

'I didn't find out the woman's name until we arrived at the house,' Mumtaz said.

'In Good Easter.'

'Yes. I only know that because she told the taxi driver.'

'Who was, in your words, "one of them".'

'Yes.'

'So why did the woman have to tell the driver where to go?'

'I don't know. Ask her.'

The man looked down at his knees.

'The woman's name was Umm Khaled,' Mumtaz said. 'That's what she told me and what Abu Imad referred to her as. When she finally took off her burqa I recognised her.'

'As?'

'As the woman who had served me at the Alexander McQueen outlet in Harrods.'

'Where you bought three Ribcage T-shirts for Abu Imad?'

'Yes.'

The extent of what this man knew was frightening. Nothing she had done had been unobserved. Nothing.

'Tell me about the first time you saw Abu Imad at the house in Good Easter.'

'Why did you think that Fayyad al'Barri wanted to return to the UK?'

'Because he sent the Tooth of Jonah to his family,' Lee said. 'One of the rules or whatever you call it that governs ISIS is that they don't do relics. Even mosques can be considered idols in their world. They blow stuff up, we all know this. So to actually save a relic is wrong, in their eyes. If they'd caught him doing it, they would've probably killed him. I served in Iraq, I know how special that relic was to people. Abbas al'Barri saw it as a sign his son had changed.'

'And did you agree with his assessment?'

247

'I wasn't sure. I told him to go to the police. But he wouldn't.'

'So why didn't you contact the police?' she said.

Was she not saying 'us' because she wasn't a police officer?

Lee didn't answer. Why hadn't he contacted the police? It was a good question. It was also one he knew he couldn't easily answer.

'Was it because you owed Abbas al'Barri?'

He shook his head. 'Partly,' he said. 'And also,' he shrugged, 'I guess I wanted to believe that Fayyad was kosher. Abbas was in such a state, drinking himself to death.'

'And yet even if you had managed to get him into the country . . .'

'Oh, we all knew we'd have to take him to the authorities,' Lee said. 'But if we could just get him here . . . He was – is a nice kid.'

'You wanted to save him.'

'Yeah. I s'pose.'

He wanted to ask her what had happened to Fayyad. Vi had told him that both Djamila and Abbas were dead. But what about Fayyad?

He said, 'Djamila, his sister . . .'

'Was radicalised at her place of work,' the woman said.

A posh designer outlet in Harrods. But then, why not? Hadn't the puritanical Wahhabi sect, from which ISIS at the very least took some of its ideas, developed in oil-rich Saudi Arabia?

'You knew?' he said. 'About me?'

Her face expressed nothing. Vi had said she'd known, so this government wonk, whatever she was, had to have known.

'Why didn't you stop me?'

It just came out. He knew. No one had stopped him because he and Mumtaz had represented a shortcut.

She said, 'Why do you think that Abu Imad chose Mrs Hakim's character for his bride?'

He had known. Through Djamila, Lee imagined. Abbas and

Shereen had always said they were keeping what they were doing from the children, but Abbas in his cups was a loose cannon. And if Djamila had been radicalised then she would have asked the right questions.

'What's going to happen to Fayyad?' Lee asked.

He'd seen him, briefly, through the smoke back in the Good Easter house.

She pushed a statement form across the table. 'You know the score,' she said. 'Every detail you can remember.'

He looked at it.

'Is he alive or dead?' he asked.

She said, 'When you leave here the incident will be at an end.'

'Hi, sweetie.'

There was a pause. The girl obviously didn't recognise the number she was calling from.

'Amma?'

'Yes.'

'Where are you? Aren't you working away or something?'

'I was.' She made a small laugh in her throat. It hurt. 'But I fell over and I've broken a couple of ribs.'

'God! How?'

Mumtaz could hear the panic in Shazia's voice. It was tinged with the disbelief that had been engendered during her young life by all the lies that had always swirled around her.

'I was late, running for the departure gate, I slipped,' Mumtaz said.

'So where are you?'

'I'm in Broomfield Hospital in Essex,' she said.

There was a pause.

'And Lee?' Shazia asked. 'Is he with you?'

'Yes,' she said. 'Just gone to get a coffee.'

'When are you coming home, Amma?'

Mumtaz looked up at the man sitting beside her bed and said, 'In the morning.'

When she'd finished the call, Mumtaz said, 'Is my daughter safe?'

He smiled.

'Is she?'

He stood up. 'She's safer than you can imagine, Mrs Hakim,' he said.

'What does that mean?'

He shrugged.

Was he deliberately behaving in a cloak-and-dagger fashion because it was expected of him or because that was how he really was? Mumtaz didn't know but it irritated her. In spite of the fact that he frightened her.

'I think I deserve to know whether we were right about Fayyad al'Barri,' she said.

'You saw him kill his own father, what do you think?' he said.

'I didn't see him kill his father. I saw him deposit his father's body on the floor in front of me,' she said. 'Read my statement.'

'I will.'

'And?' she said. 'Fayyad . . .'

'Fayyad al'Barri is nothing to you,' he said. 'You've never met him and possess no information about him or his family.'

'Yes, but is he—'

'You'll never see or speak to Fayyad al'Barri again, Mrs Hakim,' the man said.

TWENTY-THREE

Vakeel Uddin the solicitor wasn't at home when the police finally arrested him. He'd been under close surveillance since the previous morning. Now balls deep in a woman he'd met on the Tube, he was at an address in Barking. Unable to comprehend anything except his own pleasure, he'd not heard the knock on the door at 4 a.m. But the splintering of the front door had got his attention.

Aziz the tailor, on the other hand, had known they'd come. When they knocked, he'd opened his door and let them in without a murmur. He was a legitimate man who had helped Syrian refugees in good faith. How had he been expected to know that the boys Ali Huq had taken in had been radicalised? How had he been expected to know that Huq was homosexual? Old Zafar Bhatti in the electrical shop had intimated that he was, but only to that lawyer, Vakeel Uddin, not to him. He didn't personally import poisonous ideas into the country. He didn't promote them either. Not like the boxer, Taha Mirza. What Aziz didn't know when he started spilling his guts about Mirza, however, was that he was already dead.

* * *

251

'How?'

Amir Charleston was a funny colour. He looked as if he'd just seen a road accident.

'Topped himself,' Ricky Montalban said. 'Pills.'

'Why?'

'I don't know. You tell me.'

Charleston looked at his lawyer who shook his head.

Amir said, 'No comment.'

Ricky shrugged. 'If that's the way you want to play it . . .'

'My client has told you that he had nothing to do with the death of Rajiv Banergee . . .'

'Yeah, and I've told him, and you Mr Dugdale, that Banergee's blood is on his T-shirt. You were there, weren't you, Mr Charleston? Just because Taha Mirza's dead doesn't mean you're off the hook. He taught you and Mr Lewis and Mr Cranmer to box while throwing in the odd religious justification, but there's no forensic or other contact between Mirza and Banergee. He didn't kill him and Cranmer and Lewis have alibis for that night. That leaves you. That's why you've been charged.'

The solicitor said, 'And my client's motive for killing Mr Banergee, Inspector Montalban?'

'I've no idea, Mr Dugdale,' Ricky said.

'Has it occurred to you that he doesn't have one because he didn't kill him?'

'Oh, yes,' Ricky said. 'But if I look at where your client was that night, who he was with and what he was doing, oh and the forensic evidence, that doesn't really work for me.'

'I won't plead guilty,' Charleston said.

'That's up to you.'

'I'm not a Muslim fanatic. I just, I . . .'

'Please don't say any more,' Mr Dugdale said. 'You don't need to. Not at this time . . .'

Amir Charleston rubbed a hand across his face. Ricky saw the internal struggle. He'd seen it many times before. He stood up, 'I'll give you a moment, shall I?' he said.

What remained of the al'Barri family were inside the nick. Tony Bracci didn't know who they were with and he didn't want to know. Vi Collins joined him and lit a fag. Leaning against what was called the Smoking Wall at the back of the car park, they puffed in companionable silence until Tony said, 'So . . .'

'Quite a little network, as I understand it,' Vi said. 'Dunno how it's gonna shake out though.'

'What do you mean, guv?'

'I mean, Tone, you never do with go-rounds like this.'

She meant operations that involved national security. No one really knew the full facts, *they* kept those to themselves. Tony did know that SO15 had been deployed, but he didn't know where. He also didn't know why Vakeel Uddin, who had been under surveillance for months, had finally had his collar felt.

It had to do with the al'Barri family. That Tony did know. But how and why . . . As far as he was concerned the eldest son had fucked off to ISIS for reasons best known to himself. But he'd surmised there was more to it than that. Vi knew, but Tony knew better than to ask.

The mother had wept and screamed fit to wake up her whole street. Understandable given she'd just lost her husband and her daughter. How, Tony didn't know. He could tell her nothing, but then that had been the idea. She wasn't supposed to know. Or rather, that was how he interpreted it.

Her two youngest kids had just stared. One, the boy, had flashed

Tony a bitter look. But only once and who could blame him? He'd lost his dad and his sister and Tony, the only 'authority' figure in the kid's house, wasn't saying anything useful.

And what of the eldest son, the ISIS boy, Fayyad? Tony remembered when he'd been all over the papers as a missing person. Weeks later they'd found out he'd rocked up in Syria. As far as Tony could remember, the al'Barris were friends of Lee Arnold's.

He'd be mortified when he found out what had happened to them.

Mr Dugdale looked as if he'd just smelt someone else's fart.

Ricky ignored him and sat down. He looked at Dugdale's client. 'So?'

Amir Charleston glanced at his solicitor who opened his hands in a gesture of submission.

'I hit him,' his client said.

'Hit who?'

'Banergee,' he said.

'Why?'

'He disgusted me,' he said. 'I'd seen him swanning about on Brick Lane behaving like a woman. Such people are an abomination.'

Ricky crossed his arms over his chest. 'Those your words or Taha Mirza's?'

He shook his head. 'Religion is a rational choice,' he said. 'It imbues meaning.'

'What meaning?'

'To life!' he said. 'What are possessions or money if we don't have an overarching narrative that guides our thoughts and our actions? A fit body can engender a fit mind. That was my aim. Every week I was becoming fitter, stronger, more secure in my religion. Those other guys were only playing at it.'

'Lewis and Cranmer?'

'Yes. I think they just wanted to have the odd ruck to get rid of their frustrations. Working in the City isn't all it's cracked up to be. There are pressures that can make you sick, behaviours you're expected to conform to that rot your soul.'

'Like?'

'Like drinking until you pass out, doing so much coke you're awake for a week.'

Ricky tried to imagine how much cocaine that would take and how much it might cost.

'My life had become nothing. I'm not alone. There are many in the City who feel the lack of any sort of genuine meaning in their lives. The pursuit of money is entirely hollow.'

'Only if you don't have it.'

'Admittedly . . .'

'So why didn't you get yourself a colouring book and do this Mindfulness thing everybody's doing?' Ricky asked.

Charleston shot him a vicious glance. 'You think that because I'm rich, I'm silly? Such fads are simply more money-making scams. I have a connection to Islam through my mother. I was brought up a Muslim, it has meaning for me.'

'And Islam teaches that you have to go out and kick the crap out of people, does it?'

'No!'

'But Taha Mirza did?'

He lowered his head. 'The aim was to get fit for jihad,' he said. 'We fought each other.'

'And defenceless men on the street.'

'One has to get combat experience.'

'Before you fuck off to Syria.'

He said nothing.

'Taha Mirza approved this?'

Mr Dugdale looked uncomfortable. Instructed by Charleston's powerful father to get the young man off, he was rapidly losing interest whilst developing considerable disgust.

'He called it "hunting",' Charleston said. 'He'd done it. Looking for legitimate targets and making sure they stayed off the streets. Not killing, protecting the wider public. We, Cranmer, Lewis and myself, weren't Taha's only pupils.'

Ricky leant back in his chair. A fucking upmarket version of the Briks Boyz.

'Who were the others?'

'I don't know. I never met them. I think they might have been Asian lads. I'll come to that.'

'You went hunting that night?'

'Taha felt I was ready.'

'He go with you?'

'No.'

'What about Lewis and Cranmer?'

'They'd already gone,' he said. 'When we first met at the study day in south London I felt that they were only there because they were looking for something.'

'Like you.'

'Yes, but they were looking for anything. Something that made them feel alive. I don't think it mattered what it was. They wanted to be excited and challenged and . . .'

'Get rid of a load of adrenaline and act manly.'

'Yes. Whatever you think of them, modern jihadis are manly,' he said. 'They are ultimately manly. And if they have genuine belief they are like supermen. That was what attracted Lewis and Cranmer.'

'But you've got faith too, yeah?'

'I have.'

'Talk me through what happened.'

He took a deep breath. He said, 'I ran from the office to Taha's place. Cranmer and Lewis were already there.'

'You fought.'

'It wasn't like it had ever been before. We had bout after bout. Just on and on. It was exhausting but also – electrifying. We all got injured but it didn't matter. Cranmer had a really deep cut above one eye but he still carried on. There was blood on the canvass, but he only noticed later.'

'Why?'

'I knocked Lewis down and I was so elated I began to cheer. When I finished, the others were all standing in the ring watching me. I felt exposed. It was as if a spell had been broken. Lewis and Cranmer left soon after. I had a feeling they wouldn't be back. We talked.'

'You and Mirza.'

'Yes. He was a good man. He didn't like killing. He was a poor boy whose parents had come here from Pakistan and taken a lot of abuse. His dad had been a doctor back home but here he was a taxi driver. Islamophobia kills people. It does. It's been doing it for centuries. And whatever we do it never gets any better. Violence is now the only way. We get you off the streets just as you insist upon our invisibility if we don't conform to your idea of what we should be. If it's a choice between being subjugated and subjugating, the latter course is the only rational one. I was still buzzing from the bouts. Taha said I was ready.'

'To do what?'

'To hunt,' he said.

'And you found Rajiv Banergee.'

'Walking towards Arnold Circus. They go there to meet sometimes at night.'

257

'Who?'

'Perverts.'

'Is that your way of talking about gay men?'

'He smiled at me,' Charleston said.

'And so you punched him.'

'He provoked me.'

'A man on a self-confessed "hunt",' Ricky said. 'What did he have to do to not attract your attention? Hide under a bench?'

Charleston swallowed. 'I felled him with one blow,' he said. 'I grabbed him by his collar and told him to keep his filthy pursuits to himself in the future. He was alive when I left him.'

'How do you know?'

'Because he laughed at me,' he said.

'Which made you go back and kill him.'

'No!' He looked at his lawyer, then back at Ricky. 'I swear. I left him. I'd done what I set out to do.'

'And the blood on your T-shirt?' Ricky asked.

'When I held him by his collar, his mouth was close to my body and . . . It was bleeding.'

'And so you left?'

'Yes.'

'Why didn't you tell us this before?' Ricky said. 'If it's true.'

'It is!'

'Thought Mr Dugdale could get you off without you having to reveal how insecure you are in your own masculinity . . .'

'How . . .'

'Oh come on!' Ricky said. 'Blokes who have to beat up other blokes because they choose to wear eyeliner are fucking inadequate. I don't care how religious you are, if you're threatened by that, you have problems.' He shook his head. 'So you ran away, leaving Mr Banergee alive on the ground, then what?'

'Then I saw them kill him,' Charleston said.

'Who?'

Her looked down at the floor again and breathed deeply.

'Bobby Moore! Geoff Hurst! Clyde Best!'

Lee rubbed the mynah bird's silky head and said, 'Wind it in will you, Chronus?'

Weirdly the bird did. Usually when he was on a roll with West Ham United team lists, he was at it ceaselessly for hours. But then Chronus was Lee's baby. Spoilt, overfed and petted, he knew his master well enough to realise when he needed some quiet. He settled down on his perch and closed his eyes while Lee continued to stroke his head.

All Lee really wanted to do was sleep. But his mind wouldn't let him. He knew that had he been able to talk to Mumtaz maybe it would have helped. But she was back with her family on Brick Lane – with her broken ribs.

How had he allowed Abbas to put them all in harm's way like that? But then it hadn't been Abbas who had, it had been him. His guilt, his sense of being in another's debt . . . Why couldn't he deal with that? Being in any sort of debt to anyone drove him crazy. But he was in debt to Mumtaz.

Until he could talk to her, Lee wouldn't know what she'd been told. The woman who had interrogated him at Forest Gate had told him nothing about Fayyad al'Barri except that he'd been radicalised by his sister. Djamila! He'd thought she'd been all about fashion and boyfriends. Obviously not. But then his previous view of her had done her a disservice. In spite of reality television, galloping consumerism and epic levels of media narcissism, anyone with half a brain looked for meaning in life. Djamila had been a smart girl. Obviously she'd been misguided too. But then equally obvious was the fact that the radical narrative she'd become entranced with had filled a gap in her life. Maybe she felt disconnected as an exile? Abbas and Shereen had been very keen to fit in when they'd come to the UK. Perhaps they'd taken that too far?

Lee really wanted a drink. That or a handful of co-codamol. But what would being out of it achieve?

He lit up yet another fag and tried to concentrate on *Bargain Hunt*. But he couldn't. He'd always known that once Fayyad was in the country he'd have to be handed over to the authorities. But he'd just disappeared. What were they doing with him? Was he even alive? And what had the change of plan from Amsterdam to Essex really been about?

Had Fayyad turned himself in or hadn't he? And if he had, what had Djamila known about that? If anything?

For the first time since he'd served in Iraq in '91, Lee felt actively scared. Things done to and by people who thought they knew best for that country and its people always ended up exploding into violence.

TWENTY-FOUR

They looked just like any other teenagers playing football. Each trying to get the ball off the other. But if Amir Charleston was right then these kids had killed Rajiv Banergee in cold blood. While he was still down on the ground after Charleston's single, mighty punch, they'd stabbed him.

Charleston said he'd not wanted to drop two 'very decent' kids in it. But Ricky Montalban knew that was bullshit. If he'd seen those kids that night, and it was a big if, how had he known they were 'decent' kids? How had he known them at all? And what did the obvious fact that he knew of them, mean?

There was no evidence against the boys and in fact they still had an outstanding case against Ali Huq. But Ricky was also aware that Qasim and Nabil had come to the Lane via Aziz the tailor. At a level far higher than himself, Ricky knew that Tower Hamlets and Newham were now co-operating on what had been a no-go area for any coppers who didn't work for Newham – as well as many who did. This involved Aziz as well as the Forest Gate lawyer, Vakeel Uddin. Word was that others were involved in what was actually a counterterrorism investigation too. Bob Khan had heard that a whole family had been arrested in Newham.

Bringing people into the country with the intention of disrupting British life or for recruitment purposes was nothing new. Back in the seventies the IRA had slotted operatives inside perfectly peaceful, law-abiding communities with some success. But given the level of secrecy around this operation, Ricky had a feeling this was something different.

Ricky walked into the garden and the boys stopped playing.

'Lee.'

'Mumtaz.'

It was a relief to hear her voice even though he knew she was safe. He sat up and rubbed his face. He'd smoked so much he had to look like shit. It was a good job she couldn't see him.

'They took my phone,' she said. 'So I figured they'd taken yours too. Good thing we still have landlines, eh? How are you?'

He thought about pimping it up for her, but then he said, 'Shit. You?'

'On far too many painkillers,' she said.

He smiled. He was jealous.

'You still at your mum and dad's?'

'Yes,' she said. 'Mum's looking after me. It's driving me nuts. Lee, we need to talk.'

'I know.'

'Can you come over here?'

'Is that OK?'

'Of course it is,' she said. 'We've a full house, what with Shazia and Ali . . .'

'Your brother.'

'Yes,' she said. 'But we can talk in the garden. I don't know if you want to drive but Dad's got visitors' permits here.' She paused. 'I need to tell you some things.'

Lee lit another fag. 'I'll be about an hour,' he said.

'OK.'

There was something else he needed to do first.

He just stood outside the house on the pavement. He didn't knock or call the house phone. He just stared.

Shereen called up to the kids to be quiet. Hasan in particular had been crashing around up there. Packing was hard when you couldn't take everything you wanted. It was harder still when you were in grief.

What was Lee Arnold doing? They'd told her he was to have no more contact with the family. No one was. Shereen's emotions moved to their own ever-changing beat. One minute she felt tainted by what her daughter had done, the next she cried uncontrollably for her husband – and for Djamila. Whatever she'd done, she had been her child. She didn't even know how she'd died. Or Abbas.

She looked at Lee Arnold out in the street. Did he know something? Surely he had to. Had he come to tell her?

She'd wanted to tell Fazil's parents about Djamila but they'd told her she couldn't. The poor boy had to be worried sick. Unless, of course, he'd been with her when she died?

Something else that occurred to Shereen was the familiarity of the situation. The police coming to get them, the police handing them over to other people who didn't give their names. It was like Saddam's regime reborn. Her eldest brother Rauf had been taken back in the 1980s in just such a fashion. He'd never been seen again.

And what about Fayyad? The nameless people hadn't spoken about him. She'd asked but they'd said nothing. Why had he joined ISIS? He'd always been such a good, caring boy. What had happened to make him ally himself with the enemies of his own family? Living in the UK hadn't been so bad for him. In fact all the children had done well. What had she and Abbas done wrong? All she could think of was that they hadn't addressed their children's religion. But for good reasons she'd always felt. Back home, adherence to a religion had been everything, even if that 'religion' was that of the secular Baa'thists who supported Saddam. They'd both wanted their kids to be free of all that. But had that been wrong? Had their rejection of religion actually made it more attractive to their children?

She remembered how Hasan had begged and pleaded with Abbas to let him fast during Ramadan the previous year. But Abbas had been adamant. No son of his was going to fast for what he considered to be no good reason. After that argument, just like every argument any of them had had in recent years, Abbas had got howling drunk. Muslims didn't drink. Maybe that had been the attraction?

She looked out of the window again and saw that Lee Arnold had gone. Shereen shouted up the stairs, 'Finish up as quickly as you can now.'

Her own bags were packed. Just some clothes, toiletries, medicines, photographs. They'd come to the UK with so little, there were few things of sentimental value to consider. Also, what was the point? It was far more important for the children to take as much as they could. They, after all, had a future. She hoped.

Hafez, the translator, had been a documentary-maker back in his native Damascus. He'd tried not to upset the Assad regime with his films about wildlife and history. But he'd eventually fallen foul of some odious government yes-man and had finally only managed

264

to escape after the regime had rendered him sexually impotent. Now he did everything he could to oppose both Assad and those groups, like ISIS, who threatened to replace him with something even worse.

Nabil refuted what DI Montalban said. Hafez had seen many dead eyes like his in Syria and on his way into Europe.

'He says the man is lying.'

'And the man says he is,' Ricky Montalban said.

'Qasim is wondering what you are doing with the man who raped them,' Hafez translated.

'Nothing yet,' Montalban said. 'We need evidence. We found no evidence for any wrongdoing – apart from some jihadi propaganda – by either your boys or Mr Huq at his house.'

The boys said they had evidence in the form of their testimonies. Hafez explained that wasn't enough.

'The man who says you killed Rajiv Banergee also says he saw you do it,' Montalban said.

The boys exchanged a look.

'This man has given accurate descriptions of the two of you,' Montalban continued. 'DC Khan is going through your things at your foster home now.'

Nabil spoke directly to Montalban in English. 'Is it the man we showed you?' he said.

Montalban didn't answer. It was strange to hear one of the kids speak English even though he knew they had to have basic skills. Nabil, at least, had to be rattled.

It has been a long time since Lee had drunk a sweet lassi. He'd forgotten just how ruddy sweet they could be. He put his drink down on the Huq's ornate garden table and lit a fag.

Mumtaz said, 'What you did was natural.'

'What? Putting you in danger?' he said.

'No! You wanted to save Fayyad. Lee, in spite of what you might like to think, you are far more than a cynical bloke who's been there, done that and got the T-shirt. There's a part of you that's like . . . what? Well, King Arthur's knights . . .'

He laughed. 'You what?'

'You need to save people,' she said. 'You wanted to save Fayyad. If there was the slightest chance that he was reaching out to his parents you wanted to take that risk for him and it was a good thing.'

'Mumtaz, Abbas is dead, Djamila is dead . . .'

She looked down at the ground.

'Djamila was one of them,' he said. 'I can still hardly believe it. She radicalised Fayyad!'

'Umm Khaled. I saw her and her brother kill their driver and the young man I thought was her husband or boyfriend,' Mumtaz said. 'From what she said at the time it seems they never had any intention of taking the two men with them. The police—'

'Don't think the people who questioned us were strictly police, Mumtaz.'

'Whoever they were.' She waved a hand in the air. 'Lee, they asked me whether I'd seen Fayyad kill his father, but I didn't. He came into that living room with Abbas's dead body over his shoulder and then threw him to the ground. I don't know who killed him. I accept it looked as if Fayyad had done it, but I can't swear to it.'

'Did he say anything?'

Mumtaz had left her phone on so that he could hear what was happening but Lee's phone had died.

'He said my name, he smiled. I remember the woman I knew as Umm Khaled, Djamila, asking if Abbas was dead. They both spoke and acted in ways that were totally emotionless,' she said. 'Except when I was alone with him.'

'Were you?'

'For a short time, yes,' she said. 'The others were bringing cars around and organising luggage.'

'To go where?'

'I don't know. Maybe back to the airport? The man who interviewed me in hospital told me nothing,' she said.

'So what happened when you were alone? What did he say?'

'Lee, he tried to rape me,' she said.

She saw him put a hand out to her and then quickly draw it away.

'He was serious.'

He'd been aroused. Had it been by her beauty, by her helplessness or her treachery?

'Fucking bastard!'

'Yes,' she said. 'But I fought him off and then his sister came in. That was when the other men came in too, and when they died.'

'So who killed Djamila?'

Mumtaz shook her head. 'I was asked that in hospital,' she said. 'I don't know. I thought they were going to kill me.'

'Both of them?'

'They raised their weapons and pointed them at me,' Mumtaz said.

Sumita Huq came out into the garden and said, 'Mumtaz! Ask Mr Arnold if he'd like to eat with us this evening!'

Lee smiled. Life, which so often meant food, went on. Particularly in Asian households.

'That would be very nice, Mrs Huq,' he called back.

Both Lee and Mumtaz knew that he didn't have a choice. Sumita would just wheedle and bully until he agreed to stay. The guest as king as usual.

When her mother had gone, Mumtaz said, 'Sorry . . .'

'Don't be,' he said. 'Your mother's a great cook, I'm honoured.' He put his cigarette out and then lit another. 'So? What happened after they raised their weapons?'

Mumtaz shook her head. 'I shut my eyes,' she said. 'It was more a reflex than a conscious act.'

'Makes sense.'

'Then there was this noise. For some reason, unlike when the two men were killed, Fayyad didn't use a silencer. He took it off. I don't know why. The noise was horrific: explosions, gunfire, smoke everywhere. I don't know whether I screamed or not. Probably not, because I was sure I was dead.'

This time he took her hand. She let him.

'But then I realised I wasn't dead because I was in pain,' she said. 'Fayyad was on top of me. I don't, even now, know whether he had been shot or not. I don't think he was dead. I have a memory of him being taken away. But whoever questioned me didn't say anything about him.'

'Because if he is alive, and I think he is, I think I even saw him, then they'll be questioning him,' Lee said. 'I came here via the al'Barris' place.'

'Aren't you not supposed to see them?'

'Are you . . .'

'I had to agree to make no further contact,' she said.

'Well, yeah, me too,' he said.

'So why . . .'

'I didn't knock or anything. But I could tell someone was in,' he said.

'What will happen to them?' Mumtaz said.

That was why Lee had gone. To try and find that out. But Shereen too had to have been warned to make no contact. He knew that without even being told. Not for the first time he wondered whether Vi Collins knew anything. But even if she did, would she tell him? She hadn't told him she'd been involved with the al'Barri family in the first place and so it seemed unlikely.

'Lee?'

Roused from his thoughts he said, 'I dunno.'

And he didn't know. It had to depend upon what had happened to Fayyad al'Barri – whatever that might be.

'You wanna redeem this?'

He didn't even look up to see who had laid the pawn ticket down in front of him.

'No.'

'You wanna pay sumfink off?'

The pawnbroker's assistant, or whoever he was, wasn't going to look up. Absorbed in the delights of his iPhone, interrupted only by a cursory glance at the pawn ticket, he had better things to do.

Bob Khan sighed, took his badge out of his pocket and said, 'Police.'

Even that usually provocative word took a while to seep into the man's consciousness. Maybe it was because he was young? Or maybe it was just because he was bored shitless?

He looked up. Blonde, overweight and probably temporarily doomed to singledom by the many vast spots and carbuncles that littered his face and neck, he said, 'Yeah?'

'That ticket,' Bob said. 'I'd like you to tell me who took it out and what it's for.'

'Why?'

'Why? I'm a police officer,' Bob said. 'Just do it.'

Bob had been surprised to see this boy on the counter at Jones's. Usually old man Jones himself was *in situ*.

'Where's Mr Jones?' Bob asked.

The boy was opening the door to the back office. 'He's been in hospital for a month,' he said.

'I'm sorry to hear that,' Bob said.

'Cancer.'

'Sorry. And you are?'

'Tyson,' the young man said. 'I'm his nephew.'

Tyson moved quickly into the back office once he'd told Bob his name. There were few names that would have suited him less.

Bob was sad to hear that old Gareth Jones was ill. There were some good pawnbrokers and some that were not so good. Gareth was firm but fair. He was also nobody's fool and wouldn't take on any item he had reason to believe might be 'hooky'. Apparently his father had been just the same. Before that, according to Montalban, the Joneses had run a dairy on Brick Lane. Even their cows had been Welsh, apparently.

Tyson returned and put a small velvet bag on the counter.

'Says here it's a ring,' he said. 'Diamonds and emeralds, 24-carat gold.'

Bob opened the bag. The ring was clearly a product of the subcontinent. A diamond and emerald confection fit for a maharani.

'Who was the customer?' Bob asked.

Tyson Jones showed him the photograph he'd taken. The face wasn't that of either of the Syrian boys.

'I felt sorry for Mishal,' Mumtaz said.

Her mother was engaged in preparing a full-on Bengali banquet and so dinner was still hours away.

'I know she didn't exist. But girls like her do.'

Lee realised he was still holding her hand. Mumtaz saw it too and withdrew. He felt slightly bereft.

'It's hard for young people who have a legitimate interest in religion,' she said. 'Their families are so afraid of radicalisation.'

'You think? I see more kids covered up than ever before,' Lee said.

'As a white man, you would,' she said. 'There are just as many who don't cover, you just don't see them.'

Was she right? From Lee's perspective, covered girls and boys with beards seemed to be everywhere.

'Muslim women have always covered,' she said. 'The difference now is that it has come to mean something negative.'

'Why do you cover?'

He'd never asked her before. He felt nervous doing it now.

'I started when I got married,' she said. 'Out of respect for my husband. I thought that if I behaved respectably towards him, he would reciprocate. My husband was a very charming and supposedly successful man. I didn't want to give him cause to be ashamed of me. What I didn't know was that he was a hypocrite.'

Ahmet Hakim had been a drinker, a womaniser, a gambler and an abuser of his own wife and daughter.

'So when you found out, why didn't you . . .'

'Take it off?' She smiled. 'Because it made, and makes, me feel safe. Whatever horrors may be happening behind closed doors I can hold my head high as a respectable Muslim woman. I don't get hassled by men when I cover. And I don't want their attention, so it suits me.'

'Yeah, but what you said about people being afraid of radicalisation . . .'

'Oh, I've had racist abuse,' she said.

He shook his head. 'Do you tell anyone?'

'No. Why would I? To upset Amma and Abba?'

'So tell me,' he said. 'I'll sort 'em out.'

'And have you put yourself at odds with other white people?'

'Scum.'

She shook her head. 'No, Lee,' she said. She touched her headscarf. 'This is my fight. And anyway it doesn't affect my work, does it? I take off my scarf if I need to for a job.'

'Yeah . . .'

'But most of the time it helps,' she said. 'Think of all the clients we get because I cover. Women who would never go and see a PI in a million years under normal circumstances. Because of who and what I am, I can find out what their husbands are doing behind their backs, I can even sometimes give them ammunition to improve their lives. But I wasn't talking about me.'

No, she rarely wanted to do that. He wondered where she was with the crime family, the Sheikhs, now that they apparently had no further hold over her. If that was the case.

'Until genuine religious curiosity, like Mishal's, can be looked at rationally, more and more girls will be radicalised,' she said.

Lee sat back in his chair. It was a beautiful late afternoon in the Huq's idyllic garden. Spitalfields had many such secret green spaces. It was one of the many reasons why the area had become popular with artists back in the 1980s.

'The radical narrative is so feared,' she said, 'people are scared to talk about religion with their children. The women I work for—'

'Mumtaz, this martyr stuff is glamorous,' Lee said. 'It attracts the kids. Young men don't go to be soldiers just because they're young. I know, I was one. It's raging hormones too! Do you think these girls would go to Syria if they weren't gonna meet up with some handsome fighter?'

'That may be part of it.'

'That's a big part of it!'

She shook her head. 'But there has to be some genuine religious feeling too. Otherwise why put your life on the line in a country that is at war? The caliphate, and by that I don't mean this ISIS abomination, is a legitimate Islamic concept.'

'Yeah, and these kids have to know it's an abomination . . .'

'They comfort themselves that the atrocities are lies spread by the enemies of Islam.'

'Yeah?' It seemed to him as if she was acting as an apologist. 'It's all over the media. Intercepts of jihadi conversations prove these kids know what's what.'

'Yes, but I repeat, if they could have proper discussions about Islam without being made to feel as if they are being traitors to this country, then maybe . . .'

'Maybe what, Mumtaz?' Lee said. 'Maybe they'd choose the rational, un-hormone-fuelled way forward?'

'Maybe.'

He shook his head. 'Let me tell you something about my daughter, shall I?'

Jodie Arnold was the same age as Shazia. She lived with her mother, Lee's ex-wife, in Hastings. Mumtaz had only met Jodi once. She'd not been impressed, but she hadn't been horrified either. The girl was a teenager.

'Last year,' he said, 'my ex called me to tell me that Jodie had a boyfriend. I'd been expecting it for some time and thought "so what?". But then I learnt who the boyfriend was. An ex-con with a coke habit. So I went down there. What I found was a bloke who looked like a caricature of a BNP supporter, twenty years Jodie's senior. I also noticed that my daughter had some bruises from what she described as "play fighting". But my daughter loved him . . .'

'Lee, I didn't know.'

'I didn't tell anyone,' he said.

'So what . . .'

'I told Jodie I thought it was her hormones talking, not her. She of course disagreed,' he said. 'Then she told me she was having unprotected sex with this man because she wanted to give him a baby.'

Mumtaz put a hand up to her mouth. That was one of the greatest fears the parents of girls could have.

'So I gave up on her and went for him,' Lee said.

'How?'

He sighed. 'I called up a mate, and no I'm not telling you who, and we kicked the shit out of the arse'ole. I knew violence was all he'd understand and I was right. I told him if he ever saw my daughter again, I'd kill him. He left Hastings after that and Jodie fell to pieces.'

'She wasn't . . .'

'Pregnant? No, thank God,' he said. 'But she did cry all the time. Couldn't understand why he'd dumped her, said her life was over. Drama, drama, drama – then, less than a month later, she was back getting fake tans and spending money her old man doesn't have. And yet she would have "died" without this gorilla. If so many of these radicalised kids weren't teenagers, I wouldn't put so much store in the part their hormones play in all this. But they are.'

The boys didn't want to be separated. Qasim was visibly scared.

Ricky Montalban started with the other one, Nabil. He told Bob Khan his cod-psychological reason for this.

'If Qasim thinks Nabil's spilt his guts, then he'll follow suit.'

He'd surmised, rightly, that Nabil would at least start the proceedings in silence.

Ricky said, 'Our witness has described the two boys he saw attack Mr Banergee. Both of Middle Eastern appearance, one

274

slightly taller than the other. That one has got a scar on his left cheek. You've got a scar on your left cheek.'

Hafez the translator told the boy what Ricky had said. Nabil did not respond.

Ricky cleared his throat. 'How did you know the boxer Taha Mirza?'

Nabil said that he didn't know anyone of that name.

'So why'd my officers find a pawnshop ticket in the name of Mr Mirza in your stuff at Mrs Hearn's place?'

Hafez translated that the boy knew nothing about any pawn ticket. He claimed he didn't even know what one of those was. Ricky explained.

But Nabil remained silent. Then, when he did speak, he gave Ricky a right proper gift from God.

TWENTY-FIVE

Mumtaz had thought she was alone until she saw Ali sitting down beside the garden shed.

She'd woken at four and, unable to sleep any longer, she'd washed, dressed and gone to sit in her parents' garden to watch the sun rise. There, she'd seen her brother for the first time in over a week. He looked pale and haunted. She sat down beside him and tried to take one of his hands, but he wouldn't let her.

'You should've come down for dinner last night,' she said. 'It was lovely. Amma made malpua for dessert. Shazia had never had them before. You've always liked them. I guess she made them for you.'

'I doubt it.'

'She wouldn't use that much saffron if she didn't have a reason,' Mumtaz said. 'It's dead expensive.'

'Lee was here,' he said. 'Europeans like sweet pancakes. She made them for him.'

'And for you.'

'She won't even look at me.'

Mumtaz knew that her mother was struggling with her brother's sexuality. Sumita wasn't leaving the house. But this wasn't so much about Ali as about the poisonous and untrue story about him that had appeared in the local press.

'She will,' Mumtaz said.

'I didn't do anything to those boys . . .'

'I know.'

He looked at her. 'How?'

'Because I know you,' she said.

'No you don't. You didn't know I was a pervert.'

Mumtaz winced. To use such a word about oneself was weird.

'You all disagreed with my views on Islamic disaffection,' he said. 'Abba told me I had no understanding of what jihad meant . . .'

'We were alarmed,' Mumtaz said. 'To us, suddenly it seemed as if you lost your capacity for human empathy. Now we know the cause . . .'

'Sin must be atoned for,' he said.

'And love must be nurtured.'

He looked at her. She saw tears in his eyes.

'And don't tell me that what you had with Rajiv wasn't love,' she said. 'Because I know you and I knew Rajiv, and you are and were, people with big hearts.'

He began to cry. 'How am I going to live?' he said. 'How?'

'The police will find you not guilty.'

'Oh? And?'

Mumtaz knew that if and when he was exonerated, his life in and around Bangla Town wouldn't be easy. People would talk, they always did. Some may even do more than talk.

She put her head on his shoulder. 'We'll meet that when we come to it,' she said. 'As a family.'

'The dishonoured family of a pervert.'

'The family of a gay man who lost his love far too early,' she said.

* * *

The boy had been assigned the sort of duty solicitor who didn't give a shit. The translator on the other hand was concerned.

'Qasim hasn't slept,' he told Ricky just before they went into the interview room with the boy and his brief. 'He's very frightened.'

'Is he?'

Nabil had clearly been frightened at the end of his interview the previous evening. Otherwise he wouldn't have said what he did.

Ricky laid the pawn ticket down in front of Qasim and said, 'Mean anything to you?'

He could see that it did in the kid's eyes, but his mouth said no.

'Made out in the name of Taha Mirza, the boxer. Know him?'

Qasim said he didn't.

'Weird,' Ricky said, 'because Nabil told me you do know him. He said that it was your idea to take Rajiv Banergee's ring to him to pawn for you at Jones's pawnshop on Commercial Street.'

Hafez translated. As he spoke the boy's eyes widened.

Ricky continued. 'Because you knew Taha Mirza, didn't you?' he said. 'Gave you a few boxing tips, did he? Took you down that study group in south London?'

Hafez looked quickly at Montalban. Although Nabil had admitted knowing Taha Mirza 'a bit', he hadn't alluded to any boxing tips and he'd said nothing about any study group in south London. But then Nabil was, by far, the tougher of the pair. Still, he'd not hesitated to drop his friend well and truly in it.

'The pawnbroker remembers one man and two teenage boys took that ring in,' Ricky said. 'Course Nabil claims he wasn't there, it was just you.'

Qasim said, 'No!'

'Yes,' Ricky said.

'Nabil is there!'

Self-preservation was always something that could be relied upon, in Ricky's experience.

'So you're telling me,' he said, 'that you and Nabil pawned Rajiv Banergee's ring with the help of Taha Mirza?'

Hafez translated. The boy sat still, with his mouth open.

'So where'd you get the ring?' Ricky asked.

The boy said that it had been Taha's ring.

'Really? Not what Nabil said. He reckons it was yours. Not his, you understand, but belonging to you. Actually, it once belonged to poor old Rajiv Banergee. Worth a bit too.'

Ricky could see that Hafez wasn't comfortable translating that, but he assumed he'd done it anyway.

The boy began to cry.

'Good news is,' Ricky said, 'that the man who saw you in Arnold Circus with Rajiv Banergee says he saw you both stab him. In fact, to your credit, Qasim, he said he saw "the one with the scar on his face" – Nabil – cut him first.'

Lee had work to do. He didn't have broken ribs and the invoices he needed to send out wouldn't post or email themselves. Also he had to go and buy a new mobile phone. His had disappeared into whatever weird half-lit spook land the 'Emma' at Forest Gate had come from.

On his way to the mobile phone shop where he'd bought his previous handsets, he picked up a local paper. Amongst reports about summer fairs, stabbings and the joys of beekeeping he saw that a Forest Gate lawyer had been arrested under prevention of terrorism legislation. It seemed he'd been in touch with known terror suspects in the Middle East. Lee went back into the newsagents and bought a copy of *The Guardian*. Still nothing about any shooting at a house in Essex. Lee knew that the authorities could bury pretty much what they wanted, but that had been a big operation, involving multiple armed officers, road closures and ambulances.

Admittedly Good Easter was fairly remote but it wasn't in the middle of fucking Exmoor. The local people must have seen or heard something. And what about the families of the taxi driver and Djamila's boyfriend?

Lee had seen Fayyad al'Barri alive. Mumtaz had told him she had some memory about Fayyad laying on top of her, although she'd been in great pain at the time. But Lee knew. Fayyad had survived the gunfire that had killed Djamila. How, Lee didn't know. He was also pretty dodgy on the subject of why, because something at the back of his mind was suggesting to him that Fayyad al'Barri hadn't got through all that by accident.

He wanted to call Vi and just ask her outright, but he didn't. She wouldn't tell him even if she knew and, chances were, that she didn't. And much as Lee knew that for national security to have any meaning it had to be like this, it pissed him off. Because over and above everything else, Lee wanted to know where Fayyad was. More importantly, he needed to know *what* he was.

'Why'd you do it?'

Unlike Nabil, Qasim was crying. Ricky wondered whether Nabil was actually capable of tears.

The kid said they'd seen 'that man', Amir Charleston, hit Rajiv Banergee and had gone to help him out.

'But Mr Banergee was down on the ground,' Ricky said. 'Your man didn't need no help.'

Hafez the translator said something to the boy, which seemed to make him pull himself together.

'He says that where he is from, that is what people do,' Hafez translated.

'What? Attack a man when he's down?' Ricky said.

'No.' The translator shook his head. 'I know what he means, DI Montalban.'

'Tell me.'

Hafez said, 'What Qasim is describing is a phenomenon I know well from our country. I can only describe it as a blood fury or an infection of violence. When you are constantly in danger it takes very little to make you strike out against others. Two men begin fighting in a street in Damascus and this turns into a riot. People take sides. Not in an organised way but simply as their inclinations dictate. It is one of the many consequences of war. One fights to survive and then one just fights because one cannot stop.'

Ricky could see that. The violence of war could be looked upon as a communicable disease. It was a decent analogy. But it didn't reflect what Nabil had told him.

'Yeah,' Ricky said. 'I get that. But that ain't what Nabil said.'

Hafez translated.

'According to him,' Ricky continued, 'you killed Rajiv Banergee because you'd both been raped by your landlord, Ali Huq, earlier that evening.'

Hafez translated and Ricky watched the boy's face sink into confusion. He spoke.

'What's he say?'

But the translator had to wait for the boy to stop. When he did, he said, 'Qasim says that's not true. He says that although Mr Shah told them that Mr Huq was a pervert, he never touched them. It was Mr Shah who made them have sex with him.'

'When?'

'I think when they first came to the UK.'

He checked with the boy who confirmed his assumption.

'It happens many times,' Hafez said. 'When children

unaccompanied by adults come to a country, those who claim to help them sometimes take advantage.'

'But not Ali Huq?'

Hafez checked again.

'No,' he said.

'And yet Nabil and Qasim have accused him.'

'Qasim now says this is a lie.'

'Why?'

The original plan, according to Qasim, was that the boys blackmail Ali Huq.

'Why didn't they blackmail Mr Shah?' Ricky asked. 'It was him who abused them.'

Hafez smiled. 'Oh, this also is familiar, DI Montalban. They are too afraid of Mr Shah. Those who traffic these people often beat and terrorise them. I know. Such people hold power over everyone. Those they traffic and those, often good people, who want to give them a home. It is a dirty business.'

And Shah telling the kids about Ali's proclivities made it even dirtier. Ricky wondered how many other refugees Aziz Shah the tailor had abused while maintaining his outward appearance as a 'good' man, devoted to his wife, his daughters and his mosque.

But then was Qasim telling the truth? Or was Nabil?

Ricky knew who he'd put his money on.

'Ask him how he knew Taha Mirza,' he said.

Hafez rattled off rapid Arabic.

Nabil had clammed right up when Mirza had been mentioned and, looking at Qasim's face as he replied, Ricky didn't hold out too much hope. But he was proved wrong.

'He says that Mr Shah knew him,' Hafez said. 'Mr Shah recommended they go to meet Mr Mirza as he had connections to a very good study group in south London. It is called, he says, the Light of True Belief.'

Shah and Uddin's 'charity'.

'Did he ever go to any of their meetings?' Ricky asked.

According to Qasim both he and Nabil had been twice. But they'd been told to keep their attendance secret. They'd been on their way back from just such a meeting the night they'd killed Rajiv Banergee.

Ricky excused himself from the interview to go out and make a call to Newham.

Shazia was exhausted. Sleepless nights worrying about her exams were coming thick and fast now. Every day was revision day and, although she appreciated the special cramming sessions her subject tutors were putting on, she had little enthusiasm. This one had been arranged by Mr Bright to take them on a whistle-stop tour through their English Literature syllabus.

Grace stood beside her in the queue for the library where the 'crammer' was set to take place. She was wearing the type of clothes girls normally wore to go clubbing. Shazia had never seen such hot, hot pants.

'Where are you off to?' she asked her friend.

Grace said, 'Crammer, man. Like you.'

'So why're you dressed for a party?'

Grace laughed. 'Not a party,' she said. 'Just my style.'

Grace was so transparent. She always made Shazia smile. She just hoped she didn't get hurt one day.

'Well, give Mamba my best,' she said.

Grace sucked her teeth, pulled a face and then laughed again. She knew she was an open book.

Shazia felt tired and tense but she knew that she had to concentrate. Cramming sessions were only any use if you were awake. She had been worried that she might see that creepy old Wahid Sheikh outside the college or in the convenience store, which would have put a damper on her day. But he'd not appeared and Cousin Aftab had driven her all the way to the door of the college. George was going to pick her up and take her back to Brick Lane after college. It was really kind of them to do it. But Shazia was no fool. Although she'd closed her mind to it for much of the time, she knew that Wahid Sheikh wasn't wandering around after her for no reason. He blamed her for his nephew Naz's death and, in a way, he was right to do so. She could've saved Naz when she'd found him, stabbed, in that empty house in Forest Gate. But she hadn't, because she hated him for beggaring her family and abusing her amma. She knew he wanted revenge and she sensed it was going to happen through her in some way.

But she couldn't think about that now. In five minutes' time she'd be in the library.

He was sweating heavily even though it wasn't hot. Sometimes, heavy sweating could mean that a person was about to have a heart attack. He was fifty-five, overweight and terrified. He was the ideal candidate.

'What's the matter, Mr Shah? You look alarmed.'

He wanted to say *I'm in Scotland Yard, of course I'm alarmed!* But he didn't. Aziz Shah knew that if he wanted to stand any chance of getting out, he'd have to behave with the utmost respect and humility. That idiot-snake Vakeel Uddin would lay it all at his door. Maybe he already had?

He'd have to tell the truth. Well, some of it.

'What was your relationship to Taha Mirza?'

Another idiot! Recruiting men and boys for jihad! What had he been thinking? Why had neither he nor Uddin recognised the business for what it was? A business! Bringing people in from Syria was lucrative. Why hadn't they been content with that?

'Mr Mirza was involved in radicalising people. Did you know that?'

'No!'

Mirza's 'gym'. What a joke! But how could a humble tailor like Aziz have done anything about it?

'We know you recommended Mirza's gym to at least two boys.'

Aziz had nothing except sweat. Why had he done that? Because Uddin had told him to. It was all very well to pay due respect to more educated members of the family but Vakeel had always had an agenda. A lawyer *and* a religious nutter? How did that work?

'We know about the Light of True Belief study group in Peckham.'

They were only just ahead of Aziz when it came to that. When he'd found out the Light of True Belief was something other than just a money-making scam, he'd been furious.

Aziz smiled. 'We are a charitable organisation . . .'

'With no charity number . . .'

'Dedicated to rescuing people from war zones,' he said. 'I don't know of any study group.'

'Mr Uddin says you attended religious classes there on several occasions.'

Lying shit! He'd always avoided the place because it was full of fanatics!

'We also know, from a separate source, that you are alleged to have had sexual relations with some of these people you've been claiming to help.'

'Who says such a thing?'

Fuck, he was right in the eye of the shit now. What little bastard had blabbed? He knew they had those sods from Ali Huq's place in custody.

'Was it the poor boys who accused Mr Huq?' he asked.

His interrogators remained silent.

'I think you will find that they are becoming confused between Mr Huq and myself. Mr Huq has certain tastes . . .'

Zafar Bhatti had told him that Huq was a fairy years ago. Not that he'd said anything about Huq and Rajiv Banergee until very recently.

'I mean he killed poor Rajiv-ji in a fit of homo lust . . .'

'You know that do you, Mr Shah?'

'Well, I . . . Well, it's . . . You know . . . It's . . .'

'Unproven. Unlike Mr Huq's innocence in the case of the two boys who lived in his house.'

Innocent? Hadn't the boys accused Huq of sodomy and all sorts?

'Allegations of sexual abuse against Mr Huq have been withdrawn.'

How? That was inconvenient. With Huq in the frame for all sorts of homosexual crimes both real and imagined, people's attention had drifted away from Aziz completely. What had happened there?

They told him that first one and then the other boy had admitted to the killing of Rajiv Banergee. You could have knocked Aziz down with a feather. Of course he didn't know who had killed Rajiv, but those boys had not even been in his mind. Why?

Then they told him it was partly down to him.

Aziz stood up and waved his arms around. 'I never fucked them! Never! I'm a proper man, not a pervert! How dare you!'

But unfortunately for Aziz that wasn't the worst thing that his interrogators told him.

'How much, Mr Shah, do you know about this terrorist that Vakeel Uddin liaised with?'

Terrorist?

And then Aziz remembered. That terrorist.

* * *

286

Baharat Huq left his house as soon as Ali told him. Qasim and Nabil had not only admitted to killing Rajiv but they'd also withdrawn their sexual abuse allegation against him. So his son was in the clear. Baharat walked down Brick Lane with his head held high.

Of course some people looked at him as if he'd lost his mind and some others appeared disgusted. But he didn't care. He knew that his son was innocent and that was all that mattered.

'Baharat-ji!'

He hadn't noticed he'd just passed the Leather Bungalow. Susi Banergee, uncharacteristically very plainly dressed, hailed him from the doorway.

'Mrs Chopra.'

'Come in,' she said.

Inside, the Bungalow was even emptier than it had been before. But there were still chairs. Baharat had heard that Susi had been taken in by the police at one time, but he didn't allude to it. She did.

'I hit him the night that he died,' Susi said as she handed him a can of coke. There were no tea-making facilities left on the premises. She apologised for the lack of drinks choice. Baharat said it wasn't important.

'Rajiv made me so mad,' she said. 'He'd been moaning for months that he didn't want to run the business any more. I thought he'd be happy to sell. But he wasn't. He said he'd do it in his own way in his own time. I didn't have time.'

'Why?'

Susi shook her head. 'I'm a very bad woman, Baharat-ji,' she said. 'Mummy-ji would have been so ashamed.' She lit one of her Sobranie cigarettes. Blue. 'Dilip is divorcing me.'

'I'm sorry.'

'Don't be,' she said. 'We haven't lived as man and wife for many years. I could never have children, you see. Dilip regretted marrying me.'

'Ah.'

'But that isn't why he's divorcing me.'

Baharat said nothing.

'I took lovers,' she said after a pause. 'I knew it was wrong. But Dilip was unfaithful first. Not that I'm using that as an excuse. And he was far more discreet than I. That was my mistake.'

'He has some proof . . .'

'Yes. I am a silly woman. I knew I wouldn't come out of any divorce well, given the circumstances. With no children, and having not had a job since I married him, I knew that Dilip could get everything. My brother said I could come and live with him, which was kind. But I baulked at it. Back on the Lane? After all these years? Imagine how people would laugh!'

He wanted to tell her about his own recent experiences regarding his own family's reputation, but he let her carry on. She had to know most of it anyway.

'I begged Rajiv to sell. I said we could both move to wherever we wanted from the proceeds of the building and the business. Papa left it to both of us, you see. Over a million pounds each. We could have nice new apartments in Southall for half a million, or a pair of cottages in Canterbury – Rajiv always liked Canterbury. We'd have money left over, so we wouldn't have to work . . .' She shook her head. 'But he wouldn't even discuss it. He said he needed time. I said I didn't have time and then I was very rude and told him that I couldn't live in that damp old flat upstairs where we had both been brought up. I said it just wasn't good enough. Who do I think I am, eh?'

Baharat smiled. Susi Banergee had always thought herself to be a cut above. As a teenager he remembered her telling people that she was the granddaughter of a maharajah. Although to be fair her late father had put that idea in her head. There was a man who should have been on the stage.

'I was sorry as soon as I'd hit him,' Susi said. 'But by that time, it was too late. Rajiv was good about it, but I had to go. I meant to apologise in the morning. But of course by that time he was dead. I take it you now know who killed my brother, Baharat-ji?'

'Indeed. And I apologise to you that the people who committed this terrible sin were given shelter by my son,' he said.

'I am just relieved that it was not Ali-ji who did this thing, not that I ever believed that he did,' she said. 'You know, Baharat-ji, that my brother and Ali . . .'

'I know now,' he said. 'When did you find out?'

'Only after his death,' she said. 'I found some letters. I didn't tell the police. In fact I didn't tell them much, to begin with. I thought if I told them I had attacked my brother they would think that I killed him.'

He said, 'Now we all know better.'

'We do.'

They sat in silence for a few moments and then Baharat said, 'So what will you do now, Susi?'

She smiled. 'You know, after all of my raging at poor Rajiv about being stuck here back on the Lane, I am going to stay.'

'Stay?'

'Yes,' she said. 'You know, Baharat-ji, I can make enough money from renting out the shop to be able to live a decent lifestyle. Admittedly I won't be able to buy any more genuine designer handbags, but so what? Our old flat is not exactly to my taste but I can change it.'

'Are you not still worried about what people might say?'

She shook her head. 'Of course I am,' she said. 'But to do anything else is impractical. The shop will give me an income, the flat will be my home. Most people don't have such luxuries. I may be alone in the world now that my brother has died, but apart from that I am a very fortunate person.'

'You are,' Baharat said. 'And, if it helps at all, Susi, you are not alone.'

Mumtaz sat on her old bed in her old bedroom with her knees up to her chin. When she'd been a child, she'd spent hours looking down into the street, spying on the boys attempting to lure customers into the restaurants. Now she had other things on her mind.

Shazia's revision was going 'OK' according to her. That probably meant she was doing really well. When she'd been doing her GCSE revision she'd said that had just been 'OK' too. She'd gone on to get mostly A-stars. But rocking the girl's world in any fashion before her exams were out of the way was out of the question and so she couldn't say a word to Shazia until the end of July.

It had been the unexpected deaths of Djamila and Abbas al'Barri that had made her think about the last hold the Sheikh family had over her. Death could come out of the blue, at any minute, second, moment. Life was at best precarious. Mumtaz knew that if anything happened to her while Shazia didn't know the truth about her father's death, someone with ill intent, namely Wahid Sheikh, may well tell her. And he would take a certain view which would not be complimentary to her.

And so Mumtaz was decided. In just over three months she would tell Shazia her deepest, darkest secret. She would risk the girl's hatred. She had also decided not to tell Lee until after the deed was done. Then she'd risk his hatred and, possibly, unemployment. How could he, knight in shining armour that he was, employ someone who had watched coldly as another human being died in front of them?

TWENTY-SIX

Chief Superintendent Vine told Ricky Montalban to shut his office door and sit down.

'As you know,' he said, 'our own investigation into the activities of Aziz Shah and the late Taha Mirza are at an end.'

'Yes, sir.'

The tailor had been taken to Scotland Yard by counterterrorism officers. From Tower Hamlets' point of view, the matter was closed. All Ricky knew was that whatever had been gleaned from Shah's testimony so far went way beyond one single London borough.

'However, I think it's important that those intimately connected to the investigation be allowed to know whatever has been officially sanctioned for them to know. That said, what I am about to tell you cannot go outside this room.'

Bloody national security spook stuff. 'Yes, sir.'

'Know also, Montalban, that what I am about to tell you is not the definitive story. I may never know that myself.'

'Sure.'

Vine breathed in deeply. 'Right,' he said. 'I think you know that Shah, Mirza and Shah's brother-in-law Vakeel Uddin were involved with an organisation called the Light of True Belief.'

'A Muslim study group in south London,' Ricky said.

'Peckham. Well, as I am sure you will have deduced, the Light of True Belief was not an organisation sanctioned by the mainstream Muslim community. On the face of it, the Light was indeed a study group, but its aims diverged from religion into extremism. The sect, as far as we know at the moment, possessed the twin aims of identifying people likely to be open to extremist rhetoric and "developing" those individuals with a view to facilitating their passage to Syria in order to fight for ISIS. They also raised funds to help children and young people from Syria to leave that country. That would have been laudable had said youngsters not then been obliged to attend their meetings and inculcate their philosophy.

'With regard to this latter activity, it was Vakeel Uddin who identified the children,' Vine continued. 'He processed asylum applications for them and then passed them on to Shah whose job it was to secure accommodation. Not easy, you would think, amid the atmosphere of paranoia about anyone of Syrian origin these days. However, it was Shah's job to find people who were vulnerable in some way on the basis that such people will not tell if they discover that what they are doing is wrong. In the case of Ali Huq, Shah knew that he was homosexual.'

'How?'

'Shah knows the owner of the electrical shop on Brick Lane, Mr Bhatti.'

'Oh Gawd.'

'You know him?'

'Oh yes. Massive gossip, sir. Got chucked out of the committee of the local mosque for financial irregularities. The Huq family reckon it was Zafar Bhatti who contacted the local press about

Ali. Bhatti once ran a dodgy PO Box, which is where, apparently, he got his intel on Ali Huq and Rajiv Banergee.'

'We're in the process of identifying other hosts either recruited or blackmailed by Shah,' Vine said. 'To be frank, DI Montalban, this organisation was not large, but it was growing. Taha Mirza, on the other end of the operation, was involved in training martyrs for Syria using his own version of *Fight Club* to tempt stressed-out City executives. These people, we should also note, have money.'

'The Light was gonna tap 'em up?'

'Eventually, yes. It was a clever system,' he said. 'Neat, self-contained. It also made a considerable amount of money for Shah and Uddin personally.'

'From the families of the Syrian kids?'

'Exactly. Desperate parents send their children here to keep them safe, get fleeced in the process and then may or may not discover that their children are being radicalised. Or so we think. That was certainly the case with the two boys taken in by Huq. They attended meetings in Peckham and were being prepared to go and learn fighting skills from Taha Mirza. They met him before he died. They knew what he did and had observed the men who attended his gym.'

'What about the two boys, sir? What happens now?'

Ricky had felt sorry for the kids in spite of what they'd done. The poor little bastards had been fucked up by war and by evil men like Aziz Shah.

'No longer our problem, DI Montalban,' Vine said. 'But they have admitted they killed Rajiv Banergee and so they will be put to trial. However, I can tell you that they are co-operating with the investigation into the Light of True Belief. As you know, they withdrew their allegations of sexual abuse against Huq. These they have now transferred to Aziz Shah, although whether, given the boys previous record of lying about such matters, they will stick, I don't know. The good news is that across two London boroughs and one national organisation, we have been able to uncover a terrorist organisation before it managed to send those it had recruited to fight with ISIS. We should all pat ourselves on the back.'

But Ricky wondered. As he left Vine's office he knew he still had questions – like how had Uddin found these Syrian families he and Shah had exploited? Logically there had to be some sort of connection in the Middle East to act as go-between?

On the one hand Ricky knew he should have asked, but on the other he had a hunch that Vine wouldn't have told him even if he knew. What was at the 'other' end of the Light of True Belief operation would have either closed down or transformed into something else. Ricky realised he may never know. But that didn't mean he didn't want to.

Whoever had been meant to be responsible for taking kids like Qasim and Nabil and City boys like Amir Charleston into the hell that was Syria was certainly not an entity that Ricky would want to meet in the flesh. That was a person, or persons, who clearly lacked a soul.

Nothing was going to happen. In spite of his involvement with the police, not to mention a dubious Islamic organisation, Amir Charleston was going to keep his job. The current chief exec. of Vanek Brothers, a man younger than Amir by a full five years, had wanted to fire him. Not because Amir had been in trouble with the police – a lot of young men in high finance had records. It was the connection to Islam that had made him baulk.

But Amir's father had smoothed that all out with Mr Vanek senior, or Milan. Soon it would be as if Amir's small dalliance with 'meaning' had never happened. And that was a good thing. He'd been naïve and impulsive and had been swayed by his passions.

Next time he'd be much more measured – and discreet.

* * *

'Fancy falling over at the airport!' Julie shook her head. 'Poor Mumtaz! Any idea when she's coming back?'

Lee had a considerable stable of part-time and casual PIs at his disposal. Julie was one of those who was just as happy in the office as she was out in the field.

'About three weeks' time,' Lee said. 'At the moment. Depends how her ribs heal.'

'Where was she going?'

'Amsterdam,' he said.

'What, for a holiday?'

'Yeah.'

They'd decided to stick to the main facts about the trip so neither of them would make a mistake.

'I don't see Mumtaz down the coffee shops or in clubs,' Julie said. 'I may be wrong but . . .'

'She's got a cousin who lives there. They were gonna do a load of museums together.'

'Oh.'

That was what people would expect. Covered woman, in a city, with a relative, looking at art. He wanted to laugh. Oh, there was an element of that in Mumtaz's character, sure. But he knew that if she ever did get to Amsterdam, she'd be diving into the more dubious backstreets and sticking her head around coffee shop doors.

The office phone rang and Julie picked it up. 'Arnold Agency.'

Lee mouthed that he was going outside for a smoke. He'd just opened the door when Julie grabbed his arm. 'Lady says she has to speak to you,' she said.

Lee took the phone and heard a familiar voice say, 'Lee? Is that you?'

It hurt to move, but Mumtaz had to get out of the house. Her mother's constant attention was driving her mad. Every five minutes she was asking her whether she wanted to eat, whether she wanted the TV on and interrogating her about how she was feeling. Thank goodness Ali had gone to stay with Asif and Tracey! While he'd been in the house too it had been unbearable. If only her mother would talk to him!

She decided to walk as far as Christ Church. It was a bright, warm day and the district was alive with Bangladeshi traders going about their business, young hipsters looking studiously outré and the air was perfumed by the smell of spice and fresh bagels. Had she not been in so much pain she would have felt glad to be alive.

'Mrs Hakim?'

But then her blood froze. What was Wahid Sheikh doing on Brick Lane? Had he been lurking on the off chance of catching her alone?

'What do you want, Wahid-ji?' she said.

'I am simply enquiring after your health,' he said. 'I hear you had a nasty accident. Stansted Airport, wasn't it?'

'Yes,' she said.

How the hell did he know? Then she chided herself for being so naïve. People like the Sheikhs knew everything.

'I'm so sorry,' he said. 'I trust you will be healed in time for your daughter's wedding.'

She was so tempted to tell him that was never going to happen. But if she did that he'd make trouble. So she said nothing.

'Her A levels will have finished in twelve weeks' time,' he said. 'Have you told her yet, Mrs Hakim? Given her something to look forward to after her examinations.'

'No,' she said.

He smiled, doing his sweet old man act. He was very good at that.

'Shame,' he said. 'But then again I suppose if it comes as a surprise it will be better. You know I am having the finest gold and diamonds fashioned into a spectacular necklace for my bride. I know she will be impressed. Any girl would.'

Just not Shazia. She hated elaborate jewellery, she found it vulgar. Although it wouldn't be as repellent to her as he would. Not that Shazia would ever find that out.

Mumtaz began to shuffle away. If she talked to him for any longer she might tell him what she was going to do. And like him, she was rather fond of the idea of surprises, albeit only when it came to Wahid-ji and his family.

She felt his eyes on her back as she turned from Brick Lane into Fournier Street. Men were coming and going to and from the Great Mosque, so she was pretty sure he wouldn't make a scene.

And she was right. But just before she reached the church she did look back once and saw that he was still watching her.

Mumtaz smiled. She was going to enjoy disappointing that vile old man.

Lee took the call on one of the hand-held phones on the metal steps outside the office.

'What you calling me for?' he hissed. 'We're not supposed to communicate!'

'Oh, Lee!' He heard Shereen's voice catch as if she was just about to cry. 'Lee, they won't tell me anything!'

'Shereen . . .'

'How Abbas and Djamila died, where my son is . . .'

'I don't know the answer to any of those questions,' he said.

'But you were there! Abbas called me from the airport. He said that you were there with Mrs Hakim. I can't even speak to Djamila's boyfriend, Fazil . . . But then he didn't phone . . .'

Fazil was dead. But he couldn't tell her that. He couldn't tell her anything. But she deserved something, poor woman, just how much could he tell her without compromising himself?

She'd called from a mobile number he hadn't recognised. But that didn't mean much. If Shereen and the kids had been taken away by the security services then they were being monitored twenty-four seven.

'Shereen, I've nothing to say, because I don't know nothing,' he said.

'You do! You have to! You're lying!'

She was falling apart. He couldn't stand it. He felt his eyes fill up. This woman was the wife of the man to whom he owed his life.

'Lee! Please!'

What were 'they' going to do? Kill him? Maybe. But he said, 'I didn't see Abbas die, Shereen. I don't know who killed him, but—'

And then the line went dead and Lee put a hand up to his head. They knew. They'd heard his voice and now they knew that Shereen had contacted him. What would they do to her? And what would they do to him to make sure that never happened again?

Vi Collins slid her newspaper along the bar until it was underneath the nose of DI Montalban.

Ricky didn't often get out of Tower Hamlets and so being in the Boleyn, arguably Newham's finest pub, was a bit of a treat. Also, you didn't throw away an invitation to drink with Vi Collins lightly. He picked up the newspaper and his pint and led Vi over to a small table at the back of the saloon bar.

When they'd both sat down, he pointed to the newspaper headline and said, 'Anything to do with you?'

'Not directly.'

He read the article, which said that two members of staff at prestigious London department store Harrods had been arrested on suspicion of recruiting people to perpetrate terrorist offences.

'So . . .'

'FYI only,' Vi said.

'Kensington's a bit outside my area,' Ricky said. 'And yours.'

'Yeah, but Aziz Shah's on your manor.'

'Ah . . .'

'No direct connection,' Vi said, 'but, as we know, this type of investigation generally works out to be pretty wide-ranging.'

'Right. Big network was it?'

'No,' she said. 'But it had the potential to grow. Just wanted to thank you for your help.'

Ricky shrugged. 'You're welcome. But we never did that much. All I really done was find the killers of Rajiv Banergee.'

'Which helped lead us to Aziz Shah and his associates . . .'

'Who I know you was watching a long time before we got involved, DI Collins,' he said.

She smiled. 'Vi. You're not wrong . . .'

'So why the meet-up?' Ricky said. 'I can't believe you've brought me all the way here so you can listen to me sparkling conversation.'

'No. Although I might want you for your body.'

He laughed. Overweight and with a face, some said, that looked a bit like a bull's, Ricky had never considered himself attractive. Nor, as far as he was aware, had many other people. Nearly forty, he was still single and hadn't been on a date for a good five years.

'But as well as that,' Vi continued, 'there's also said Aziz Shah the tailor.'

'What about him?'

'Thought you'd like to know that sexual abuse charges by your two Syrian boys against Shah will be dropped,' she said.

'What? How do you know that?'

Shah's collar had been felt by Tower Hamlets, not Newham.

But then Ricky knew that 'another' agency had been involved too.

When she didn't answer, he said, 'Is this because he didn't do it?'

Vi shrugged.

'So . . .'

'You know Shah, probably better than I do,' Vi said. 'So you'll know that he's by way of being what could be described as a useful idiot.'

Aziz the tailor had always had a way of being able to get himself out of the bad situations he frequently put himself into. It was said that with his loose tongue and obvious delight in anything salacious, he was an easy channel through which information could be broadcast.

'Some people feel that Shah's best off out in the world,' Vi said. 'His brother-in-law's another matter.'

All Ricky knew about Vakeel Uddin was that the Forest Gate lawyer had been responsible for bringing people from the Middle East into the country under guidance, so he had deduced, of the Light of True Belief organisation. Whoever they were . . .

Vi, as if reading his mind, said, 'Uddin was directly involved with that Light of True Belief mob. Shah wasn't. He just did the day to day.'

'Which included abusing those two boys?'

'I dunno,' she said. He almost expected her to follow this with *And I don't care*. But she didn't. All she said was, 'Them kids murdered a man.'

'I know.'

'They admitted to it and were proud about it.'

Yes, they had confessed, but Ricky hadn't been aware they'd been proud of what they'd done. Where had she got that from? But then Ricky knew he'd probably never find that out. Vi Collins was one of those local, old-fashioned coppers who, nevertheless, moved between worlds. On the face of it she was simply a cynical, middle-aged detective. But with her easy contacts all over the Mct and beyond, who really knew what she did when, from time to time, she appeared to move out of her role for a while?

'The Light of True Belief won't be seen again,' Vi said. 'But Shah will. I believe he's staying on in your manor.'

'But didn't he find homes for kids . . .'

'He ain't doing that now,' Vi said. She smiled. 'Back to tailoring, I think, for Mr Shah.'

Ricky was angry. A nonce, admittedly unconvicted, on his patch! He said, 'And kiddie fiddling.'

'No evidence for that, Ricky,' she said. 'Hearsay only. Have to be careful what we say.'

'Yeah, but . . .'

'Yeah, but nothing,' she said. 'Get used to seeing Shah back on your streets.'

Obviously someone had some sort of need to keep him there. Ricky hated these games ordinary plod was sometimes obliged to play on behalf of 'secret' plod. Aziz Shah was a nonce, Ricky had seen it in his eyes.

Vi said, 'And keep your ear to the ground. Like I say, he's got a loose gob, which he's got very little control over.'

So he was being kept on the loose, as Vi had said, as a useful idiot.

TWENTY-SEVEN

Three Months Later

Lee wasn't the same. But then neither was she. They'd shared an experience that neither of them could talk about. It could have brought them closer together. But it hadn't.

Mumtaz kept on telling herself she'd only been back at work for eight weeks. It would take much longer than that for them to get back to 'normal'. Whatever normal might be. What it wasn't, was a quiet Lee who jumped whenever the phone rang. That wasn't him any more than she was the person who now took tranquillisers.

Wahid Sheikh had, so he said, assembled an impressive amount of jewellery to give to his prospective bride. He'd told Mumtaz all about it. Of course it had been done to humiliate her. What he was saying was *Look at all these lovely things I'm giving your daughter! It's more than you ever could.*

She'd wipe that smile off his face. She'd do it that evening when she went home and told Shazia everything.

The girls celebrated the end of their exams with a slap-up meal in the chicken shop. As well as Shazia there were five girls, including her best friend, Grace. Mamba, the gangsta object of Grace's affections, sat outside smoking weed.

Rabia, a very neat and clever girl whose parents came from Saudi Arabia said, 'So what are we all doing now we've finished college?'

Grace automatically looked out of the window at Mamba. Shazia rolled her eyes. 'Work in my cousin's shop to get some money and wait for my results, I guess,' she said.

'I've gotta go on holiday with my mum,' Mary said.

'Where?'

Mary shook her head. 'Skegness,' she said. 'In a caravan like last year. It's shit. Mum fancies this bloke up there and so we have to go to be with him. When they have sex in the caravan it's like trying to sleep next to elephants shagging.'

The girls laughed. But Banveet, who came from a very religious Sikh family, blushed. 'How do you put up with that?' she asked.

'I don't,' Mary said. 'Tell 'em to shut the fuck up. But they don't take no notice. I usually go out.'

'Where?'

'There's sand dunes,' Mary said. 'I just muck about in them.'

Mary had always been a tomboy. All the girls could imagine her rolling about in sand and getting really dirty. Mary didn't give a toss how she looked.

Kym, on the other hand, gave far too much of a toss. Whenever she moved her head, her blonde extensions almost had someone's eye out.

'What, at night?' she said. 'On your own?'

'Yeah.'

'I could never do that. Not without my Manny.'

Only Grace and Kym had boyfriends – and Grace's relationship with Mamba was open to question. She seemed to be a lot more keen than he was. Shazia watched him suck hard on his joint. Not once did his eyes flicker in Grace's direction. But he did look at Kym. In spite of all the false hair, false eyelashes and fake tan, she was a very pretty girl. But she was also the girlfriend of a boy who was very high up in a rival gang. Manny Nwogu was a hardman who everyone knew carried a knife as long as his forearm.

'Well, I'm going to Saudi,' Rabia said.

'To see your family?'

'Yes, but also something else,' she said. 'Something, er . . .' She laughed. Then she blushed.

Shazia frowned. Rabia was a really brilliant girl who would probably get straight A-star results. She really hoped she wasn't going to say what she thought she was going to say.

'Mum wants me to meet this boy,' she said.

Kym squealed. 'Oh, honey, that's amazing!'

More subdued, Banveet said, 'To marry?'

'Of course. Apparently he's really handsome and really rich and he'll let me have a career and everything!'

Shazia, the only other Muslim at the table, pondered on the words 'let me' as she picked at her fried chicken. A girl as bright as Rabia should make her own decisions.

'Have you seen a picture? Kym asked.

'No. But I know that he's handsome because my brother Salman has met him,' Rabia said.

Shazia and Banveet exchanged a look. Ban's dad had tried to arrange her marriage once but she and her mum had refused to even think about it. Ban was lucky, her mum was a doctor as well as being the one who wore the trousers in their household.

'What about you, Shaz?' Rabia asked.

'Me?'

'Yeah. Aren't your family looking out for someone for you?'

304

Grace answered for her.

'No, she's going uni, ain't you?'

'Yeah.'

And she probably was. Amma had banged on about university so much Shazia had sort of given in. It was probably a good idea to follow through with her place at Manchester. Hendon could come later.

The shop door opened and a man came in. Asian, probably in his early twenties, he was clean-shaven, smart and extremely handsome. All the girls stared.

'Two pieces of chicken and fries, please,' he said to the boy behind the counter.

Shazia consciously looked away.

When he'd gone, Rabia said, 'My Turki is more handsome than he was.'

Mary said, 'Ya think?'

The other girls laughed. Shazia watched the man go to his car, a green Corsa, and drive off.

'Don't like his car much,' Kym said.

But Shazia did. Having a 'normal' car meant that he might just be a 'normal' boy, as in not flash. She liked that, mainly because it meant that he probably wasn't like her dad.

Newham was somewhere Bob didn't know well. He had relatives in the borough but he rarely visited. On this occasion, however, his reason for being in the manor was work. After he'd stuffed some chicken and chips in his face, he was off to Forest Gate nick to see the formidable DI Violet Collins.

Collins and Montalban had a bit of cross-borough working going on with regard to Aziz Shah the tailor. It seemed that now that Taha Mirza was dead, Aziz was taking it upon himself to train up young Muslim lads for the boxing ring. As far as anyone knew he had no qualification to do this. He hadn't even known Mirza that well. So what was his angle? If any? His brother-in-law, Vakeel Uddin was in prison on remand pending trial for terror offences and so it would be reasonable to assume that Aziz would keep a low profile. Clearly he wasn't.

But then Bob was aware he didn't know everything about the counterterrorism operation that had spanned Newham and Tower Hamlets. All he was really sure about was that Uddin, who had been a member of some dodgy Islamic study group in south London, had brought people, mainly kids, into the UK from Syria. Once in the UK they had been placed with families by Shah and then radicalised. Concurrent to this, another member of the dodgy group, Taha Mirza, had been training men up to fight for ISIS in Syria. Everything they'd done channelled into radicalisation.

But there had been other players too. Not just the Light of True Belief people down in Peckham. Rumour had it that there were further connections that counterterrorism were keeping to themselves. Vakeel Uddin, it was said, had been to Syria. But no one seemed to know who he'd met there, if anyone. Bob, like his boss, Ricky Montalban, sensed that counterterrorism were still working on this network, in one way or another.

In the meantime he'd report Shah's latest activities to Vi Collins and hope she didn't spend too much time trying to seduce him. Not that her approaches were aggressive, they were just persistent.

'Jodie?'

Ever since Shereen had phoned him that one time, Lee had taken to contacting his daughter every day. Knowing he'd, albeit unwillingly, broken the rules imposed on him by counterterrorism, he wanted to make sure that his mistakes didn't rebound on his family.

He heard the girl sigh.

'You there?' he asked.

He knew she was, he just needed to hear her voice.

'Yes,' she said. 'What do you want?'

'Just making sure you're OK.'

'Well, I am,' she said. 'Not with a man twice my age, if that's what's bothering you.'

'Babe . . .'

'Nobby no-mates as usual. The way you like it.'

She was bitter. Her mother said she'd admitted she still had feelings for 'Jase' the racist ex-con. Last Lee had heard he was in Birmingham.

'And yeah, I am looking for a job,' Jodie continued. 'But there's nothing except selling sticks of rock to tourists or hideous Goth clothes to losers.'

'So do that,' Lee said.

'You don't understand,' she answered. Then she ended the call.

Mumtaz had gone home early so she could cook a special meal for Shazia now her exams were over. Lee envied their relationship. He envied the way Shazia, however difficult she could be, always knuckled down to work and study. But then she wasn't mesmerised by bling and plastic tits. According to Mumtaz, what floated Shazia's boat these days, was a desire to work in policing. Lee hoped that if she did go into the job she would not be disappointed. Asian women didn't get an easy time of it. Casual racism was the least of it, as Lee well knew. Was it any wonder so many Muslim kids turned to the dark side of their religion when the word 'Paki' was still such common currency in so many places?

However, not for the first time, he wondered what, specifically, had turned Fayyad al'Barri's face towards Islamic State. Djamila had been instrumental in his conversion but something other than sibling fellow feeling must have been involved. Had his defection to ISIS been sparked by one particular incident or just a build-up of many slights and insults over the years? He'd had a good career going in banking, as far as Lee could remember. But sometimes, often, a good career wasn't enough. Also Fayyad hadn't had a girlfriend, or anyone significant in his life. Had he perhaps been secretly gay? Had joining ISIS been his way of atoning for that 'sin'? And what about Djamila?

Both Fayyad and Djamila had seen more violence in their lives than most. Growing up on the Plain of Nineveh, they'd seen many, many violent men attempt to take over their home. In the end the violent men had won. And had that been at the root of their divergence from the world of their parents? That winning violence? Had they really learnt that, in the end, hate, violence and barbarity always won?

If they had, it was hardly surprising. But what still puzzled Lee was why Abbas had died. Someone had killed him – either Djamila, Fayyad, the taxi driver or Fazil. He knew he'd never know who had actually done the deed. But that didn't mean he couldn't speculate. Assuming that either Djamila, Fayyad or both of them had killed Abbas, then why? Abbas had been a devoted father, he would have done anything to protect those children, whatever their crimes. And why had he had to die? Had he perhaps tried to leave the house again to go and get help? Had he tried to persuade his children to stop following Islamic State? As he went back over the events of that day, the time he had spent waiting outside that house after Abbas had left him seemed very short. But had it been?

He wondered whether Shereen knew. Surely she would have to be told at some time. Abbas had been her husband, Djamila her daughter. And, he thought, Fayyad was her son. Lee had seen the young man in that room with those counterterrorism officers. He

308

had been alive – then. Djamila was dead, although he hadn't seen her body, but Fayyad had lived.

Lee couldn't help wondering whether there was a reason for that.

Although she could hardly eat because her stomach was so constricted, Mumtaz waited until after their meal to tell Shazia the truth about her father's death. The girl had been so happy to have finished her exams, Mumtaz felt she had to give her at least a few hours of joy.

Shazia had suggested that they both spend the evening watching 'daft DVDs'— kids films and superhero movies. Mumtaz said she wanted to talk to her first.

The girl was tall and slim, like her father, but she had the gentle features of Ahmet Hakim's first wife, her mother. Although they'd had an awkward start to their relationship, she was a good kid and Mumtaz loved her. The last thing in the world she wanted to do was hurt her.

But then if she went to Wahid Sheikh as his wife, she'd be more than hurt. She could very easily end up dead.

When Mumtaz had finished the washing-up she came back into the living room where Shazia was draped over one of their battered old wing chairs. She sat down on the sofa. Then she said, 'Shazia, I need to tell you something.'

For a moment Shazia looked confused, even a little worried. But then her face brightened and she said, 'Are you finally going out with Lee?'

She smiled. Shazia had long entertained the hope that her amma and Lee would get together romantically. And Mumtaz was no fool. She knew that Lee was attracted to her. But she also knew that she was way too damaged by her relationship with Ahmet to let another man into her life for the foreseeable future, even if she was attracted to him. And she was . . .

'No, sweetheart,' she said. 'It's about your father.'

Shazia frowned. She didn't like talking about her dad. He'd hurt her so badly she preferred to pretend, for much of the time, that he'd never existed.

When she did speak, she said, 'What about him?'

Mumtaz swallowed. 'Well,' she said, 'you know he was murdered . . .'

'By the Sheikhs,' she said.

'Although there is—there has been no proof.'

'Yes, but everyone knows they did it. He owed them money.'

'Yes.' She felt sick. How was she going to do this?

'So? That's over. There's nothing we can do. There's no . . .'

'Shazia, when your father was stabbed I told the police that I didn't see who did it,' Mumtaz said. She paused for a moment. Her chest felt tight. God almighty she felt light-headed!

'Amma?'

'I lied,' Mumtaz said.

For a moment, Shazia did nothing. Then she sat forward in her chair. 'Lied?'

The room was spinning now. The stress was going to kill her!

'Why?'

'It was Naz,' Mumtaz said. 'I saw him do it. Shazia, I saw him stick the knife into your father and then I watched as . . . as my husband bled to death in front of me.'

The girl was white.

'But you called an ambulance and . . .'

'Too late!' she said. 'I called it too late and I knew it! I waited until I knew he couldn't be saved! Do you understand! I let your father die!'

Nothing happened. No tears, no recriminations, no movement.

In the end, Mumtaz said, 'Do you understand, Shazia? I killed your father!'

And then there was another pause. Mumtaz held her breath.

The girl folded herself up on Mumtaz's lap like a cat.

'I would give anything to go back in time,' Mumtaz said.

'To my father's death?'

'No. To when you repeated my mistake. So I could have stopped you.'

Shazia had told her everything. That the girl should have suffered the same terrible experience that had scarred Mumtaz's life was almost unbearable.

'Naz Sheikh would still be alive.'

'But you would be free of guilt.'

'I never said I suffered from guilt,' Shazia said.

Mumtaz felt cold. 'I do,' she said. 'Ahmet was your father. I should have thought how much his death would hurt you.'

'It didn't.'

Mumtaz couldn't see her face and she was glad. She liked to think that Shazia was crying, but she knew that she wasn't. Ahmet had taken so much from her. Her virginity was almost a detail. He'd killed her love all except, it seemed, for her. But was that real?

'Shazia, I did a terrible thing . . .'

'Why didn't you tell me before?'

It seemed obvious. 'Why didn't you tell me about Naz?'

There was a silence. Then Shazia sat up. Her eyes were quite dry, her face, emotionless. 'I thought you might go to the police.'

'Why?'

'Because you're a good, moral person.'

'Yes, well now you know I'm not . . .'

'You are!' She hugged her. Then she cried. 'Only my mum ever loved me like you!'

'Oh, Shazia.' She put her arms around her.

They both sobbed. Mumtaz's phone rang twice but she ignored it. She hadn't been expecting what Shazia had told her. When the girl had followed Naz Sheikh to that empty house in Forest Gate, not only had she watched him die, she knew who had killed him. She refused to say who. All she would say was that the killer was a good man who had been persecuted by the Sheikhs. He was a husband and a father and he was protecting his family. Mumtaz knew how he must have felt.

Once she'd composed herself, Shazia said, 'Anyway, why are you telling me this now?'

Mumtaz took a deep breath. 'Because the Sheikhs know,' she said, 'that I let your father die. They also know I have been keeping that knowledge from you. Over the years they have used many things I would rather people didn't know against me. They threatened to tell the police that Uncle Ali had given a home to those Syrian boys. In fact the police knew already. More importantly, they were going to tell you what I've just told you.'

'But I wouldn't have cared!'

'They didn't know that and neither did I.'

And to be honest, Mumtaz was still not sure whether she had done the right thing. Shazia had accepted what she had done far too easily. Ahmet, for all his wickedness, had been her father. But then what did Mumtaz know of child sexual abuse? She'd been an adult when Ahmet had abused her, an adult who had experienced an almost charmed childhood.

'I couldn't risk losing you,' Mumtaz gasped. Her breath was coming short and painfully now. Shazia hugged her again.

'Oh, Amma! You would never lose me, never!' Then she said, 'So do you pay them money to keep quiet?'

And then she told her about the 'arrangement' Wahid Sheikh had forced her to accept. Now she was shocked. She got up and whirled across the room as if she was having a fit. There was a change in the atmosphere in that room, which Mumtaz feared.

'Marry him! Are you crazy?'

Weak at the knees, she sat down on the floor and put her head between her knees.

'I would never have let it get that far,' Mumtaz said. 'I just needed to—'

'You took a risk with my life!'

She knew she had. 'I did it because I couldn't risk your knowing . . .'

Shazia raised her head. 'That is the most selfish thing I've ever heard!' she said.

'No, I—'

'So what happens now I know? What will he do when this "wedding" he has arranged is cancelled?'

'He has no further hold over us, Shazia! Now you know, we are free.'

Shazia jumped to her feet. 'No we're not!' she said. 'That old bastard who has been following me around will go mad. You know he will! He will punish both of us! I will have to marry him!'

'No!'

And yet she had a point and Mumtaz knew it. Cousin Aftab had tried to warn her and she'd closed her eyes to it. Wahid Sheikh wouldn't take the loss of his bride lying down.

'Not that I will marry him,' Shazia said. 'I'd rather die! You'll have to sort it out!'

And here was her hard shell of self-preservation again. What had Ahmet unwittingly created in this girl?

'I'll go and stay with Lee until my A-level results come through and then I'll go straight to Hendon,' Shazia said. 'When I tell him what you've done he'll probably give you the sack!'

Mumtaz wanted to say *He knows!* Not that he knew what she'd done to Ahmet, he didn't. He knew the Sheikhs had tried to get her to give up Shazia, although he didn't know why. But if Shazia was going to go anywhere, that was probably the most sensible place for her to be. The Sheikhs would think twice about taking on an ex-copper and also Lee was probably the best person to explain what Mumtaz had done and why.

But then the hardest blow of all arrived.

'I hate you!' Shazia said. 'How dare you play with my life! You're no better than my dad!'

She left the room. Mumtaz heard the key turn in the lock on her bedroom door. There was a pain in her chest that was so bad, she felt as if she'd been stabbed. Minutes later she heard the girl unlock her door and run out of the flat. She knew she had to call Lee before Shazia turned up at his flat. In whispers and through tears, she told him everything. He arrived twenty minutes later and, when she opened the door to him, he took her in his arms and kissed her with an urgency she had never experienced before. When it was over, he said, 'No more secrets, Mumtaz. None.'

She put a hand up to his face. 'Is Shazia at your flat?'

'Yes.' He kissed her again. 'I've told her I've had to go out to get milk.'

'Oh Lee, what am I to do? She said she hated me!'

He guided her back into her hallway and shut the front door behind him. He said, 'She'll get over it. It's a shock. Trust me, I wouldn't lie to you. Not to you.'

She felt his arms around her waist and although she knew that she should push him away she also knew that that first, impulsive kiss he'd given her had changed things. What had been an insurmountable obstacle between them had simply melted away.

Crying, she kissed him and, when he caressed her body, she didn't try to make him stop.

TWENTY-EIGHT

There were Jews next door. Not the ordinary type, these were like the ones who had lived in Stamford Hill. The ones who wore the big hats and sidelocks and had loads of kids. In themselves they were harmless enough. On the other side there were a load of Pakistanis. The father had a greengrocer's business where most of them worked.

Nobody bothered him.

When he'd first moved in they'd all come out to have a good look at him. Of course they had. The Irishmen who lived in the squat opposite had stared out of their top windows. One of them wasn't all that he seemed. His curiosity was beyond idle. His presence was no accident. His new British masters didn't yet trust him.

They'd given him a Greek name, Filippo Aristide. The first letters of each name were the same as his own and he could speak Greek – albeit not brilliantly. He'd learnt because his father knew the priests on the Plain. They had taught him. His father had wanted them all to be educated. He'd thought that was the key to success.

He'd never been to Manchester before. The part where he lived was called Cheetham Hill, which was a very multicultural place. Not unlike East Ham, it had a lot of Asian grocers, halal and kosher butchers, shops where saris could be purchased and where Turks would cut your hair. It also, in places, had another life, which was why he had been sent there.

He'd proved himself in London. He'd been believed when he'd said he wanted to change sides. Now, in place of the Light of True Belief, there was a small, but efficient group bringing young men from Syria and Iraq to Cheetham Hill. Some of them were really good speakers, so he'd heard from the Irishman. But he couldn't get involved too quickly. That would look dodgy.

The debrief, after Essex, had gone on for months. He didn't know how long exactly. Some events he'd had to repeat and write about over and over. When Djamila had killed their father was one example. He'd cried every time he'd told it. She'd been so brainwashed she'd executed Abbas with a smile on her face. Not that she had. She had been glad he'd died, of course, but it was doubtful she'd have actually been able to do it. Djamila had always been her daddy's best girl and, although she knew he was a lush and an unbeliever, who claimed to hate him, she couldn't have killed him. Abbas would have pleaded with her and, in spite of everything, she would have crumbled. He'd had to do that. The old man with his screaming and shouting would have messed everything up. As would Djamila. But then he'd always known that she would have to be dispensed with eventually. It was odd to think that initially she'd got him involved. In doing so she'd colluded in her own death.

Djamila had more than suspected him. If he'd let her live she may have turned her gun on him after she killed the Hakim woman. The stupid Turkish boyfriend had told him as much when he'd arrived. Djamila had said she doubted her brother's loyalty. She'd said she'd seen him meet people that he shouldn't.

Had she? It was unlikely. The only person she'd ever seen him meet was that stupid lawyer Vakeel Uddin. A useful idiot if ever there was one. A fool he'd first met out in Syria and then made contact with on one of his many trips to London. Why did some people visit war zones when they had no intention of fighting? Was it simply to convince themselves that their betrayal of their own country was worth it?

Filippo Aristide was a photographer. He even had a studio on Cheetham Hill Road. He worked alone, which was good, and already had a list of clients when he arrived. Very considerate of his new masters. Filippo was divorced – his ex-wife and kids still lived in London. He'd lived up north for a while. He liked it. But while not in the market for another wife, he did want a girlfriend, just as long as she wasn't feisty.

He'd laughed with the Irishman about that one. He, the Irishman, had said that he couldn't imagine anything worse than a woman who just lay on her back and didn't feel a bloody thing when you fucked her. How they'd laughed at that! And he knew what the Irishman meant. An unmoving plank of a woman wasn't much fun. But one who screamed and hurt and sometimes died, was. He wondered what the Irishman's views on that would be?

He'd probably kill him.

That amateurish network back home had needed to be closed down. What was happening in Manchester was far more professional. He'd have to tell his new masters the job wasn't going to be easy. He was pretty sure the Irishman would disagree. He'd kill him.

His old masters in Syria were waiting to come and shop at the

Trafford Centre. He had to be ready to welcome them. Winners in the land of the kaffir. Not like his parents.

One day, Fayyad al'Barri knew, he'd get the Tooth of Jonah back from his mother – the police had given it to her. How he had enjoyed imagining the pathetic hope on his mother and father's faces when they had received the tooth – and then he'd crush it in front of her stupid face.

'That,' he would say to her as it disintegrated, 'is for forcing your children to reject their culture and their religion.'